Puppet Dreams

a novel for children

by Jose Sevilla Ho

HydeAway Press

4313 Glenridge St.

Kensington Maryland 20895

U.S.A.

http://hydeawaypress.net

ISBN 978-0-9982971-2-5

To Nadia and Marie

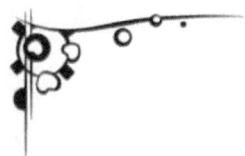

Chapter 1

'Paul! I know you're here! Come out right now!'
When he heard his mother's voice, Paul knew he was in bigger
trouble than he'd ever been. There was a man and a woman
with her, and for one terrified moment Paul wondered if she
had brought the social worker and a policeman. They were
looking in the wardrobes of the empty room, opening the
cupboards and calling out for him.

'Paul! Last chance!' his mother shouted again.

'Maybe we should come out,' whispered Dum Dum
near his shoulder.

'Sssh!' hissed Paul, moving closer to the vent to hear
what was going on below them. He could feel the dust and
cobwebs all around them, the rough, rickety wood of the
ceiling, and the pipes that were cold in the long abandoned
building. Thank God for the vents snaking all around the
walls. It allowed them to hear everything his mother was
saying to the people with her.

He heard the word "sleepwalking" and knew right away she was spilling out his most embarrassing secrets. Her mouth was like a broken flush valve that was gushing out everything Paul wanted to keep private. 'The doctor said it's not that uncommon,' she was saying. 'Says it might be something to do with Paul missing his dad. Wanting some kind of father figure.'

Where did she get that idea? Paul thought.

'That might explain the stuttering, too', added the other woman. Paul recognized the voice of Tiffany, the neighbour from two floors below them. Soon everyone in the building would know that he sleepwalked and used to wet his bed until he was six.

Shut up, mother! He screamed in his head. He could see Dum Dum looking wide eyed at him in the shadows, listening to this public humiliation of Paul. It was enough to make him want to come out of hiding. Anything just to make it stop.

The man spoke up. 'Where'd he get that dummy anyway?'

Paul was relieved. The man wasn't a cop after all. It was Jeremy something or other. Paul had never actually met him, but had answered the phone to him a few times.

'He says he found it,' Paul's mother replied to Jeremy's question.

'Found it?' Paul could hear the sneer in Jeremy's voice. 'Where?'

'At the puppet theatre,' Paul's mother said. 'His class went there on a field trip, and when he came home he said he found that the puppet had stowed away in his bag.'

Tiffany laughed. 'What imagination!'

Sounds to me like he filched it,' Jeremy declared. From his voice, Paul knew this Jeremy was fat and probably bald. The kind that didn't like kids.

'My son wouldn't do that!' Paul' mother snapped. 'He may have a few problems, but one thing he doesn't do is steal!'

Paul was pleased at his mother's defence. He smiled to himself in the dark. He turned to see Dum Dum smiling at him, too.

'Well maybe the dummy helps him talk to himself,' Tiffany tried to change the subject.

'That's right,' Jeremy followed her example, trying to be amicable. 'It might just be his way of coping with his problems. At least he can talk to his dummy without being laughed at.'

'But he really believes the dummy is talking to him,' Paul's mother protested. 'He says it begged him not to take it back to its owner.'

'Well, why don't we just buy him a new one?' suggested Jeremy. His use of 'we' disturbed Paul a little.

3

'He doesn't want any other one,' Paul's mother replied. 'His heart seems set on this puppet. He seems to feel they've become real friends…'

Their voices grew fainter as they went out the door and walked to the other room. He kept his eye on the trapdoor, worrying they might find a way up to the ceiling. After a few moments, they were back again.

'I'll have to admit, Paul's mom was saying, ' 'Having the puppet seems to have done him some good. I noticed he's started to stutter a little less since he's had it.'

Maybe it's his psychological crutch,' put in Jeremy the know-it-all. 'Like some kids have a security blanket or a rabbit's paw.'

'But other kids' security blanket don't tell them to run away,' countered Tiffany.

'Or keep them from seeing their friends,' added Paul's mother.

'Why doesn't Paul want to see his friends?'

'He says the puppet is afraid its old owner might see him.'

'What's wrong with that?' Tiffany countered. 'If the owner wants it back then he should have it.'

'But the dummy swears its owner was awful to him. That's why it ran away.'

'According to Paul?' said Jeremy.

Paul's mom seemed at a loss. 'I know. I know it sounds strange. That's why I tried to take the puppet away.'

'That, I suppose,' inferred Tiffany, 'is why we're here?'

Paul's mom didn't answer, but he could picture her nodding. He still smarted from the memory: he was just about to show Dum Dum his memory box when his mother finished talking on the phone and suddenly barged into his room.

'Dr. Balding says you'll have to get rid of that puppet,' she had said through clenched teeth. 'Right now!'

Paul had straightened up to defy her, but she strode in and grabbed Dum Dum by the neck. She didn't even seem to hear the dummy yelp or cry out in pain as Paul fought to grab him back from her. Then he bolted down the stairs with Dum Dum under his arm, running into the street and dashing through the traffic until he had reached this empty building.

Now he heard them conferring in a conspiratorial murmur below them. Paul's heart was beating fast as he and Dum Dum pressed their ears to the ceiling to hear what was being said.

'You have to send that puppet back somehow,' Jeremy stated with certainty.

'If I can't find the owner,' Paul's mother said, 'I might just have to throw the damn thing in the bin!'

Dum Dum's eyes glistened with terror as they listened to the grownups. Paul had to put a reassuring arm around him.

At last his mother spoke up in a loud voice. She said it to her companions but intended it for Paul's ears: 'He'll come out soon enough! When it's dark and they come to lock up this dump!'

'Did you hear that?' Dum Dum muttered at Paul's knee. His eyes looked big enough to light up the shadows around them. Paul held up his finger and counted to one hundred. Before he got to ninety, he heard the door downstairs slam shut.

'Let's go!' The inched forward on their stomachs until they reached the trapdoor.

With a creak, the trapdoor flew open and Paul poked his head out. The coast was clear. He lowered himself and swung from the edge of the opening before jumping onto the floor. A puff of dust rose up around him, making him cough. He was a frail-looking boy with curly chestnut brown hair. He looked up as another head poked out of the opening. Dum Dum looked around timidly before fixing his glance on Paul. 'Is it safe?'

'Yes! Come on down,' Paul held his arms out to catch him.

'Wait, wait,' said Dum Dum.

'What's the matter?'

'I think one of my strings is caught.'

Paul looked up as Dum Dum struggled to free himself. The dummy screwed up his eyes as if he was pondering a very deep question. Then at last he smiled,' 'There!'

He wriggled out of the opening and swung by his hands like Paul had. Then he leapt down a foot or two from Paul. He patted his knees and had a good look around. 'Nice. We can stay here all night if we have to.'

Paul shifted his weight from one leg to the other. 'We're not staying here. We have to go.'

'Go where?'

'Home.'

Dum Dum glared at Paul like he thought he was being really stupid. 'Didn't you hear what your mother said? She's either going to send me back to Marc or throw me in the trash!'

'I won't let her do that.'

'You know I can't go to Marc,' pleaded the dummy, his big eyes almost welling up with tears. 'It'd be awful. You might as well throw me out the window now.

'No! That'll never happen,' Paul patted the dummy on the shoulder. He walked to the window and looked out at the street below.

'What do you think we should do?' he said after a while.

Dum Dum walked over to join him at the window. 'We'll have to run away,' he replied.

'I don't want to miss school,' Paul objected.

'We can find another school where we're going!' argued Dum Dum.

'But how are we going to get money?'

'We'll find a way,' said Dum Dum. 'You could sit me on your knee and pretend you're making me talk.'

'Is that how your old owner used to make money?'

Dum Dum nodded with a big smile. 'When he wasn't gambling or boxing my ears.'

'I'd never box your ears,' vowed Paul.

'That settles it, then,' Dum Dum nodded. 'Let's go run away.'

Paul made no move to leave.

'What's wrong now?' Dum Dum pulled at his wrist.

'It's just the other thing my mother said,' Paul remarked.

'Which one?' Said Dum Dum. 'Your mother said *a lot* of things.'

'She said I'm probably just imagining you.'

Dum Dum took Paul's hands and pressed them against his chest. 'Feel me. You think I'm our imagination?'

'You feel real enough,' uttered Paul. It's not that.'

'Then what is it?' Dum Dum put his hands on his hips.

'She said I'm probably just imagining that you're talking to me. What if we run away and I can never go back to school? And in the end it turns out I was just talking to myself?'

Dum Dum glanced around the room with this big eyes for several moments.

'Well?' he said at length. 'Do I stu-stu-stutter?'

No,' admitted Paul.

'If my voice was just you talking to yourself , wouldn't I stutter, too?'

No,' sighed Paul. 'I guess you're right. Come to think of it, I don't stutter as much when I talk to you.'

'Well?' Dum Dum spread his hands to show he'd made his point. He was a rare dummy. He didn't have one of those weird frozen features that never changed. His face was incredibly alive. His lips were not the stiff line that went up and down like a duck's bill when he talked.

Paul had never seen such a real looking puppet. If not for the strings, Dum Dum really would have passed for a very small boy.

Paul looked at his watch. 'It'll be safe to go home now.'

'But what about your mother? Dum Dum held back.

'She'd have left for her second job by now,' Paul calmly told him. 'I just need to grab my bag and a few things.'

Wow! *He'd said that without a hitch. Eleven words in two clauses.* His mother was right. The dummy was good for him.

'Come on, then,' Paul gestured with his head and Dum Dum followed him out to the corridor. They hurried down the stairs. They walked for a block until they reached Paul's building. He kept looking around to check if people noticed Dum Dum trotting after him.

'What now?' Dum Dum said.

'Paul sidled up to him and spoke softly. 'Can other people see you?'

'Of course they can,' uttered Dum Dum.

'But can they hear you talk?'

'Most of them will think it's you talking through me,' Dum Dum replied. 'Some will be able to see I talk for myself.'

They reached the entrance to Paul's building. There was no one else around.

'But if you keep treating me like a real boy,'
Dum Dum continued, 'before long others will start doing the
same. It's all about what you believe.'

Paul chuckled. 'I can't believe I'm hearing this from a
puppet.'

'See?' smiled Dum Dum. 'That proves you're not the
one making me talk.'

An old lady came out the door and Paul saw their
chance. They darted inside before the door shut again. But
the lift was full, so Paul steered Dum Dum towards the
stairway. They climbed seven floors to reach Paul's flat.

Several minutes later, Dum Dum staggered out of the
stairwell after him. 'That's one thing I was never made to do,'
he struggled to catch his breath. 'I'm a sit down puppet!' he
cried in outrage. 'Didn't I tell you that? We were never meant
to climb stairs!'

'Quiet!' Paul murmured as he bent down to find the
key under the doormat. He found it and unlocked the door.
'Quick!' he shooed Dum Dum in and locked the door once
more.

They ran into the kitchen and looked in the
cupboards.

'You hungry?' asked Paul.

Dum Dum looked at him as if he didn't know what that meant.

'I'll bring some bread and cheese,' said Paul, laying out their supplies on the counter. 'You want some milk?'

Dum Dum shook his head.

Paul poured himself a glass and gulped it down.

'There is something I would like though,' Dum Dum said.

'What's that?'

The dummy leaned forward a little bit and said, 'This thing in my back is killing me. You have something that could break it off?'

Paul walked around to look at it. It was a large piece of wire sticking out of the dummy's back.

'Stay here,' he said and ran out. A few minutes later he came back with a pair of pliers. He braced himself against Dum Dum's shoulder while he cut off the wire.
'Ah!' Dum Dum turned his head around to smile at Paul. 'Thank you.'

'Does it hurt?' asked Paul.

'Don't worry,' Dum Dum answered. 'Nothing hurts me.'

'How'd it get there in the first place?' said Paul.

'That's how they used to roll my eyes and move my mouth,' said Dum Dum. 'Till I learned to do it all myself.'

'How did you learn to talk?' said Paul. 'And walk and move like a real boy?'

The puppet spread out his hands as if it were really obvious. 'I guess it was meant to be.'

Again, Paul was sure he didn't say those words. Even his mother didn't talk like that. Either the dummy was real or something really weird was going on. Paul patted himself on the stomach, on his arms and legs.

'You're trying to see if you're dreaming, aren't you?' Dum Dum asked him with a smile.

'How'd you know that?' said Paul.

'I've been wondering the same thing,' the puppet replied. 'If I'm dreaming you or you're dreaming me.'

Paul laughed again. He looked down on the floor and saw the wires he had just cut off from Dum Dum's back. There was no going back. Dum Dum couldn't go back to being a dummy again.

'Well?' Dum Dum leaned forward. 'Are we going or no?'

'We are! Give me one minute!'

Paul ran into his room to get his backpack. He scooped the food from the counter into it. Then he arranged them inside so he could easily get to his maps, the brochures, all the things he'd been gathering for months. Dum Dum walked towards him with a limp.

'Why are you limping?' asked Paul. 'Is it because I cut off your wires?'

'No,' Dum Dum waved his hand. 'I've always had this limp.'

'Okay,' said Paul and they went to the door. He suddenly stopped.

'What's the matter?' said Dum Dum.

'But what if I'm really just imagining you?' fretted Paul.

'So what if you *are*?' Dum Dum threw up his hands. 'It wouldn't be possible to live without imagining some things.'

Again, Paul shook his head. He was sure the words weren't his, so the puppet must be real.

'Let's go,' he said.

They walked to the train station.

'Where should we go?' Dum Dum asked.

'I don't know,' shrugged Paul. 'Cyprus, maybe.'

'Why Cyprus?'

'I think my dad is there.'

'Does he know we're coming?'

I haven't seen him in years,' answered Paul. 'But he wouldn't turn us away.'

When they got to the station Paul looked for the Departures Board. As they waited for the right train numbers to appear, Paul took out the brochures and maps he'd been collecting about Cyprus. He read the posters on the walls and suddenly exclaimed,

'Oh shoot! We can't get to Cyprus.'

'Why not?' said Dum Dum.

'The fare is thirty pounds.'

'How much money have you got?

Paul took all the money out of his pockets. 'I've got thirteen pounds forty six pennies.'

'You don't have any more?' said Dum Dum.

Paul shook his head, his empty pockets hanging on either side of him like the ears of a forlorn dog.

'We can go beg,' suggested Dum Dum. Some travellers walking by heard him and laughed.

'Don't talk so loud, will you?' admonished Paul.

'Why not?'

'People are looking.'

'So what?' argued Dum Dum.

'They'll think I'm batty. Talking to myself with my dummy.'

Dum Dum stomped his foot on the ground. 'I'm *not* your dummy!'

He crooked his finger and beckoned Paul to come closer.

'What?'

'The more you talk to me,' Dum Dum said seriously, 'the more others will. And soon they'll start treating me like a real boy.'

Paul nodded and they walked around. To his surprise, it seemed to work. He spoke to Dum Dum and treated him like a real person, and little by little, others did the same. The dummy was right. It really *was* a matter of what you believed.

'What are we looking for?' Dum Dum piped up after a while. 'I thought the trains to Cyprus were back there.'

'We have to go with a family,' Paul explained. 'We can just pretend to be with them and maybe we won't need to pay the fare.'

Paul stopped and listened to him for a moment. Now he was wondering if the dummy was making *him* talk. He'd never thought of doing such a thing before.

'There's a big family!' Dum Dum pointed. There was a ragged group of travellers waiting to board the carriage.

'Quick!' said Paul. 'Let's hide behind the older kids!'

A booming announcement rang over the speakers and reverberated around the cavernous station. It was followed by an even louder one, and Paul didn't hear the voice shouting.

'Oi! You, two! Come back here!'

The station guard was bearing down on them. Paul thought fast for an explanation.

'We were j-j-jju -jusst....'

16

He could barely get the words out. As soon as he addressed other people, the spell was broken, and he became the stuterrer again. *Stu-tu-tuterrer.* He couldn't even say the word in his mind.

'Hey you!' the ticket inspector was pointing at them. 'Where are your tickets?'

Jesus!' uttered Paul. One word. No stutter. Now he needed just another word. Starting with a T, or an S, or a P. T-t-t-t....top! St-to-to Stop! 'Dum Dum stop!'

Dum Dum was racing down the platform. Paul took off after him.

'Dum Dum, don't run!' Paul yelled again.

The station guard spun around to glare at him. 'Who you calling Dum Dum? Stop right there! I'm warning you!'

'No!' howled Paul once again and sprinted forward. Another station worker was just a few paces behind Dum Dum now. Paul surged forward faster than he'd ever run. He had no choice. He had to grab Dum Dum by the neck. He made it to the lockers before they corralled him with outstretched arms.

'Come now,' the oldest man put a hand on his shoulder. 'Let's take you to the office.'

Paul glanced around as they marched him up to the first floor. None of them seemed to notice that Paul's accomplice was missing. No one mentioned Dum Dum, and they seemed intent on dealing only with Paul. He let out a sigh of relief, hoping they wouldn't find Dum Dum.

They got to a small, untidy room with cluttered desks and several phones ringing endlessly. The old man sat down and picked up one phone. Paul was terrified he might call the police. But the man did something worse. He called Paul's mother.

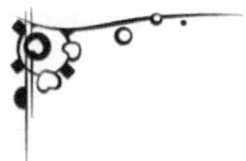

Chapter 2

A week after he came back, Paul got up and found his mum frying eggs.

'You've got a doctor's appointment on Friday,' she said.

'What for?' whined Paul.

'You know very well what for!' his mother slammed the pan on the table.

'But I don't sleepwalk anymore,' groaned Paul.

'You might,' said his mum. 'That's why you have to go on seeing him.'

Paul was going to argue some more, but his mother abruptly sat down. 'You know what the social worker said while you were off trying to stow away somewhere?'

'What?'

'She told me how kids like you can end up in an institution.'

'There's nothing wrong with me!' yelled Paul.

'Then show me a normal kid who runs away with a puppet!' his mother taunted. 'Show me a healthy boy who'd rather spend days talking to himself in his room than go out and play with other children!'

'I don't sit in my room and talk to myself!' Paul asserted.

His mum held her thumb and forefinger an inch apart. 'I was this close to saying *maybe* about the institution. Push me some more and it'll be a yes!'

`Paul hung his head and muttered, 'Okay.'

They finished their breakfast in silence.

At length, his mum pushed back her chair and got up. "All right then. Now we can all go back to normal. You go back to school and I go back to my job.'

She went out the front door, leaving Paul in the kitchen thinking about it. He knew nothing had changed, but the flat felt emptier than before. Something was missing. The thought of going back to normal was *awful*. There was no way he could face that. He had to go find Dum Dum!

As soon as he had left school, he sneaked back into the train station. When he got to the lockers, he waited until the old man with the mop had left the room before he went in. Then he got behind the first group of lockers and reached under the bottom. His hand found a little shoe, then the leg wriggled and he pulled Dum Dum out.

'Where've you been?' Dum Dum sputtered, brushing off the dust and fur from his face. 'Some kids found me and tried to pull me apart! Thank God that old man saved me.'

'That's good of him,' said Paul.

'He said his grandson had always wanted to be a ventriloquist,' replied Dum Dum. 'So he tried to take me home.'

'Then what happened?' asked Paul.

'I had to jump out of his bag and hide under the bus seat to get away.'

'Why? Paul asked. 'You might have been better off with his grandson. At least I'm sure his mum wouldn't have kept telling him to get rid of you.'

'He wanted to be a ventriloquist,' protested Dum Dum. 'He would have kept trying to make me talk.'

'But you are a ventriloquist dummy,' pointed out Paul. 'That's what ventriloquist's dummies are for, so people can make them talk.'

'I hate being made to talk!' spat out Dum Dum. 'I've got my own voice!'

Paul put his hand over his own mouth.

'What on earth are you doing?' Dum Dum tilted his head.

'I want to make sure I'm not the one saying all these things.'

Dum Dum threw his head back with a laugh. 'Ha! As if you could say things so well!'

Dum Dum made an almost Shakespearean gesture. 'I'm so weary of people making me talk. With their meagre vocabularies and their hackneyed emotions. As Shakespeare said, *We know what we are, but not what we may be.* Who knows what I could be if people just stop trying to make me some silly character they imagine?'

He puffed himself up and spread out his hands, as though he were addressing a full auditorium. 'I'm me, the once and future Dum Dum! My old owner used to dress me up as a girl and make me sing *My Heart Belongs to Daddy* and awful stuff like that. Yuck!'

Paul took his hand away from his lips. Now he was sure he wasn't just imagining Dum Dum's voice. He'd never seen a dummy that quoted Shakespeare before. Or move without wires, or look at him with such intense eyes.

'So is that why you want to come home with me?' Paul asked.

'Yea!' Dum Dum nodded. 'I know you're not interested in making me talk. You've got enough trouble making yourself talk.'

Paul smiled. 'That's true.'

'All right,' Paul decided. 'I *will* take you home again. But remember. You stay out of sight! My mum gets an inkling you're back, it's curtains for Shakespeare.'

Dum Dum blinked his eyes and nodded.

They walked the two blocks to Paul's home. When they got to Paul's room, Dum Dum exhaled, 'Ah. It's nice to be home!'

'For good this time,' said Paul. 'I hope.'

'Now where were we?' Dum Dum looked around. 'Before we got so rudely interrupted?'

Paul bit his lip and tried to recall 'Oh yeah! I was showing you my memory box.'

'That's right!'

Paul opened the closet and looked for the chest. He grabbed it and lay it down in front of Dum Dum.

'You showed me that, that, and that,' Dum Dum pointed to the various items in the box. 'But you never told me who that boy is.'

He was holding up a picture.

'That's me and Daniel,' Paul said. 'My best friend in first grade. My best friend *ever*.'

'Are you still friends?' Dum Dum quizzed.

For the first time, Paul had difficulty answering Dum Dum. 'He-h-he h-ha-had to go away.'

Paul had to look away from the picture when he said that.

'Did something happen?' Dum Dum said softly.

'He he he was sick,' Paul managed to say.

Dum Dum leaned forward to peek at Paul. 'You miss him a lot, don't you?'

Paul nodded, but couldn't speak.

'How do you know?' he said when he had recovered.

Dum Dum gave him a knowing smile. 'Dummies know what you're thinking before you even say it.'

Dum Dum took the picture and looked at it closely. 'He has big eyes,' he observed.

'Yes,' smiled Paul. 'He's a bit like you really.'

Dum Dum put the picture back in the container. 'I'll take that as a compliment.'

Paul felt sad as Dum Dum rummaged among the mementoes.

He looked up to see Dum Dum holding a book. 'What's that?'

'It's a book of nursery rhymes,' Paul revealed. He took it and fingered the gilt edge of the cover lovingly. 'Daniel gave it to me.'

'Read me one,' asked Dum Dum.

Paul read one of his favourites out loud:

A Friday night's dream on a Saturday told

Is sure to come true be it ever so old.

Dum Dum looked charmed.

'I like reading it to myself sometimes,' Paul remarked. 'It's like having Daniel here with me again.'

Dum Dum flipped to another page. 'What's that one say?'

Paul read it out loud in turn:

When I was a little boy my mammy kept me in

But now I am a great boy

I'm fit to serve the king;

I can hand a musket

And I can smoke a pipe,

And I can kiss a pretty girl

At twelve o'clock at night.

'What's a musket?' Dum Dum asked.

'It's a kind of gun they used in the old days,' explained Paul.

'Have you smoked a pipe?' Dum Dum posed further.

Paul shook his head. 'No. Why would I want to?'

'But you're a big boy now,' Dum Dum remarked.

'Not quite a great boy yet,' said Paul. 'Like it says in the rhyme.'

Dum Dum got on the swivel chair and spun himself around. 'Wheeeeeeeee!'

By the time he stopped spinning his eyes were rolling around in his head. 'I like your room,' he said with a dizzy smile.

'It's our room now,' Paul declared, putting the memory box away.

'Should I sleep in the closet tonight?' Dum Dum asked.

'Why would you want to sleep in a closet?'

'I thought you wanted me to keep out of sight, Dum Dum said. 'Besides. I've always slept in closets.'

'My mum won't be coming to my room all the time,' Paul said. 'And if you're going to become a real little boy, you better get used to sleeping on a bed rather than in a closet.'

An hour or so later they heard the front door opening. Paul turned off the light and pretended to be asleep. 'Mum's home,' he Paul whispered. 'You have to be quiet, ok?'

They talked in whispers as Paul's mum moved around and got ready for bed. But Paul was too excited to sleep. In the dark, he asked Dum Dum, 'So why did you really run away?'

'Marc would throw me against the wall sometimes when he lost money at cards,' Dum Dum answered. 'And once when I

26

said he was nothing but a drunk, he said he was going to sell me to a carpenter for parts.'

Paul heard his mother moving around in the next room. He held a finger to his lips.

'That's the worst thing for a puppet,' Dum Dum continued in a whisper. 'They'd take you apart to repair other dummies. You'd be scattered in hundreds of different places. And no one could ever put you back together again.'

Paul's mum pounded on the wall. She said, 'It's late. Who're you talking to? Go to sleep.'

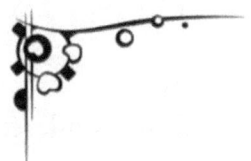

Chapter 3

What had seemed strange at first seemed so natural now. Paul came home from school every day and took Dum Dum for a walk.

'People don't even stare at us anymore,' said Paul.

'See? I told you,' Dum Dum smiled at him. 'You just have to believe.'

Why did they call you Dum Dum?' Paul asked one day.

Dum Dum turned his round friendly face with a grin. 'My owner wasn't very smart. He called me the first thing he could think of. Besides, it made people laugh to hear him calling me Dum Dum.'

'What did you call him?' Paul wanted to know.

'Oh, lots of names children aren't supposed to hear,' said the puppet. 'But his real name was Marc. Marc Gascoigne.'

'Did he buy you in Blackpool?' Paul asked.

'I have no idea how he got me. Either he stole me or won me at cards.'

'Did Marc win much at cards?' Paul wondered.

'No,' shrugged Dum Dum. 'He loved it too much to keep anything he won. Once he lost so much money he pawned me.'

'What was that like?'

'I was lucky the pawnbroker knew me from the pub. He locked me in the store room with some of his best stuff.'

'That must have been awful.'

'Not really. I got a chance to talk to some old watches and a few antique clocks. The music boxes entertained us all night, putting on all their best pieces until we fell asleep. And there were some pretty cute dolls on the same shelf as me.'

'Were they nice?'

'Nice to look at,' said Dum Dum. 'But not much to talk to. They were the ceramic ones with their lips sealed shut. They just sat there staring into space as if the rest of us weren't there. It was spooky.'

'Didn't anyone try to buy you?'

'A little girl and her brother asked to try me out. The didn't know how to make me talk so I said a few words to them.'

'What happened?'

'The girl squealed with delight,' chuckled Dum Dum. '"It works! It works!" she shouted, jumping all over the place. "I made him talk!" She put her arms around me and it felt so good. I wished they would buy me.'

'Why didn't they?'

'When the pawnbroker saw how much the kids wanted me, he asked for the highest price he could get. I knew how much he had given Marc for me, so I knew he was just being greedy.'

'Then?'

'Then I said, to the kids' mother, "He only paid eight quid for me. You can have me for twelve or fifteen.'

'What did the mother say?' asked Paul.

'The pawnbroker intervened. He said, '"Don't listen to him. He's just a dummy."'

'So the kids went away?'

Dum Dum nodded sadly. 'They were both in tears,' he said. 'I wished I could run out and join them.'

They sat for several moments without talking. Then Dum Dum took something out of his pocket and held it out to Paul. 'This is the map one of the puppets gave me.'

'Which puppets?' asked Paul.

'The ones at the pawnshop.'

Paul unfolded the piece of paper. It looked faded and hard to read. 'What's it for?'

'That shows the entire V-X-V Line,' Dum Dum told him.

'What's the V-X-V Line?'

'The Vierris-Xircupolis – Valta Line,' Dum Dum replied. 'That's the route puppets take for the Carnival.'

'What carnival?'

'The famous Valta Carnival, you dope.'

'I've never heard of a Valta Carnival,' Paul scratched his head. 'Or any place called Valta for that matter.'

Well, you're not a puppet, are you?' said Dum Dum. 'Though you *are* a bit of a dummy.'

'But how is this map going to help us?' uttered Paul. The chart hovered between being very vivid to being just a ghostly image, depending on how he held the paper.

'It's one way for us to run away where they'll never find us,' Dum Dum smiled.

Paul took another look at the creased sheet in his hand. Now he wasn't sure this adventure was taking him where he wanted to go. 'I'm not sure I'm ready to go somewhere and never come back,' he said.

'Don't worry,' Dum Dum patted his arm. I'll be with you.'

They walked until they reached the park and sat on a bench. Paul looked at passers-by quietly for a long time. Daniel came to his mind again. They used to talk for hours about adventures they were going to have. But then Daniel went away, and Paul thought he would never go on any quests.

But now Dum Dum was here. Could they do all those things he never got to do with Daniel? Where would it take them?

Dum Dum intruded into this thoughts 'What are you racking your brains about?'

Paul looked at Dum Dum's map again. 'You think that map can really take us somewhere?

'Of course,' Dum Dum nodded.

'What if it's not real? What if Valta doesn't exist?'

'It better do,' Dum Dum said. 'Last I heard that's where Ginger was going.'

'Who's Ginger?' asked Paul.

'She was this puppet I met on the way to a show once. We were in the luggage compartment together. My, she was very pretty. We stretched out on the suitcases and boxes, and she cheered me up with her songs. She knew all the words to *Zing Went the Strings of my Heart*. And it's true. She really did make my strings go Zing!'

Dum Dum hummed and then sang the first verse of a song:

> *Dear when you smiled at me, I heard a melody*
> *It haunted me from the start.*
> *Something inside of me started a symphony*

Zing! Went the strings of my heart.

She looked like she glowed in the dark,' Dum Dum recalled wistfully. 'Her skin was like ivory.'

'Where is she now?'

'Somewhere between here and Valta, I guess.'

'You don't know where exactly?'

Dum Dum hung his head sadly. 'No.'

They carried on walking. After a while, Dum Dum remarked,

'She had a mean owner, too. And we talked about running away together.'

'Why didn't you?'

'We almost did!' moaned Dum Dum.

'What do you mean almost?'

'Well, our bus stopped at a gas station,' Dum Dum recounted. 'It was taking so long I had time to work the latch loose. I jumped out and waited for Ginger. She ran towards me and suddenly stopped.'

'Why?'

'She forgot her ostrich feather dress. She said she couldn't go anywhere without it.'

'So?'

'So she ran back in the compartment and searched through the bags. By the time she found it her owner was back from the coffee shop.'

'What did she do?'

'She chased Ginger around until she caught her.'
Dum Dum put on a woman's voice. "What you doing out of
the sack, you little tart!"

Dum Dum continued with his own voice, 'Then she
grabbed Ginger by the neck and threw her back into the
compartment.'

Paul noticed a little glint in Dum Dum's eyes.

They ambled to a square and sat down on a bench.

'I told Marc about Ginger,' Dum Dum revealed.

'What did he say?'

'He just laughed. He said dummies can't run away
together.'

'But you did!' said Paul. 'You escaped.'

'He didn't believe it at the time.'

'You think he believes it now?'

'I hope he does,' Dum Dum spread out his hands.
'Cause I'm here, aren't I?'

'Yes,' Paul put his arm around him, while Dum Dum
looked around greedily with those big eyes of his.

After a while he added glumly, 'Ginger's not with me,
though.'

'No, ' said Paul. 'But she can be.'

'Yes. I can go find her,' Dum Dum smiled. 'I can do
anything now. I'm free!'

36

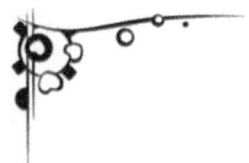

Chapter 4

Mr. Carver was in the middle of doing fractions when Paul turned towards the window. He saw Dum Dum on the ledge outside, staring at him. Paul gestured frantically for him to get out of there. But Dum Dum seemed fascinated by everything that was going on in the classroom. He shook his head at Paul, crossed his arms and pouted. Finally, after the most ferocious scowl Paul could muster, Dum Dum gave in. He climbed down and disappeared.

Paul turned his attention back to the math teacher. But out of the corner of his eye he could still see Dum Dum's head bobbing up at one window then another, his eyes wide with curiosity. Paul gestured even more wildly for Dum Dum to stop. He made a walking motion with his hand and mimed the act of going in the closet, closing the door and going to sleep.

But Mr. Carver suddenly stopped in mid sentence and said, 'Paul. Is something bothering you?'

Paul put his hands under the desk. 'No, Mr. Carver. I was just…'

But some of the other kids had already caught a glimpse of Dum Dum. Paul's friend Charlie turned and let out a whistle. Everyone became excited.

'Paul, I'm warning you,' said Mr. Carver. 'This is important. We're going to have a test on Friday.'

He went back to the board and resumed talking about nominators and denominators.

Dum Dum suddenly stuck his head outside the corner window. Paul blurted out, 'Go away! I'm tired of you!'

Mr. Carver stopped writing on the board and turned around slowly. 'I beg your pardon?'

Paul tried to explain. But Mr. Carver had already opened the door. 'Right, that's it. You're getting too disruptive. Off with you. Go sit in Mr. Scottsdale's office. That'll teach you to shout and carry on!'

Paul got up to go. He stole one last glance at the window. Dum Dum was gone.

Hours later, Paul came out after everyone in his class had gone home. He walked sadly towards the street corner. He heard someone running up from behind him.

'What took you so long?' he heard Dum Dum say.

'I could have been out hours ago, ' Paul told him. 'No thanks to you.'

'Where were you?' demanded Dum Dum.

'I was in detention.'

'What's that?'

'That's where they send you if you've been disobedient.'

'Why?'

'That's what it means to be a real boy,' Paul tried to enlighten him. 'Most of the time you just do what you're told. If they tell you to do sums you do sums. If they tell you to shut up you shut up.'

'What if you don't want to?' challenged Dum Dum.

'You're not supposed to do what you want when you're a kid,' said Paul. 'You should get used to being told you're wrong all the time. If people yell at you, you keep quiet. You let them think they know everything and you don't.'

'That sounds terribly dull,' said Dum Dum.

'I know,' agreed Paul. 'That's why I need a friend like you.'

He watched as Dum Dum limped along beside him.
'Say, how *did* you get that limp?'

'Once Marc was hiding from people he owed money
to,' explained Dum Dum. 'They came to the house to collect.'

'What happened?'

'They couldn't find any money, but they found me in
one of the drawers. *Eureka!* one of them said.'

'What did they do?'

'One of them threw me out the window. Then the
other caught me and whirled me around like a lasso. Then
they stomped on my legs, set me on fire and threw me down
an abandoned mine shaft.'

'How did you get out?' asked Paul.

'Marc came and fished me out,' said Dum Dum.
'Cleaned me up just in time for the show at the pub.'

'Was that all he did?' said Paul.

'Oh, he tried to fix my leg as best he could. Then he
was nice to me for a few days, and soon he was back to being
his nasty old self.'

Paul stopped to look at him with a horrified face. 'I'm glad you
ran away from him.'

Dum Dum looked around happily. 'So am I.'

It started to get dark and they headed home.

'I know someone who might be able to do something about your limp,' mentioned Paul.

'Who's that?'

'My uncle Matthew is a carpenter,' answered Paul. 'He's worked in theatres and stuff. He might be able to fix you.'

When they got home, Paul's, mum was still out. They went into the kitchen.

'You sure you're not hungry?' said Paul. Dum Dum shook his head.

'Because I am,' said Paul, taking out some bread and making himself a sandwich. As he ate they heard something hit the window softly from outside. Paul got up and looked out.

'Oh great!' he put down his sandwich and took some paper out of the cupboard. He wrote something quickly and held it up.

'What are you doing?' inquired Dum Dum.

'That's Sayna,' Paul replied. 'She lives upstairs. We talk to each other with signs.'

Dum Dum stood next to him. He saw the girl holding up a piece of paper at the window above them. Paul put his arm around Dum Dum. He scribbled another sign and held it up: 'Meet my friend Dum Dum."

The girl upstairs looked delighted. She held up a sign that said, 'Come up and see me."

Paul and Dum Dum hurried out and ran upstairs. When they got there Paul rang the bell. A tall man with dreadlocks opened the door.

'What is it?' he said.

'Where's Sayna?' Paul tried to see around the door.

'Who?'

'The girl at the window,' Paul explained. 'We talk to each other with signs.'

'There's no girl up here,' said the man. 'Never has been.'

Paul grabbed Dum Dum by the wrist and they ran home.

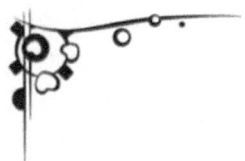

Chapter 5

It wasn't long before they wound up in another train station. Paul wanted Dum Dum to share his love of trains. It was the thing he and Daniel had loved doing the most together. But as soon as Dum Dum saw the carriages, he hid behind Paul.

'That old man with the mop is going to take me!'

'This is a different station, silly. No one knows us here.'

They spent hours walking around and watching people. They even made some friends. One was a big beefy boy named Cy, who had dark curly hair, and eyes that seemed to look in different directions.

With him was a much smaller boy called Luke, with bright red hair and a scar over his left eyebrow. They didn't seem to treat Dum Dum any different to any other boy. Paul was amazed at how Dum Dum's magic was working.

Cy narrowed his eyes to size him up. 'Want to play a game?'

'What's that?' piped up Dum Dum.

'A game, well,' Cy looked at Paul. 'Is he slow or something?'

'No he's not,' answered Paul. 'His parents were just...er very strict. They never let him play with other kids.'

'Shame,' said Cy. 'It would have been much more fun if he *was* slow.'

Paul seldom stuttered when it came to defending Dum Dum. 'He's just a little, uh, different.'

'He looks ok for a retard,' put in Luke.

'He's not a retard!' snapped Paul.

'Well, he's something,' said Luke as he and Cy walked away. 'I don't know what it is. But it's something.'

When they were gone Dum Dum turned to Paul with a smile. 'They had no idea I'm not a real little boy.'

'They had no idea I normally stutter,' answered Paul.

A week later they saw Cy and Luke again. 'Wanna play 'Hunt the Thimble?' Luke suggested. Paul and Dum Dum nodded their heads.

Cy took a gleaming cigarette lighter out of his pocket. 'Now you two cover your eyes while I find somewhere to hide this.'

He looked around for a suitable location. At length he decided to go behind the notice board. He was bending down to reach behind the pillar when he caught Dum Dum peeking. 'Hey!'

'Tell him he's not supposed to look!' he turned angrily to Paul.

Paul made amends for Dum Dum. 'He didn't know.'

'He don't know Hunt the friggin thimble?' yelled Cy. 'What planet's he from then?"

'He's...he's not from around here.'

The two ruffians exchanged glances. Luke whispered something into Cy's ear, and they snickered secretly, throwing sly glances at Dum Dum.

Dum Dum became intrigued and came closer.

'Hey, listen,' whispered Cy. 'You want to play tag?'

Dum Dum wasn't sure what it was, but he nodded.

'Come on then,' gestured Cy and started to run away. Luke followed suit. Dum Dum took off after them.

'Dum Dum, stop!' Paul cried out. But it was too late. The three of them quickly disappeared into the crowds.

Paul walked around worriedly, going up the escalator and looking behind columns. He even searched under the benches for a sign of Dum Dum. He shouted at the top of his lungs, 'Dum Dum!'

People turned around and gave him strange looks.

He had gone around the station dozens of times before he finally caught sight of him. Dum Dum was barrelling across the station hall. At his heels was an old woman, shouting, 'Stop! Thief! Help! Police!'

The next thing he knew there was a shrill whistle and Paul saw two fat policemen racing after Dum Dum. Paul bolted down towards them. There was a thick milling throng near the booths and Paul got a chance to grab Dum Dum, while the old lady and the policemen thundered past them. They ducked behind a vending machine.

'What happened?' Paul hissed.

'I was chasing Luke and Cy, ' accounted Dum Dum. 'Then they bumped into an old lady and made her spill her bags.'

'Then what happened?'

'While Cy was helping her up, Luke handed me a yellow purse and said, 'Tag!'

Paul shook his head. 'But why did you run away?'

'Because I wanted to tag one of them back.'

Paul clucked his tongue and shook his head. 'Next time, you play only with kids you know.'

'But I don't know anyone else but you!'

From that moment on Paul tried to steer clear of the two ruffians. But it wasn't easy. No matter how they tried, Luke or Cy always found them. One day they were standing near the entrance when Cy stuck his head out and said, 'Want to play Knock Knock Ginger?'

'I'd love to!' said Dum Dum.

'No, Dum Dum,' Paul tried to pull him away. 'Not today.'

'Aw don't be such a party pooper,' said Luke. 'The fella wants to play.'

'He doesn't know the game,' Paul told him.

'Yes I do,' insisted Dum Dum. 'I love anything to do with Ginger!'

'See?' said Cy. 'The kid wants to play. You're not his muvver. Let 'im do what 'e wants!'

Dum Dum wriggled out of Paul's grasp and joined the pair.

'We'll play a different version, okay?' explained Cy in a whisper. 'See that red thing on the wall?' he pointed to the fire alarm. 'you break the glass and pull it down. Then everyone will go running out screaming.'

Dum Dum nodded and walked towards the wall. When Paul saw what he was doing, he dashed towards him.

But by the time he reached him the deafening fire alarm was already pealing all over the station. The throngs surged all around them, shrieking, 'Fire ! Fire! Get out! Everybody out!'

Paul and Dum Dum were swept along to the street outside. They stood around until somebody realized it was all a false alarm. Fire trucks heading for the station stopped and turned around. People finally started trickling back into the building. They met Luke and Cy coming out with boxes of cupcakes and abandoned packages from the deserted platforms. Luke grinned at Dum Dum, "See? Isn't that a great game?'

One day Paul made up an excuse not to go to the station. They went to the docks instead. Paul showed Dum Dum the fishing boats and vats of fish in the warehouse. 'Aren't you supposed to be in school today?' asked Dum Dum.

'I'll give it a miss,' said Paul. 'It's too boring.'

'But I thought school was important for little boys,' said Dum Dum.

'It is,' admitted Paul. 'But other things are more important.'

'Like what?'

'Like watching trains,' answered Paul. 'And watching people.'

'Why did your mum say you have to see the doctor?' quizzed Dum Dum.

'That's another part of being a real boy,' Paul informed him. 'Seeing doctors, dentists, getting flu shots.'

'Would I have to see doctors if I became a real boy?' Dum Dum said.

'Only if you sleepwalk.'

'What's that?'

'I used to walk in my sleep,' Paul explained. 'But I'm cured now.'

Dum Dum gave him a probing look. 'Do you think you'll do it again?'

'I hope not.'

On the way home they walked past the station. Paul saw Cy waving to them, but he ignored him.

'Come on, let's go in,' Dum Dum stopped walking.' It's going to be fun.'

Paul gave in.

A train had just come in. It let air out of its vents, producing a loud hiss that carried across the distance.

'We just came in on that train,' Luke said.

'From where?' asked Paul.

'Brighton.'

'How?' Dum Dum hopped excitedly towards Cy.

Cy gave a toss of his head. 'Come on. We'll show you.'

They looked for a spot away from the gates and climbed down onto the tracks. They were invisible to anyone on ground level, and walked right up to the parked train. Luke and Cy showed them all the handholds, the spaces between carriages where a kid could hide. Luke lifted himself onto the ledge next to the coupling and said, 'you could sit here and the conductor would never see you.'

"You think I can do it, too?' Dum Dum wanted to know.

'Of course,' said Cy. 'The smaller you are the better. But you have to keep your hands warm.'

'Why?'

'Otherwise, you won't be able to hold on and you'll fall.'

They crawled between the wheels and moved to the restaurant carriage. Luke crawled into a little space above the sleepers.

'This is the best spot,' he said.

'Why?'

'It's right under the stove. So it's warm. And you can slip your hand in and grab yourself a piece of ham.'

They walked over to the other end of the tracks. Luke took out a pack of cigarettes. 'You won't believe the things people leave behind on their seats.'

He lit a cigarette and let out several puffs. He held it out to Dum Dum.

Dum Dum took it and sucked on the tip like he saw Luke doing. He watched the smoke curl out of his mouth and beamed, 'I like that!'

Cy kicked at the pebbles on the ground around him, spitting here and there. He slapped the dust off his trousers and said, 'Well, be seein' ya.'

Paul and Dum Dum climbed back onto the platform and headed home.

When they got to their street Dum Dum started spitting.

"What you doin'?' asked Paul.

'I'm doing like Luke and Cy,' answered Dum Dum.

'You don't have to do that!' scolded Paul. 'You don't have to act like them to be a real boy.'

When they got to Paul's room, Dum Dum took out the remnants of the cigarette packet.

'Where'd you get that?' demanded Paul.

'Luke gave it to me.'

'Get rid of it!' Paul ordered.

'No!' resisted Dum Dum. 'I like it. A real boy can smoke if he wants to!'

A week later they bumped into the pair again. 'Fancy a game of Jingles then?' Cy suggested.

Paul couldn't stop Dum Dum from agreeing.

'Hey, let's ask that kid to join,' said Luke, nodding towards a boy standing by himself at a bus stop.

They walked over to him, and Cy did his best to entice the boy.

'You bounce your coin off the wall, see?' Paul heard him saying. 'If yours lands closer to the wall you win.'

'Okay!'

They all give it a try, landing their coins a few inches from the wall.

'Here,' coaxed Cy. 'Why don't you use a pound coin? It's heavier and you're more likely to win.'

The boy searched in his pocket. His eyes lit up and he held up a pound coin. They took their positions and started slamming their change against the wall. It tinkled and scattered in every direction. Cy got on all fours to scoop them up, then gave them back to everyone.

'Ready?' he said, preparing to hurl at the wall again.

But the boy suddenly stopped to look at his hand. 'Hey! Where's my coin?'

'I gave it back to you!' Cy said with complete innocence.

'No, you didn't!' shouted the boy. 'I gave you my pound! You gage me back 20p!'

Cy got down on the ground again to look. 'Must be here somewhere...'

'Give me back my pound!' wailed the boy as he burst into tears. Just then his father came out of a shop and bellowed at him. 'Oi! What you carryin' on about?'

'They took my money!' the boy pointed at Luke and Cy. The two bolted down the street in the blink of an eye. The angry father turned towards Paul and Dum Dum, who took off after the two hooligans.

When they came back to the corner, the boy and his father were long gone. Dum Dum bent down to hunt under the seat of the bus stop.

'There it is!' cried out, holding up the pound coin. He looked from side to side. 'Where's that kid? We should give it back to him.'

'Put it away,' Paul said softly.

'Why?'

'We might need it. In case I have to hide you in one of the station lockers again.'

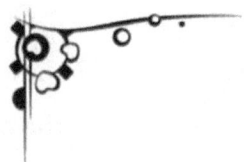

Chapter 6

Through Paul and the two roughnecks, Dum Dum came to understand the importance of money.

'You need money for everything,' Paul avowed.

Dum Dum scratched his head. 'But how do you get some?'

'You have to have a mummy and a daddy,' said Paul.

'But I don't have a mummy or daddy,' Dum Dum lamented. 'There was only Marc. And he never let me touch his money.'

'Don't worry about that,' said Paul. 'I'll think of something.'

They both pondered for a moment, then Dum Dum blurted out, 'I know how!'

'How?'

'You have to learn to play cards.'

'Why?'

'That's how Marc used to do it. He'd scoop up handfuls of money from the table, and people just let him.'

At first Paul wouldn't hear of it, but Dum Dum told him a story. 'Marc never used to play cards without me,' he recounted. 'He'd leave me in the corner, behind the other players. If the dealer had a Queen, I'd blink once with my left eye.'

'And if he had a king?'

'I'd give two blinks on the right.'

'What if he had an ace?'

'Two blinks with both eyes.'

Paul was intrigued. 'Did it work?'

'Most times. But one night one of the other players caught me.'

'What did he do?'

'He grabbed me and tried to throw me in the fireplace.'

'What did the others do?'

Dum Dum chuckled. 'They just laughed at him. Said that he was just imagining it. That he was just sore for losing so much.'

So Paul let Dum Dum teach him a few tricks at cards. In addition to poker and Black Jack, Dum Dum demonstrated remarkable expertise in dice, horse racing, and other forms of wagering.

But Paul also had a few things to teach Dum Dum. He coached him on football, trains, airplanes and other important branches of knowledge. They went to a toy shop and Paul named all the model locomotives in the window, quoting their freight capacity and top speeds.

'Where'd you learn all that?' Dum Dum asked.

'From my dad. He knew all about trains.'

'Your dad?' Dum Dum smiled. 'You mean your owner?'

'No. I mean my father. He and my mum had me. But they're not my owners.'

As they walked away from the shop Dum Dum asked, 'What's it like to have a mum and dad?'

'I don't really know,' Paul replied.

Dum Dum walked quietly beside him for a while, watching everything with his big eyes.

'There's really just my mum and me,' Paul remarked at length.

'Does she spend much time with you?'

'No. She's busy most of the time. She leaves the house early and I'm asleep by the time she gets home. So usually I'm just by myself. But now I have you.'

He put his arm around Dum Dum and they went inside.

As they were going up in the lift Dum Dum let out a contented sigh, 'I've had a great day.'

'Good. Which part did you like best?'

'The fact that nobody realized I'm not a real boy.'

Paul agreed. 'You're doing a really good job. Soon no one would ever know you were once a dummy. But there's still work to do.'

Paul unlocked the door and they ran to the kitchen. Paul poured two glasses of milk and offered one to Dum Dum.

Dum Dum looked confused. 'What's that for?'

'Part of being a real boy is eating food and drinking milk,' Paul explained. He looked inside a pot and spooned out some broccoli left over from the night before.

Dum Dum forked a floret into his mouth. He immediately spat it out. 'Yuck! That's horrible!'

'Now you're acting like a real kid,' chuckled Paul. 'One of the hardest things about being a real boy is eating vegetables.'

Paul washed the saucer and put it in the rack. 'And there's another thing.'

'What's that?' Dum Dum turned to look at him.

' You need to go to the bathroom once in a while.'

The next several weeks were filled with lessons of that kind. Paul took Dum Dum to different places and showed him how to act like a real boy.

One day they came home to find Sayna waiting for them at her window. When she saw Paul she held up a sign, 'Where you been?'

Paul scribbled out numerous signs in reply until he ran out of paper. Dum Dum tried writing his own signs. But his spelling and handwriting were atrocious.

'*Yu want to kam daun end pley?*' said one sign.

Sayna held up her response: 'What language you speaking?'

'I thought she could read English,' Dum Dum complained to Paul.

'She can,' said Paul, 'But...'
They sat down at the table and Paul tried to correct Dum Dum's spelling. Then he showed him how to make his letters more legible. It was all too much for Dum Dum.

'See?' Paul put down the pencil finally. 'We still have some way to go.'

Paul's mother came home early that day and she saw the paper scattered all over the kitchen. She picked up each one and read. *Ar Yo bai yursilf?*

Ar yu hangry?

Yu wont sam melk?

She called Paul and he came out of his room.

'What do you mean wasting paper like this?' she shook the clutch of signs in his face. 'And what kind of spelling is that?' her voice started to rise. 'Haven't you learned anything in school? That's worse than a second grader's!'

Paul tried to explain, but he didn't want to mention Dum Dum.

'I thought you were getting better!' his mum continued her rebuke, 'I've already hired tutors and asked all your teachers for extra help!'

Paul went back to his room. He stayed there until his mum called out, 'Well? Are you coming for dinner or not?'

Paul stuck his head out the door. 'I'm not hungry yet. Can I eat later?'

Paul went back and sat at hhis desk. Dum Dum chimed from behind him, in the exact same voice as Paul's mother, but in a much sweeter tone, 'Okay, if you have to, sweetheart!'

Paul spun around. 'How'd you do that?'

'I've always been good with voices,' smirked Dum Dum. 'It's easy if you have different voices go through you all the time,'

Paul beamed, 'I like that.'

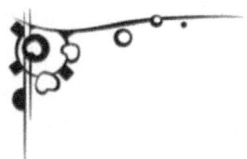

Chapter 7

The more Dum Dum learned to be like a real boy, the more Paul worried about his limp. One day he asked his mother, 'Does Uncle Matthew still live in the same place?'

'I suppose so,' said his mum. 'Why?'

'I might go see him.'

'What for?'

'I haven't seen him in a while,' replied Paul.

'You'll be lucky if you find him,' said his mum. 'He'll either be in jail or out drunk with one of his crummy girlfriends.'

After supper, Paul went back to his room to play with Dum Dum. They were shuffling cards when they heard someone knock on the front door.

Paul's mum answered and they heard a man's voice. Dum Dum suddenly froze.

'I'd know that voice anywhere,' he whispered.

They listened to the man Paul's mum was talking to, and Dum Dum murmured, 'It's Marc! He's found me!'

Paul opened their door a crack to see what was going on. He saw Marc standing in the hallway outside, flanked by two large men.

'I don't know what puppet you're talking about,' Paul's mum was saying.

'Listen lady,' Marc's voice began to rise. 'I know my property's been stolen. And I've been told that he's here!'

'There's no one here but me and my son,' insisted Paul's mum. 'And neither of us have stolen anything. Now get out or I'll call the police!'

'I'll go for now, lady,' hissed Marc, retreating. 'But you'll see me again!'

Paul's mum slammed the door.

In Paul's room Dum Dum leaned weakly against the wall. His jaw started to rattle. 'What're we going to do?' he put his hands on his head. 'We might have to run away. Will you come with me?'

Paul locked his door. A few moments later, Paul's mum rapped on it. 'You in there? Come out. I need to talk to you.'

'I'm sleeping!' Paul lied.

'Sleeping?' his mother answered. 'Ha! At this hour? Come on! Open up!'

They heard the key turning in the lock. Dum Dum switched off the light and pulled Paul towards the closet. 'Come on, help me with this!' he said.

They moved the mirror and created some space behind it. They both squeezed in just before Paul's mum burst in. She turned on the light and looked around. 'Paul? Paul?'

She poked her head into the closet and called out again. 'Paul? Where are you?'

After a few moments she left the room. They heard her pick up the phone.

'Jane?' they heard her say. 'Have you seen Paul? I can't find him anywhere. He's not in his bedroom. There's no sign of him at all.'

Paul and Dum Dum snickered to each other in the dark. At last Dum Dum gave Paul a nudge and Paul went out to see his mother.

'Wait a minute,' she said into the receiver. 'He's here now.'

She hung up and yelled at him, 'You little rascal!'

As they were getting ready for bed, Paul asked Dum Dum. 'That was a neat trick with the mirror,' Paul remarked. 'Where'd you learn that?'

'From one of the magicians in our show,' Dum Dum said. 'I've picked up a lot of tricks over the years. I can make fans with cards, make them jump up by themselves, shuffle them and always find the one I want.'

'Can you show me some?' said Paul.

'Of course!' exclaimed Dum Dum. 'This is the one that drove audiences wild.'

He put his head into his hands, and when he opened his palms his eyes were in them.

'That's disgusting,' frowned Paul. 'But it's impressive.'

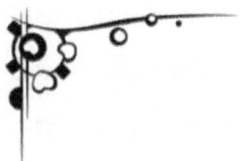

Chapter 8

At last Paul decided it was time for his friends to meet Dum Dum. On Friday at the playground, he gathered Albert, Ryan and Charlie. Charlie's sister Nadine noticed and ran up to join them. She had dark brown hair with a tinge of red, whereas Charlie was blonde and round - faced.

'I've got something to show you,' Paul revealed to the group. 'But it's a…s-s-secret.'

'Se*cret*?' Nadine's eyes opened wide. 'Can I come, too? Can I come, too?'

Paul looked at each boy in turn, and they all nodded.

So at Charlie's house that weekend Paul arrived with Dum Dum. Everyone was astonished by the sight of a puppet that could walk and talk without strings. At first they were sure it was some kind of trick.

'Who taught you ventriloquism?' asked Nadine. 'Our uncle Rupert is a ventriloquist, and he's shown us some tricks.'

'Well, I'm sure he hasn't shown you this one,' Paul confidently looked around. 'Anyone have some tape?'

Charlie ran out and brought some back. Paul cut a length and placed it over his mouth. He nodded to Dum Dum, who walked to the centre of the room.

All eyes were on him as he spread out his hands and started singing:

When marimba rhythms start to play
Dance with me, make me sway
Like a lazy ocean hugs the shore
Hold me close, sway me more
Like a flower bending in the breeze
Bend with me, sway with ease
When we dance you have a way with me
Stay with me, sway with me.

He boogied around the room, his feet making loud thumps on the floor boards. The children started clapping along. Nadine skipped forward and danced with him.

At the end of the performance the kids were speechless. They all had to pinch themselves to make sure they weren't dreaming.

Paul peeled the tape from his mouth and told them: 'Remember, it has to be a secret. No one can know about him but us.'

They all nodded solemnly.

'All he wants is to become a real boy,' continued Paul. 'If he succeeds he'll never have to go back to being a dummy.'

'But he's wonderful as a dummy!' protested Nadine.

'There's nothing wonderful about being forced to work in a pub every night!" answered Paul. 'Surrounded by drunk, sad people. Once someone grabbed him and tried to pull him apart just for laughs.'

'Is that so?' Nadine looked at Dum Dum with sympathy. 'We mustn't let him go back to that!' she stomped her foot on the floor. We simply mustn't!'

She leaned down to give him a tight hug.

But their mum suddenly walked into the room. The kids froze in panic.

'Why, what are you all doing here so hush-hush?' she said. 'Come out to the front and have some tea.'

While Paul's friends were groping for the right reply, Charlie's mother noticed Dum Dum. 'Why hello!' she bent down to speak to him. 'I've never seen you before. I'm Charlie and Nadine's mother.'

Dum Dum shook her hand.

'What school do you go to?' she asked him.

Dum Dum looked around stupidly.

'He's between schools, mum,' Charlie answered for him.

'Is he now?' chuckled Charlie's mother. 'Isn't it a bit late to be switching schools?'

'They, they just moved here,' made up Paul.

The kids racked their brains for a way to get rid of her.

'Fire!' Albert suddenly shouted.

'I beg your pardon?' Charlie's mother straightened up.

'Something's burning in the living room!' pointed Albert. 'I can smell smoke!'

'Oh dear,' said Charlie's mother. 'I guess I'd better check.'

As soon as she left, Paul and Dum Dum said goodbye and ran out the door.

Charlie watched them through the window.

'However are we going to help him?' he said.

'We'll have to find a way,' said Albert. 'He's our friend now. Even if he's just a dummy.'

'He's not just a dummy!' uttered Nadine. 'His cheeks were wet when I hugged him. A dummy doesn't cry real tears.'

It was almost night When Paul and Dum Dum got home. They saw Paul's mum on the street talking to some policemen. 'Quick,' Paul whispered to Dum Dum, 'Hide in that corner while I talk to her.'

'And where've you been all this time?' she turned around to accost him.

'What happened?'

'Someone tried to break into our flat,' she informed him. 'They broke the window to your room.'

Paul rushed upstairs with Dum Dum. They saw Paul's broken window.

'I'm sure it was Marc,' Dum Dum shuddered. 'He won't stop until he gets me back.'

'He won't get you back,' Paul promised.

'He might,' Dum Dum eyed the cracked glass. 'If you don't fix that.'

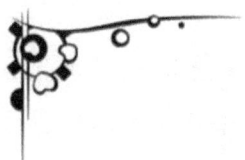

Chapter 9

Dum Dum kept pestering Paul about the broken window until one day he gave in. They went to see his Uncle Mathew.

'Maybe he can take a look at your leg while we're there,' said Paul as they walked to the bus stop. 'He's worked in toy factories and other places. He knows all about puppets and stuff.'

Soon they reached Matthew's stop. Paul took Dum Dum aside before going in. 'Don't say anything while you're there, okay? I don't want my uncle to suspect you're more than just a dummy.'

Dum Dum gave him a big grin. 'Thanks a lot.'

'No, I mean it,' pleaded Paul. 'He might tell my mum. Then we'll both be in hot water.'

Paul led the way inside.

'Why, hello!' called out Matthew, a tall pale man with a salt-and-pepper goatee. 'I haven't seen you in a while.'

Paul fumbled for a way to explain his problem. 'I was w-wondering if I could borrow some tools.'

'What for?' asked Matthew.

'We've got a broken window at home,' Paul replied.

Mathew came out from behind the counter and squatted in front of Dum Dum. 'And who do we have here?' he said. 'I never knew you liked puppets.'

'I uh, just found him,' mumbled Paul. 'He's got a bit of a limp.'

'Does he now?' Matthew lifted up Dum Dum onto his glass counter. He gave him a thorough check. He found the problem right away.

'Somebody put in different bits of wood just to make up the length in his knee,' he told Paul. 'I guess he wasn't meant to be walking at all. He's just a sit down puppet. You plunk him down on your leg and most of the action is with his mouth.'

'That sounds about right,' Paul quipped.

Paul snickered as Dum Dum shot him an angry look.

'It's true,' said Matthew, starting to sand off bits from Dum Dum's knee. Dum Dum gritted his teeth and struggled not to scream in pain. Paul looked around the shop while his uncle cut some pieces of wood. At last he fitted them into the gap in Dum Dum's knee and pounded them into place. When he was done, he lifted the dummy again up and examined him more closely.

He made a puzzled observation, 'But there *is* something funny about him.'

Paul looked up nervously. 'What is it?'

'Well there's this part,' said Matthew, feeling around Dum Dum's back. 'It doesn't seem to have any function as far as I can tell. I've never seen it in a dummy before.'

'Oh, I wouldn't worry,' Paul told him. 'He was pretty smashed up when I found him.'

'Shame,' commented Matthew. 'He's a pretty good puppet.'

From behind Matthew, Dum Dum turned his head to wink at Paul. Paul gave him a ferocious scowl.

'I can't imagine anyone throwing out something like him,' commented Matthew. 'He's in pretty good nick, considering.'

Dum Dum waited until Matthew's back was turned, before nodding smugly at Paul.

'Now did you see that?' Matthew suddenly said.

Paul looked up in panic. 'See what?'

'There's this piece of wire over here,' Matthew pointed out. 'Just under his shoulder. Now why would anyone cut that wire off?'

'I did that,' answered Paul, relieved.

'You did? Why?'

'He asked me to,' shrugged Paul.

Matthew raised an eyebrow. 'He *asked* you to?'

'I mean, I thought he didn't really need it any more.'

'But that's how you control a puppet's movements,' Matthew showed him. 'You use that to make it look like they're alive and doing things by themselves.'

'He doesn't need wires for that,' stated Paul. 'He's a bit too good at doing things by himself, if you ask me.'

Matthew laughed. 'Is he now?'

He lifted Dum Dum's good leg and let it fall. 'Where did you find him? I know they don't make this kind much any more. Most of the stuff you get these days are all plastic and microchips. These were the real ones.'

'Yeah,' Paul shrugged. 'I guess I was lucky to find him.'

Dum Dum made sure that Matthew wasn't looking before he gave Paul an approving nod.

Then someone started tapping on the window from outside. Paul turned to see three women grinning and making gestures at Matthew through the glass, their faces garish with makeup. Paul's uncle slid the window open and one of them poked her head in, 'Oi! You coming out with us or what?'

'Just finishin' up here, luv!' Matthew told her.

'Oh, a cust'mer!' slurred the woman, looking at Paul and Dum Dum. 'Jeez! Haven't seen that in a while!'

She giggled and staggered away to rejoin her friends. Matthew shut the window and turned back to Paul.

'There's one thing I don't mind telling you, though,' he told Paul. 'His joints look a bit run down. I've got a few parts lying around. We could spruce him up if you like. Make him good as new.'

Paul looked behind his uncle to see Dum Dum secretly shaking his head.

'No thanks,' he demurred. 'I think I'll keep him as he is for now.'

'There's one thing I noticed, however,' added Matthew.

Paul stopped. 'What's that?'

'His left ear is a little loose.'

'Oh,' Paul waved his hand. 'His old owner used to box him around the ears a lot. That's why he still goes deaf once in a while.' He flashed an evil smile at Dum Dum, who scowled back at him.

'Well, take care of your little friend now,' counselled Matthew. 'If he gets any more dings or dents just give me a call.'

Paul grabbed Dum Dum, thanked his uncle and left.

Paul carried him all the way to the corner.

'Put me down!' ordered Dum Dum. 'I can walk by myself!'

'I can't put you down!' said Paul. 'Uncle Matthew might still be watching. It'd look terribly odd if he saw my puppet walking by himself.'

It wasn't until they had rounded the corner that Paul finally put Dum Dum down. As soon as his feet touched the ground, Dum Dum threw his head back to let out a mighty howl. '*Ow! Ow! Ow!Oooooooooooooooowwwwww!*'

Paul covered his ears. 'Stop that! People are looking. They'll think I'm hurting you.'

Dum Dum staggered around like a wounded old man. 'Do you have any idea how much I wanted to scream in there?' he whimpered. 'You ever had someone drive a chisel into your knee then scrape off bits with sandpaper? You try that and see if you can keep from screaming out your tonsils!'

'I know, I know,' said Paul with sympathy. 'You were very brave in there.'

Dum Dum smiled and patted himself on the stomach.

'I know it wasn't easy,' continued Paul. 'But look! You've lost your limp!'

Dum Dum glanced down on his legs. He tried doing a little jig. 'You're right. It was worth all that agony.'

He walked around. 'I'm good as new! I can sway! I can dance!'

He did a tap dance on the pavement and started to sing:

Just in time, I found you just in time

Before you came, my time was runnin' low

I was lost, the losin' dice were tossed

My bridges all were crossed, nowhere to go

Now you're here and now I know just where I'm goin'
No more doubt or fear, I found my way.

He jumped on Paul's shoulder and they cavorted around the deserted alley.

You found me just in time

And changed my lonely life that lovely day

Then Dum Dum suddenly stopped singing.
'What's wrong?' Paul put him down again.
'Aren't we forgetting something?' Dum Dum prompted.
'What's that?'
'I thought you were going to borrow some tools.'
Paul slapped himself on the forehead. 'Oh!'
They resumed walking until they reached the bus stop.

'Anyway,' said Dum Dum. 'Marc would never recognize me now.'

'That's right.'

Dum Dum spread his arms to gaze at himself. 'I was all beat up and miserable when he owned me. Well, I'm a different person now.'

'No, you look like one happy little boy now.'

Dum Dum nodded with a big smile.

'It's one thing to steal a puppet,' stated Paul. 'If Marc stole you now he'd be in big trouble with the police.'

'That's right.'

'That'd be kidnapping.'

'Yeah! I hope he knows that, though. Maybe I should write him a letter.'

'No. Don't do that!'

They waited some time before their bus showed up. When it did they dashed up to the top deck and grabbed the front seat.

'Hey, isn't it interesting, though?' said Paul.

'What is?'

'Uncle Matthew thinks you're unique.'

Dum Dum gave him an offended look. 'You needed your uncle to tell you *that*?'

'No. But I think it's neat,' Paul explained. 'He says there are parts of you he's never seen on any other puppet.'

Dum Dum opened his eyes wide. 'Thank God he didn't look at all my other parts!'

'But maybe that's what makes you special,' added Paul. 'You got all these things that don't make sense to anybody. But maybe they're the things that make you, you.'

Dum Dum looked at the road ahead with that big smile on his face.

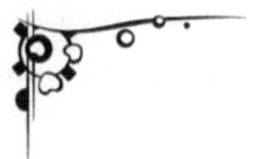

Chapter 10

When Charlie's birthday rolled around, Paul saw his chance to take Dum Dum to his first birthday party. They went to a toy shop to get Charlie's present. Paul marched up to the large cabinet full of locomotives.

'He's already got a Bachmann Durango,' he told Dum Dum. 'But he's been wanting a Spectrum.'

So they bought a Spectrum and had it gift-wrapped.

'What are you supposed to do at somebody's birthday?' asked Dum Dum as they walked to the corner.

'You play games, ' said Paul, 'eat lots of cake and just horse around till they tell you to go home.'

'Can't we just stay the night?' suggested Dum Dum.

'You don't usually on birthdays,' replied Paul. 'But I'll ask Charlie.'

'Good.'

Paul faced him. 'You still scared of sleeping at home?'

'I won't feel right until you get that window fixed,' Dum Dum admitted. 'I don't fancy ending up back in Marc's closet.'

'Don't worry,' Paul put his arm around Dum Dum. 'We won't let that happen.'

At Charlie's party Paul's friends were delighted to see Dum Dum again. Charlie's mother and his uncle Rupert were going around the room, making sure everyone had a place to sit. Albert and Ryan waved from different corners. Nadine did a little jump when she saw Dum Dum.

But as soon as Dum Dum entered, all the children started asking, 'Is there going to be a show? Is someone going to perform? Will there be magic?'

Their excitement grew so much Charlie came over and whispered to Paul, 'Should we let them know?'

There was a bunch of other kids Paul had never met before.

'No,' he decided. 'It's too risky.'

Albert and Ryan started suggesting all sorts of games to distract the other children, who were all gazing expectantly at Paul.

'No,' Charlie told his guests. 'He doesn't really know how to make the puppet talk.'

There were groans of disappointment.

'But I do,' Charlie's uncle Rupert walked in front of the gathering. 'In fact I have a little surprise for Charlie.'

He bent down and took out a rather menacing puppet from his case. Charlie and Nadine looked at each other in surprise. Rupert raised his arm, 'Chair please?'

Someone brought a chair and Charlie's uncle sat down to give a performance. 'This is Fyodor,' he announced.

'Hi Fyodor! Hello!' several voices pealed in greeting.

But the nasty-looking puppet on Rupert's knee ignored them all and turned his head to scan the room. His gaze fell on Dum Dum.

So Fyodor,' Rupert began his act. 'Why don't you tell everybody where you were yesterday?'

But Fyodor wasn't interested. He kept turning his head to look at Dum Dum.

'Now, look this way, ' admonished Rupert. 'Pay attention.'

'I thought I was going to be the only dummy in this party!' Fyodor growled.

'But you are,' said Rupert.

'Then what's *he* doing *here*?' Fyodor pointed belligerently at Dum Dum.

The kids laughed.

'Don't be rude now,' frowned Rupert. 'That's one of Charlie's guests. He came here to eat cake. Just like you.'

'I don't eat cake!' responded Fyodor. 'Yuck! Who wants a gooey, creamy lump stuck in their throat for days?'

'Mind your manners now, Fyodor,' Rupert reproved. 'It's a very nice cake. Charlie's mother made it.'

He turned to his audience. 'Isn't it nice?'

They all shouted, 'Yes!'

Fyodor started trying to wriggle out of Rupert's grasp.

'What are you doing?'

'Let me go!' cried Fyodor. 'There's something I need to settle here.'

He shook his fists at Dum Dum. 'Let's you and me fight! I'll knock those dimples out of that silly face of yours!'

Paul moved in front of Dum Dum to protect him.

'Now, now,' said Rupert, struggling to restrain Fyodor. 'You know you can only stay in the party if you behave.'

He got up and opened his suitcase. 'And you know what happens to badly behaved boys. They're sent home until they learn some manners.'

He put Fyodor still struggling in the case. Fyodor's shouts could still be heard even after Rupert had shut the lid. The children laughed and applauded.

Rupert took a bow, picked up his valise and walked towards the door. He stopped briefly to talk to Paul. 'That's very strange,' he muttered. 'I've never seen him act like that before. Usually he does exactly what I say.'

Paul and Dum Dum exchanged glances.

Charlie's mother lit the candles and they all sang Happy Birthday. Charlie blew out the candles and the party erupted into chaos.

After a while Nadine made a suggestion. 'Anyone want to play Chinese Whispers?'

'I don't speak Chinese,' objected Dum Dum. The other kids laughed and pointed. Paul slunk back into the crowd to hide.

Nadine explained the rules. 'Somebody writes down the message and whispers it to somebody, then that person whispers it to somebody else and so on and so forth.'

Nadine wrote down a message to start the game. She whispered it to Paul, who whispered it to Charlie, who whispered it to someone else, who whispered it to someone else.

In the end, Ryan whispered it to Albert, who whispered it to Dum Dum.

'Well?' Nadine quizzed him at last. 'What was the message?'

Dum Dum tried to remember what Albert had mumbled. 'The bird flew away from the cake on the window.'

'No, silly!' Nadine laughed. She read the note she had written. 'The message was "The cat on the window sill ate the bird on the cake."'

Dum Dum repeated the message in ten different voices.

All the kids were awed.

The next day they went to the park for a picnic with Charlie and Nadine's parents. It was a beautiful day. For the first time, Dum Dum knew what it was like to be with a family. He asked Paul what he should do.

'Nothing,' shrugged Paul. 'Just be yourself.'

'I don't know how to be myself,' Dum Dum worried. 'I always needed Marc to be myself.'

'Forget Marc,' sighed Paul. 'Just have a good time.'

'But I've never gone on a picnic before,' said Dum Dum.

'Me, neither. This is what normal families do.'

'I'll need to do this when I become a real boy,' decided Dum Dum.

'Why wait?' answered Paul. 'You can do it now.'

Dum Dum got up and ran around, doing cartwheels and rolling on the grass. Paul watched him laughing.

Then one of the kids came and tagged Paul. Paul jumped up and ran after somebody else to tag. Dum Dum watched them run this way and that, his head swivelling from one direction to the other.

He saw Paul almost catch someone but stopping abruptly at the edge of the pond.

Go on!' rooted Dum Dum from where he was. 'Jump in after him! You'll catch him easy!'

But Paul just shook his head and walked away from the edge of the water. As Dum Dum watched him loping along, he felt a tap on his shoulder, 'Tag!'

He looked for someone else to tag, but everyone bolted away from him.

'How'm I supposed to tag you if you keep running away?' hollered Dum Dum. 'Stand still will you!'

Paul ran up to him and tried to explain, 'That's the point of the game. They're supposed to run away when you're trying to tag them.'

'But that's stupid!' spat out Dum Dum. 'How can anybody get tagged when they're all running away?'

'You're not supposed to get tagged,' stated Paul. 'That's why you run away.'

'But somebody tagged me!' bawled Dum Dum in outrage.

Someone ran up to them and threw a ball at Dum Dum, 'Catch!'

'Thanks,' Dum Dum tucked it under his arm and walked away.

'What's wrong with him?' said the boy to Paul. 'Tell him he's supposed to throw the ball back.'

'Go and tell him,' countered Paul. 'He doesn't listen to anything I say.'

The boy took the ball back from Dum Dum and threw it to Ryan. They ran around passing the ball back and forth until they disappeared behind the trees.

Later Paul and Dum Dum were sitting with Nadine and Charlie when Nadine's uncle Rupert walked up.

'Why, if it's not my fellow ventriloquist!' he greeted Paul cheerily.

'He's really good, you know,' blurted out Nadine, earning her a filthy look from her brother.

'Well as for me,' said Rupert, lowering himself on the grass beside them, 'I'm afraid I muffed up the job last night,' 'Maybe your friend here can give me some tips?'

Paul looked at Charlie, who gave him a secret wink. Paul picked up Dum Dum and sat him on his knee.

'Well, I was just telling my friend Paul here,' Paul started, tilting the dummy's head clumsily from side to side. 'He insists on pretending that my voice is really his. No wonder I keep saying such stupid things.'

'His lips are moving!' one of the boys pointed at Paul.

'I don't like to say stupid things,' continued Paul in Dum Dum's voice. 'I want to *ge* a *good goy*.'

Paul turned his head each time Dum Dum did, and when his lips stopped moving Dum Dum stopped talking. It was the worst ventriloquist act any of them had seen.

'He wants to be a *good goil*!' laughed one boy. They all jeered at Paul. He was such a big disappointment, they were all booing and holding their thumbs down.

'I can't do it,' Paul gave up. 'I'm not really a ventriloquist.'

He put Dum Dum down on the grass and went off to sit by himself.

After a while Rupert joined him.

'Don't worry, lad,' he cajoled. 'You just need to avoid words that need you to put your lips together. Like *box*, and *bottle* and *boy* or *parcel*. See? You ended up sounding like you wanted to be a *goil*. But don't worry. I've made mistakes like that too. Everybody does. You can't always control everything.'

'I noticed that,' agreed Paul. He exchanged looks with Dum Dum behind Rupert's back. Dum Dum winked at him. Paul glowered back at him to stop it.

Luckily one of the kids came running up. 'Let's play hide and seek!"

Paul was only too glad to be rid of Rupert and jumped up, 'Hurrah! Who's *it*?'

The kid pointed to Dum Dum, 'He is!'

Dum Dum was puzzled. 'Me? Why? What did I do?'

Paul took him by the hand and led him to a nearby tree. 'You cover your eyes and count to ten. Let everyone go and hide. Then you look for them.'

Dum Dum found a place to position himself and Paul stepped away. 'Now cover your eyes and start counting. And don't peek!'

Dum Dum began counting, '1, 2, 3...'

All the kids spread out to hide.

One of them stopped in his tracks and howled, 'Hey!'

'What's the matter?' Charlie asked.

'He's looking!' the kid gestured at Dum Dum, who was still counting, '7, 8, 9..' but with his eyes open wide.

'Tell him he's not supposed to look!' Albert told Paul.

'Do it again, you dummy!' bellowed one of the other boys.

'Count slow and close your eyes!' ordered another kid. 'What's wrong with you? Haven't you ever played this before?'

'Why are you all shouting at me?' Dum Dum screamed back. 'What's the matter with you, you little runts?' He began shrieking and cursing, saying all the horrible things he used to hear from Marc.

'Dum Dum! Stop!' Paul pleaded.

But it was too late. Dum Dum was already letting out a stream of expletives even Charlie's father had never heard before. Nadine and the other children had to cover their ears. They all withdrew from him, hurt and a little afraid.

'It's all his fault!' one of the smaller boys pointed at Paul.

'I didn't do anything!' yelled Paul.

'You didn't, did you?' the older boy defended his brother. 'But you're the one making him talk!'

'I *don't* make him talk!' Paul retorted.

'Liar!' blubbered the little boy. 'How could he talk if it wasn't for you?'

All the little kids started crying. Charlie's mum had to come and intervene.

'Now, now, we're all getting a bit tired and fractious,' she said gently. 'It's been a long day. I think we'd all better go home.'

And so the party broke up in a gloomy mood. Paul and Dum Dum left the park, feeling that a beautiful day had been ruined.

They sat on the bus without talking for a long time. Then suddenly Dum Dum remembered something. 'Why didn't you jump in the pond to tag that boy?' he demanded. 'You would have got him for sure.'

Paul seemed to struggle with something before he answered. 'I..I'm a little afraid of the water.'

'Why?'

'I can't swim. I've always been a bit scared of drowning.'

The bus went over a bridge and Dum Dum looked around at the street lights coming on.

'It's like the marquees outside our old pub,' he smiled. 'By this time Marc would be dressing me up and practicing our lines.'

'Do you miss that?' said Paul.

Dum Dum cocked his head to think.

'Nah,' he said at length. 'It was the same old jokes over and over again.'

They rode in silence or a few moments. Then Dum Dum recalled something else, 'You *sure* did a terrible job being a ventriloquist for Rupert.'

'I was doing it to protect you,' Paul revealed. 'We can't have Charlie's uncle thinking you're more than just a dummy.'

Dum Dum threw up his hands. 'But how am I going to become a real boy if everyone keeps thinking I'm just dummy?'

They reached their stop and they got off.

Paul mounted the steps wearily into their building. 'That was one long picnic.'

'I'm sorry I broke it up like that,' Dum Dum said.

'It was time to anyway,' Paul assured him. 'But there *is* one thing you'll have to learn.'

'What's that?' Dum Dum turned to him eagerly.

'Part of being a real boy is minding what you say.'

'I never had to do that before,' Dum Dum admitted. 'I just said whatever Marc wanted me to.'

'Well, you're not with Marc now. said Paul. 'People have feelings. They're not just an audience who'll laugh at everything you say.'

Dum Dum nodded contritely.

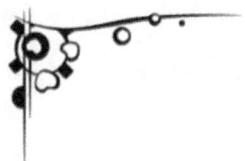

Chapter 11

For the first time Paul knew what it was like to be
blamed for someone else's actions. All his friends blamed him
for what had happened at the picnic.

'I bet you've been busy teaching your dummy awful
words!' snapped Ryan when Paul walked past him at school.

'I didn't teach him anything!' howled Paul.

'Then where does he know them from?' countered
Albert. 'You keep telling us he's not the one saying all that
terrible stuff. Then it must be you!'

'I told you it's all from his old owner,' Paul reasoned.
'He was a very nasty character. Made Dum Dum say all sorts
of horrible things.'

'How could a dummy remember all that? ' Charlie
taunted. 'Eh? Eh? He hasn't been with that owner for months.
If it's true he really ran away.'

'*If* it's true you didn't just pinch him from somewhere,'
Albert chimed in.

Paul was shocked. 'You know I would never steal anything! He asked me to save him. I swear! D, d--don't you believe me?'

The boys exchanged mocking glances and walked away.

Later Paul saw them standing together in the playground. He walked over to join them.

'What're you guys up to?'

'We're planning to go fishing with Ryan's dad next weekend,' Albert revealed.

'Ooh, Can I come?' begged Paul.

'You can,' Ryan told him.' But not your dummy.'

'Guys, he's just a dummy.'

'So you stick with him then,' said Charlie, walking away with the others. 'After all, you're birds of a feather.'

They all laughed.

Things weren't any better when Paul got home. He opened the front door and was confronted by a terrible mess in the kitchen. His pills are scattered on the floor, one plate was broken, and there was flour everywhere. He wondered if someone had broken in.

He ran into his room to check on Dum Dum. But he wasn't there.

'Dum Dum!' yelled Paul at the top of the voice. There was no answer.

He ran around shouting. 'Dum Dum! Where are you? Answer me! Dum Dum!'

He heard a noise in his mother's room. Frightened of intruders, he tiptoed to the door and opened it a crack. Something fell to the floor and Paul nearly jumped out of his skin.

'Oops!' Paul heard from somewhere above him. He gazed up to see Dum Dum rummaging on top of the wardrobe.

'What are you doing up there?' Paul demanded.

'I was looking for paper.'

'What for?'

'That girl upstairs,' Dum Dum replied. 'She came to the window and held up a sign.'

'What did it say?'

'I don't know,' shrugged Dum Dum. 'I don't go to school, do I?'

Paul put his hand on his head. 'Lord! Is that what why there's all that litter everywhere?

Dum Dum nodded. 'I had to get some paper to say something to her.'

'I told you,' Paul said. 'We don't have much paper in this house.'

'I know,' Dum Dum peeked over the edge. 'I checked. If I'd known I would have used toilet paper instead.'

'Don't worry,' Paul threw up his hands. 'She'll turn up again.'

He helped Dum Dum get down and they went to the kitchen. 'Quick!' Paul handed Dum Dum a broom. 'Help me tidy up before my mum gets home.'

Paul tried to scoop up the pills while Dum Dum flailed the broom around, scattering the flour even more. Paul had put most of the pills back in heir bottle when they heard the lock turning in the front door.

'Go!' hissed Paul. Dum Dum dropped the broom and ran into Paul's room, leaving footprints in flour across the living room.

When Paul's mum saw all the disorder she went white with horror. 'What's all this?'

Paul picked up the broken plate and threw it in the bin.

'What are those pills doing there?' his mother pointed under the table.

'They fell,' said Paul.

'I can see they fell!' she barked. 'I mean why are they still here? You were supposed to have taken them months ago. There shouldn't be any left.'

She sat down. 'Haven't you been taking your pills?'

'I *have!*' Paul whined.

'Well, it sure doesn't look like it!' she slapped the table. 'I keep paying for them, and you leave them in there to rot!'

'I told you I'm taking them,' Paul assured her, trying to sweep the remaining flour off the floor.

'You better be,' she retorted. 'Because if you start sleepwalking again, it's your own fault!'

'I don't sleepwalk any more,' whinged Paul, getting angry. 'The doctor said it's stopped.'

His mum got up and walked to the trail of Dum Dum's footprints in flour. 'Then what do you call that?' she challenged. 'What child in his right mind scatters flour on the floor and walks around in it?'

Paul finished cleaning up and went to his room. He found Dum Dum sitting under the desk, looking through a magazine.

'You'll have to learn to say sorry!' he hissed.

Dum Dum shrugged, 'Okay.'

'That's not enough!' cried Paul. 'You've got to learn to make up for bad things you've done!'

Dum Dum's eyes flared and he began to shout.

'Okay, okay! I'm sorry!' he jumped up and down. What do you want me to do? I said I'm sorry! Is that enough? I'M VERY, VERY SORRY!'

'The door suddenly opened. It was Paul's mum. Paul held the closet door shut to hide Dum Dum.

'If you're sorry you should come out and say it,' she said to Paul. 'You don't have to rant and shout to yourself in here. Anyway, I forgive you. Now come have supper.'

Paul went out to join her.

While they were eating mum said, 'Suppose I went to Cyprus for a couple of months, would you be okay? You like seeing Uncle Matthew don't you? He could teach you carpentry or something.'

Paul looked up at her. 'You trying to get rid of me?'

'No. I just thought it might be good for you to spend more time with other people. With other boys like you.'

'But I do! I spend all my time with another boy.'

Mum stopped eating. 'You do? Where?'

Paul realized his blunder. 'I mean…I meant Charlie and Albert.'

His mum drank from her glass. 'Uncle Matthew's a bit more like a dad though, ain't he? Someone who could teach you something.'

They sat eating quietly for while.

'I think I might be going fishing with Ryan and his dad this weekend,' Paul mentioned.

'That's good,' his mum nodded. 'Where you going?'

'I don't know yet....Can I have some money?'

'What you need it for?'

'For lunch and stuff. There's nothing left in the box.'

She thought about it. 'Go look in my purse.'

Paul got up to do as she said. He found an opened packet of cigarettes inside.

'Since when did you smoke?' he demanded.

She seemed flustered for a moment.' Those aren't mine. They're Jeremy's.'

'What's his cigarettes doing in your purse?'

She mumbled something and got up to do the dishes. Paul went back to his room.

A while later they heard the phone ring. Paul opened his door a crack so they could listen.

'Well, I've never worked in a bar before,' they heard his mum say. 'But I hear the money's not bad. What with tips and everything. I could certainly use some right now.'

She was quiet for a moment.

'Yeah, I hear Jeremy's keen to go,' she resumed. 'That'd be wonderful. But I think I might spoil it if I brought a kid along.'

She turned around so it was hard for Paul and
Dum Dum to hear what she was saying. Paul shut the door.
'Could you hear what she was saying?' Paul murmured to
Dum Dum.

Dum Dum shook his head. 'My ears seem to have gone a little
deaf again.'

'That's because they're coming loose,' said Paul before
grabbing Dum Dum's head.

'Ow! What do you think you're doing? Stop that!'
Dum Dum tried to wriggle out of his grasp. But Paul held on
tight until he could push Dum Dum's ears back in.

'What did you do that for?' the dummy protested.
'How would you like it if I did that to you?'

'I had to,' said Paul. 'We can't have you losing both
your ears.'

After staring at them for a moment, Paul asked, 'What
did Marc used to box your ears for?'

'He used to say that when we were onstage I often
blurted out things he didn't want anyone else to know.'

'But wasn't he saying them himself?' wondered Paul.
'Pretending it was coming from you?'

Dum Dum shrugged. 'I don't know.'

'Maybe he was guilty about them,' mused Paul. 'That's
why he needed someone else to say them.'

'Maybe. Anyway it was getting too creepy living with him,' Dum Dum concluded. 'That's why I had to run away.'

When they were getting ready for bed, Dum Dum asked, 'You think your mum will take us to Cyprus?'

'I don't know about that,' answered Paul, getting into bed.

After a long silence, he added, 'I wonder if she's planning to see my dad.'

Dum Dum lifted his head to look at him. 'You think he wants to see her?'

'I don't know.'

'What if they see each other?' suggested Dum Dum. 'Would you like that?'

Paul thought about it. 'It'd be nice if they got back, in a way. Then I'd have a mum and dad. Like Charlie and Nadine.'

'*We'd* have a mum and dad,' smiled Dum Dum.

'Yes,' Paul turned to look at him. 'We would.'

Paul turned out the light. Several moments later Dum Dum opened his eyes to see Paul lying wide awake, staring at the ceiling.

'What's wrong?' Dum Dum whispered.

'I can't sleep,' said Paul.

'Maybe you're hungry.'

'No,' Paul put an arm under his head. 'I just feel funny.'

Dum Dum looked up at the ceiling for a few moments. After a while he said, 'I know what you're feeling. That's exactly how I felt when I found out Marc was thinking of throwing me out.'

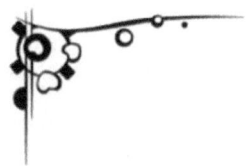

Chapter 12

Paul never stopped trying to reconcile Dum Dum with his friends. So when Charlie invited him to his home, Paul saw his chance. He spent the weekend teaching Dum Dum how to make the kites and paper planes he used to make with Daniel. Then he made Dum Dum sign them and took them to Charlie's house.

But Paul friends were sceptical. 'How do we know he did any of these?' Charlie said.

'Well, who else would spell like that?' Paul opened one of the cards.

They all crowded around to read the writing. They giggled at the mistakes.

'I believe it,' decided Nadine. 'I think he's sweet, really.'

'You would,' scoffed Charlie.

'No, I wouldn't!'

'Look at all those square *s*'s and the pointy *p*'s!' Ryan pointed out. 'They'd send you back to first grade for writing like that!'

'Those are the letters he never gets right,' Paul told them.

'Why?' Nadine asked.

'Because his fingers can't bend far enough.'

'Besides,' added Paul. 'Has any of you ever seen me make cards for anybody?'

Charlie considered for a moment. 'I guess not. Your mum would kill you for wasting so much paper.'

'Oh!' Nadine scooped up the paper flowers Paul had brought. 'They're lovely!'

'I tell you,' he's trying his best,' Paul implored them. 'Please give him a chance.'

Nadine clasped her hands beside him, until all the others grudgingly nodded their heads.

So a week later, Paul arrived with Dum Dum, who was overjoyed to see everyone again, 'What are we going to play?'

'Anything but hide and seek,' quipped Charlie with a wink at Paul.

'Come round to the back,' he herded all of them down the hall. 'I've got something to show you.'

They found Charlie's gleaming new bike outside, still covered in plastic. They hurriedly tore off the wrapping and took turns riding it up and down the garden, ringing the bell and tearing around the hedges.

Whenever his turn came, Paul kept making excuses.

'It's Albert's turn,' he stalled when Nadine finished and passed the bike on to him.

'I've already been on it five times,' said Albert.

'Then let Ryan have a go,' dawdled Paul.

'I've been up and down and round and round,' Ryan said. *You* go.'

'Let's take a turn!' Dum Dum urged him.

Paul shook his head.

'Give it to Dum Dum them,' suggested Charlie.

'But I can't!' Dum Dum said.

'Well, neither can I,' answered Paul and walked away.

'Come on!' Dum Dum kept at him. 'I've never been on a bicycle before. It's easy! Monkeys in our show used to do it all the time!'

'Well, I'm not a monkey,' Paul resisted . 'But you can be if you want to.'

After lunch Charlie's uncle Rupert arrived. He opened a suitcase and Dum Dum saw the foot of a dummy. He quickly got behind Paul.

'Don't worry,' Rupert smiled at him. 'Fyodor isn't with us today. He's at home practicing how to be well-behaved. What we have in his place is Lupita.'

He held up a pretty little puppet with glowing eyes and raven coloured hair. Dum Dum's eyes almost popped out of their sockets.

Rupert sat down to demonstrate his skills. Lupita introduced herself in her charming Spanish accent and batted her eyelashes at everyone in the room. 'And now I will perform some music from my native Tijuana!' she declared, and started singing Mexican songs while accompanying herself on castanets.

Several times Dum Dum's eyes did pop out of their sockets. They clattered under the chairs, and he had to crawl between everyone's legs to retrieve them. Thankfully Rupert interrupted his own performance frequently to explain his techniques to Paul. Charlie and Nadine rolled their eyes. But Dum Dum couldn't stop himself drooling at the sight of Lupita.

That night Paul and Dum Dum slept in the guest room. While the whole house was quiet, Dum Dum slipped out of bed and tiptoed out to the hall. He went from door to door until he was right outside Rupert's room.

The door opened very softly and no one heard the soft patter of feet as Dum Dum led Lupita through the shadows. They went out the side doors to sit out in the patio.

The next morning Rupert woke up in a panic. He came to breakfast all dishevelled. He ignored everyone and poked his head into every corner and got down on his knees to look under the table.

'What's the matter?' asked Charlie's mother.

Rupert wheeled around and burst out, 'Lupita's gone missing!'

His alarm spread through the house, and a flurry of maids ran from room to room searching for Rupert's puppet.

At last one of them shouted from the children's wing, 'Here she is!'

Everyone calmed down. The maid came into the dining room holding Lupita. Rupert grabbed her with great relief. 'Where was she?'

'She was on Charlie's bed,' the maid disclosed.

All heads turned to Charlie, but he looked completely innocent, and just as puzzled as they. At last Rupert sat down to drink his coffee.

'Next time,' he chided Charlie, 'you really must ask permission if you want to play with someone else's property.'

'But I didn't take her!' Charlie cried.

His glance fell on Paul. 'Maybe Paul did it while he was sleepwalking.'

'I didn't take her!' Paul also protested.

Dum Dum appeared in the doorway. 'It wasn't Paul or Charlie,' he confessed. 'It was me.'

Rupert nearly dropped his cup. 'How on earth…?'

He grabbed Lupita and ran up to his room. A few minutes later he ran through the living room saying goodbye to everybody.

When he was gone the children looked at each other and laughed.

'Maybe it's time we left, too,' said Paul.

On the way home, he told Dum Dum, 'You should be more careful.'

'What did I do wrong?' argued Dum Dum. 'She was bored in the house, she said Rupert's snoring was keeping her awake. So I took her out for a walk.'

'I don't mean that,' said Paul. 'I mean you're starting to show off too much.'

'How?'

'You didn't have to show Rupert you could really talk.'

'But I had to tell him you and Charlie didn't take Lupita. *I* did.'

'Even so,' insisted Paul. 'We don't want anyone to suspect the truth.'

'What's the truth?' Dum Dum threw up his hands. 'I'm just a little boy. Why should I hide that?'

Paul nodded and they walked in silence for a while.

At length Paul turned to him. 'So what did you and Lupita talk about?'

'Oh, she told me a lot of things,' Dum Dum chuckled.

'Like what?'

'She told me Rupert really hates Charlie's father. He's only nice to him because of his sister, Charlie and Nadine's mum.'

'How come he keeps coming around then?' asked Paul.

'Because he likes performing with his dummies,' Dum Dum said. 'When he's at home he makes fun of Charlie's dad.'

'How?'

'He makes Lupita play Charlie's mum. And Fyodor plays his dad.'

They both laughed.

When they got to their building, Dum Dum said, 'Charlie's new bike is beautiful.'

'It is.'

'Why didn't you ride it?'

'I don't know how.'

Dum Dum twisted his neck around to look at him. 'You never learned?'

'Where would I?' Paul countered. 'How could anyone learn to ride a bike in this place?'

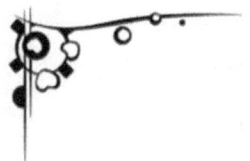

Chapter 13

One night at dinner Nadine told her brother, 'I've decided.'

'Decided what?' Charlie asked.

I'm going to teach Dum Dum how to become a real boy.'

Charlie checked to see if anyone had heard. 'I'm not sure that's going to be very easy,' he muttered.

'I know. But I'll try very hard,' vowed Nadine. 'I won't give up till I've succeeded.'

So the next time Paul came around with Dum Dum, Nadine immediately took charge.

'This is how you go to school,' she told Dum Dum.

She ran off and hurriedly washed her face in the bathroom, then wolfed down her food before jumping up with a shout, 'I'm going to be late!'

Dum Dum tried to copy it exactly, stuffing food into his mouth before washing his face and yelling, 'I'm going to be late!'

'Slightly in the wrong order,' giggled Nadine. 'And you're not supposed to talk with your mouth full.'

'Even if you're late?' Dum Dum asked.

'Never mind. It's good enough for a start.'

Next she made him sit down with a notebook and pencil. 'This is how you do homework.'

She scribbled on the notebook, stared at the ceiling, puffing up her cheeks and looking really bored.

'That's easy,' Dum Dum said. He sat in the chair and copied Nadine's actions right down to the puffed cheeks.

'Why, homework is peanuts!' he sneered. 'I don't know why Paul has so much trouble doing it.'

They all laughed.

A few days later day Nadine declared, 'We're going to do sums.'

Dum Dum seemed at a loss. 'What for?'

'Do you know how to count?' she questioned him.

'All the way to 21!' Dum Dum proudly answered.

Even Charlie was intrigued. 'Why only 21?'

'Because if you go over 21 you go bust,' Dum Dum enlightened him.

Nadine scratched her head, but the older boys smiled and exchanged knowing glances.

'Now let's forget about 21 for the moment,' Nadine tried again. 'What's 6 plus 5?'

Dum Dum thought briefly. 'Good hand! Hit me!'

'I'm not going to hit you,' said Nadine. 'Why ever would I do that?'

'No, I mean give me another card,' Dum Dum held out his hand. 'And make sure it's not higher than 10.'

Nadine threw up her hands in exasperation. 'Can we *please forget* about *cards*?'

Dum Dum sat quietly and waited for her to say something.

'What's 25 divided by 5?' Nadine quizzed him some more.

'How should I know?' Dum Dum shrugged.

'Okay, I'll give you an easy one,' Nadine relented. 'You write the answers on these.'

She gave him a piece of paper. Dum Dum bent over it, humming. After a while, he held it up and waved it in the air, 'Done!'

Nadine looked at it.

'That's terrible!' she cried out. She passed it on to her brother. He started laughing. 'How would he ever finish school?'

'Why would I want to do that?' Dum Dum asked him. 'I like going to school.'

'You're beginning to sound like a pretty dumb boy,' said Nadine.

'Well, it sure beats working in a pub every night,' Dum Dum retorted.

'You worked in a pub?' Brian came forward.

'I worked in *dozens* of pubs.' Dum Dum waved his hand. 'I almost didn't go anywhere else.'

'What did you do?' Nadine wanted to know.

'Insult people. Pretend to be a little boy. Poke fun at my owner.'

'That's not very nice,' Nadine reproved.

'Well, when people are laughing they buy more drinks,' reasoned Dum Dum.

'I suppose,' conceded Nadine.

Another time Nadine brought all sorts of costumes to the playground. 'We're going to do school plays,' she said.

'Great,' cheered Dum Dum. 'Can I be the king?'

'Of course!' Nadine replied,' putting a crown on his head. Charlie and Paul ran off to play somewhere else.

Dum Dum tried to position the crown on his head. 'What am I supposed to do?'

'You're supposed to say important things and give orders to everybody,' spelled out Nadine. 'You'll have to look strong and scary, though.'

'Good,' said Dum Dum. 'Can I make fun of you?'

'That wouldn't be nice,' Nadine objected. 'Kings don't really make fun of people or do things that aren't very nice.'

'Can I make jokes instead?'

Nadine shook her head. 'You don't really make jokes if you're a king. You have to be really serious and act a little angry all the time.'

'Akh!' Dum Dum flung the crown to the ground. 'Being a king is *boring*!'

Nadine looked in her box of costumes and pulled out a Lady's cape. 'You could be a countess instead.'

Dum Dum took several steps back. 'No, no, thank you. I think I'll go find the boys!'

And he ran off to find the others.

The next time they came to Charlie's house, Nadine was waiting. She lead Dum Dum to her father's study and handed him a book. 'Here. Read that.'

Dum Dum stared at it, not knowing what to do.

'You're supposed to read it, silly!' Nadine said.

'How do you do that?'

'Here, I'll show you,' she took the book and held it in front of her, moving her head slightly from side to side.

She gave it back to him. 'Here, you try it.'

Dum Dum held it in front of his face and moved his head from side to side, like he had seen Nadine doing.

She laughed. 'you're supposed to go from left to right.'

He scratched his head. 'Always?'

'Always,' Nadine nodded.

'But I like starting from the right,' grumbled Dum Dum.

'Well, it's not allowed,' Nadine held.

'Why not?'

'Because that's the way it's supposed to be.'

And so Dum Dum learned that part of being a real child is knowing how things are supposed to be and how things are not supposed to be.

That day, when they were going home on the bus, Dum Dum started moving his head from side to side.

'What're you doin'?' asked Paul.

'Shut up!' Dum Dum snapped. 'I'm reading.'

Paul laughed.

'What's so funny?' Dum Dum whined. 'What you laughin' about? I don't laugh at you when you're reading!'

'But you can't read with nothing in front of you!' shouted Paul.

'Who says?' Dum Dum shouted back.

'Hey, keep it down!' the bus conductor yelled at them.

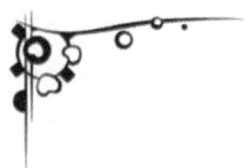

Chapter 14

It was just before the holidays and Paul's school was planning a costume party. Paul's friends asked him to take Dum Dum along.

'I'm not sure it's time to let others see him,' wavered Paul.

'But everyone will be wearing costumes,' Albert tried to convince him. 'They'll think he's just one of us.'

'It'll be full of kids in weird outfits,' added Charlie. 'He'll look normal for once.'

'Thanks,' Dum Dum gave him a grudging nod.

On the day of the party, Paul's gang managed to smuggle Dum Dum in with them. He mingled with all the other kids wearing all sorts of disguises. Some were dressed as turtles, others as superheroes, still others as lions, vampires and crocodiles. Dum Dum had come as he was.

As they were leaving one of the teachers bent over Dum Dum. 'Why that's a cute little costume!' she gushed. 'I really thought you were a ventriloquist's dummy!'

Paul and his friends exchanged smiles as they left.

Dum Dum was very happy on the way home. It was the first time he'd been in a roomful of kids other than Paul and his group.

'I really felt like a real boy!' he rejoiced. Paul put his arm around him as they walked to their building. When they were inside Dum Dum said, 'Why don't we go upstairs and say hello to Sayna?'

Paul agreed and they went up several floors. But when they knocked on the door, they found it open. They walked inside, calling, 'Sayna? Hello? Anybody home?'

But the flat was empty. Sayna's family had disappeared.

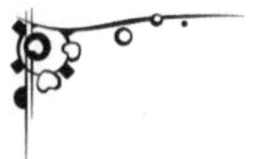

Chapter 15

Paul was hoping Dum Dum had forgotten all about Luke and Cy, but one day they spotted them at the park.

'Let's go say hello,' pleaded Dum Dum. 'We haven't seen them for a while.'

'No,' Paul tried to pull him in the opposite direction. 'I'm not sure that's a good idea.'

'Why not?' Dum Dum pulled back. 'I want to show them all the new games I've learned. I didn't even know what hide-n'-seek was before.'

Paul tried to walk away as fast as he could. But the ruffians ran up to them. They were both breathless and seemed in a big rush.

'You in the mood for a game?' Cy grinned at Dum Dum.

'*Hunt the Thimble*?' Dum Dum eagerly replied.

' No, no,' said Cy. It's a bit different this time.'

He took something out of his pocket and slipped it in Dum Dum's hand.

'Don't take it!' Paul cried.

'Go on,' cajoled Cy. 'Just a little game.'

He gave Dum Dum a wink. 'You can even take a little for yourself.'

Suddenly they heard a man yell, 'That's them!'

He was pointing to Cy, who shot off, followed by Luke. The man and two others darted after them.

'What shall we do with this?' Dum Dum held up the wallet Cy had given him.

'Quick!' Paul ordered. 'Hide it!'

When they were near their building, Paul turned to Dum Dum. 'You'll have to throw away that wallet.'

'No!' Dum Dum defied him.

That's stolen goods!' hissed Paul. 'The cops are gonna think we stole it.'

'It's not stolen,' argued Dum Dum. 'Look. It's got a picture.'

Paul examined it. 'That's definitely not their picture,' he concluded. 'Unless they've got grey hair and missing teeth. We got to get rid of it!'

'No! ' Dum Dum stepped back, refusing to yield. 'I want to play *Hunt the Thimble*.'

Paul threw up his hands and they went inside.

Later that night Paul was woken up by someone knocking on his window. He and Dum Dum sat up in a fright, thinking it was Marc.

Paul went to the window. He saw Luke peering through the glass.

Paul opened the pane. 'What do you want?'

'Remember that thing we gave you this morning?' Cy tried to put on a sweet smile.

Dum Dum jumped up to see his friends. He was eager to play. 'You got to hunt for it,' he teased them. 'That's the rules.'

Luke brought up a dirty brick from somewhere and snarled, 'Why, you filthy dummy! You give that thing back or I'll smash this on yer face!'

'Sssshh!' Paul tried to quieten them down. 'You're going to wake up my mum!'

He went to the closet and rummaged until he found the wallet. He put it in Luke's outstretched hand.

The ruffians went away happy, while Paul and Dum Dum went back to bed.

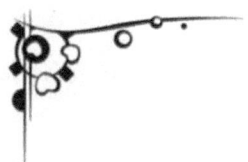

Chapter 16

With each day, Paul noticed more and more changes in Dum Dum. He seemed to be acting more and more like a real boy. One day a candy bar fell out of Paul's pocket.

'What's that?' Dum Dum leaned forward to see.

'It's candy,' Paul unwrapped it and took a bite. Then he offered it to Dum Dum.

He looked at it curiously for a moment, then, for the first time, bit off a piece. His face lit up. 'Ooh! That's nice!'

'Finally!' Paul raised a triumphant fist. He explained to Dum Dum how part of being a real boy was feeling hungry and loving sugar and all sorts of sweet things.

'That's the difference between you and Fyodor,' he patted Dum Dum on the shoulder. 'You understand that. But Fyodor never will.'

In time, Dum Dum began asking Paul about other places. Paul didn't know what to tell him because he'd never been anywhere else.

'I'd like to go somewhere far away,' breathed
Dum Dum. 'Somewhere I can learn more about being a real
boy.'

'I suppose you'll have to one day,' conceded Paul.

'I'd like to go to school with you,' Dum Dum
proposed.

Paul seemed to think that was going too far. 'You
can't!'

'Well, I got to do something,' Dum Dum pondered.
'You go to school everyday. Your mum goes to work. How will
I ever become a real boy if I just stay here in your room
everyday?'

Paul shrugged, 'I guess you're right.'

So Dum Dum started disappearing for stretches at a
time. Paul would come home and find him gone. He'd wake
up the next morning to find Dum Dum sleeping on the floor
near his bed.

But one day Paul woke up in the middle of the night.
Dum Dum still wasn't back.

He got up and looked in the closet. Everything was
quiet.

From somewhere across the city he heard a siren wail.
He lay down again but couldn't get back to sleep.

Finally he crept out quietly and went upstairs to
Sayna's flat.

But it was still deserted. This time there was police tape stretched across the entrance. Paul was even more frightened. He went home and got back in bed. But he still couldn't sleep.

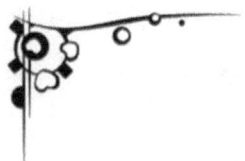

Chapter 17

One day Paul came home to find Dum Dum waiting at the front door.

'Where've you been?' Paul demanded.

'Where else?' retorted Dum Dum. 'I've been learning all the things you can't teach me.'

Once they were inside Dum Dum went to the kitchen and took out some bread. He showed Paul not only that could eat real food now, but he could also drink.

After he had finished a sandwich, he produced a packet of cigarettes. He put one in his mouth and lit it.

'Stop that!' Paul snatched it out of his mouth and crushed it underfoot.

He looked up to see Dum Dum dangling a gold watch near his face.

'Where'd you get that?' Paul snarled.

'None of your business!'

'Tell me!' shouted Paul.

'I don't want to!' Dum Dum shouted in return.

Paul took a step towards him. 'Give that back!'

'No!' Dum Dum retreated, putting the watch away.

'You hear me?' Paul yelled even louder. 'You're going to return that watch to whoever you took it from!'

'Why should I?' Dum Dum defied him. 'I don't have to do anything you say! You're not my only friend now. I've got lots of other friends!'

'You wouldn't know any of them if not for me! You'd still be stuck in that children's theatre with Marc!'

'That doesn't make you my owner!' responded Dum Dum. 'In fact I don't have an owner anymore! So I can do what I want!'

'That doesn't mean you don't have to follow rules!' Paul asserted.

'What's the matter?' Dum Dum changed tack. 'You want one, too?'

He took a winning stub from his pocket and produced some cash.

'I've had a good day at the races, you know,' he said, counting out some bills. 'I could buy you a watch if I want.'

He threw the money at Paul.

'I don't want your filthy money!' Paul flung it back.

At last Paul suggested going for a walk so they could both calm down. When they were just outside the park Dum Dum disclosed, 'I've seen Sayna.'

'Did she talk to you?'

Dum Dum nodded with a gleam in his eye.

'Why is there police tape where they used to live?' Paul inquired.

'Must be because of all the stolen goods,' Dum Dum said. 'That's why they moved out.'

'What do you mean, stolen goods?' Paul said.

'Her parents got caught selling drugs and buying stolen stuff, Dum Dum explained.

'Where did they go?'

'Oh, just a few streets away,' Dum Dum replied. 'I've been there several times. She's taught me more things than I learned at the train station.'

Paul looked at him. 'So Sayna's one of your new friends, is she?'

'Yes,' Dum Dum grinned. 'She's a way better teacher than you.'

Paul had to accept that Dum Dum was changing. He couldn't remain the same as when Paul first found him. Even Dum Dum seemed surprised at his own transformation.

One day his stomach growled.

'What's that?' he asked Paul worriedly.

'It means you're hungry,' Paul told him.

Dum Dum patted his stomach with a smile. 'I like that. It's like there's something alive inside me.'

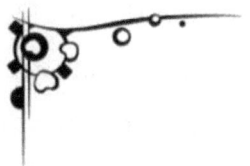

<u>Chapter 18</u>

One day Paul came home from school to find
Dum Dum waiting at the corner. 'I've got something to show
you,' he motioned for Paul to follow. They crossed several
streets until they reached a derelict building.

'This is where Sayna lives now,' Dum Dum led him up
a worn out flight of stairs. 'They're on the top floor.'

'Are we going to see them?'

'Not yet. I want you to see this first.'

They kept climbing up to the third landing.
Dum Dum put a finger to his lips and walked down a narrow,
dirty passage. At the end of it they came to a door. Paul raised
his hand to knock.

'Don't bother,' said Dum Dum. 'There's no one here.'

He threw the door open and they walked into the large
empty room.

'This is where I've learned a lot of things,' Dum Dum looked around proudly. It was all bare pillars and a concrete floor, strewn with empty bottles and cigarette butts. In a corner was a large black spot where someone had lit a fire.

Suddenly they heard noises from outside. There were several voices coming down towards them.

Paul looked at Dum Dum. 'I thought you said there was no one here!'

'Quick!' hissed Dum Dum. 'Find somewhere to hide!'

They ran inside and found even more vacant rooms. There was one with tattered bits of wall paper still clinging to the sides. In another room they saw a big fireplace all black on the inside. It gaped like a dark mouth out of the wall. Paul ran into that.

Dum Dum looked around for something to shield him. In the end he just lay down on the floor and didn't move.

Finally a group of young men burst in. Paul retreated further into the fireplace. He heard the youths talking and looking around. One of them found Dum Dum. 'Hey! Who left that doll there? I thought no one else knew about this place!'

The tallest of the group grabbed a shorter one by the collar. 'You been telling anyone else about this spot?'

'No!' came the fearful answer. 'I haven't breathed a word! I swear!'

'He's a snitch!' cried another voice. 'Let's cut him and leave him here!'

'No, I'm not!' howled the accused teen. 'You're the snitch! Can't keep your stupid mouth shut!'

From where he was hiding, Paul saw the gang spread out and pull knives on each other. Some of them picked up bars or one of the broken bottles scattered on the floor. Paul retreated deeper into his sooty cavity.

One of the group walked over towards Dum Dum and said, 'Now, I might just use this dummy to set this damn place on fire.'

Paul wanted to come out and save Dum Dum, but he was too scared.

'Don't touch him!' someone suddenly yelled.

'Why not?'

'Look at all these needles lying around,' a chubby boy came forward. 'That doll could be infected with AIDS or something. Maybe that's why it was left here.'

'Okay,' said the large tough. 'Let's do this quickly and get out of here.'

Something was taken out of their pockets and given to the other group to examine. Then money was counted out and passed from one hand to another.

'Let's go!' shouted the leader and they all scurried out.

Paul waited several moments to make sure they were quite alone before he came out. He looked at himself and gasped. He was all black with soot from head to toe. He ran over to the corner and whispered to Dum Dum, 'They're gone!'

With that Dum Dum jumped to his feet. 'You run along,' he said. 'I'll go upstairs and see Sayna.'

Paul ran home. To his surprise, his mum was already there.

'What happened?' she screamed as soon as she saw him. 'Where on *earth* have you *been*?'

'I was just playing,' Paul tried to act casual.

'Just playing!' she hooted. 'Nobody gets all black and filthy like that just playing!'

She stood up and planted herself in front of him. 'Have you been next door?'

'What do you mean next door?'

'Next door?' she pulled him towards the sofa. 'Don't pretend you don't know! I mean those empty buildings around the corner!'

'Of course not!' refuted Paul. Why would I do that? There's nothing there!'

'Don't get all coy with me!' she pointed a finger in his face. 'I know what goes on in that place. And so do the bloody cops! If you know what's good for you, you stay away from there!'

She turned around and marched into his room. He tried to stop her but she pushed him aside. She started looking in every corner, under the books scattered on the floor, behind the bookcase, even under his mattress. Paul held his breath when she stopped in front of the closet. But something suddenly caught her eye.

She crossed quickly to the window and bent down.

'And what is this?' she held up the empty cigarette packets Dum Dum had left behind. She hurried out and came back with a broom. Under the bed she found more damaging proof Paul hadn't thought to get rid of: the winning stubs, a pair of dice, an empty flask of whiskey Dum Dum had left there.

'What's all this?' she bawled. 'And *this*! And *this*! And *this*!'

Paul struggled to explain.

'So this is what you've been doing!' she said quietly.

'They're not mine!' Paul managed to blurt out.

She was shaking her head. 'This is why I got a letter from your school the other day.'

'What letter?'

'They say you haven't been to your classes.'

'But I have!'

'Well the evidence says otherwise don't it?' she lay down he flask and cigarette packets on his bed.

'Are you running around with that crowd next door?' she put her hands on her hips.

'What crowd next door?'

'Those drug dealers and those pimps, don't think I don't know. I've been through all this already with your dad!'

Mum, 'you don't understand,' pleaded Paul.

She snatched up one of the cigarette packets ad crushed it in her fist.

'What don't I understand?' she shook it angrily. 'This? That my little baby is smoking already? Hiding little flasks of liquor under his bed? Going off to the races instead of going to school?'

'They're not mine,' Paul whimpered in defeat.

His mum straightened up. 'Then *whose* are they?'

'They belong to another kid.'

'Another kid!' Her eyes opened wide. 'Well, how am I supposed to believe *that*? You mean there's *someone* else living *here* with you that I haven't *seen*? Someone responsible for all these filthy things in my house?'

'I swear!' Paul implored. 'They're really not mine!'

'Now there you go again!' his mum heaved her chest. 'Lying and making things up. When are you going to learn to just own up to what you've done? That's why we had all that trouble before. You can't keep imagining things and blaming others for what you've done!'

She went outside. Paul followed her.

'Mum, you've got to believe me,' he entreated. 'There really *is* another kid.'

She threw up her hands. 'You know, up to about the time you were five years old, I let you say whatever you wanted. Because kids can say anything they want. As long as they're *wrong*. And they *know* they're *wrong*!'

'But I'm not wrong this time, mum!' Paul insisted. 'I really *do* have a friend you don't know about.'

His mum put a hand on his shoulder. 'All right. I'll let you believe that if you want. But this is the last time! In a couple of years, you know what it's going to be called? *Perjury*. That's what they throw you in the slammer for. That's exactly the kind of trouble I had with your dad!'

After they'd had dinner, Paul tried to go out again to get Dum Dum.

'You're not going anywhere,' his mum ordered. 'You're going to sit in your room and read.'

After his mum had left for her second job, Paul heard a knock on the door. When he opened it, he found a note on the floor. It was from Dum Dum. The letters were written exactly the way Nadine wrote her letters, and it told him

Dum Dum had gone off with Sayna so he could learn more about life.

Paul closed the door. He went back to his room and started sobbing.

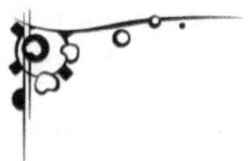

Chapter 19

After many weeks, Sayna accosted Paul at the bus stop.

'I thought you were hiding from the police,' he said to her.

'Oh things get hot until they get cool again,' she laughed. 'You can only lie low for so long. Then you have to come out again.'

'You don't have to drag Dum Dum into your mess.'

'Who's dragging him?' Sayna pouted. 'He likes it with us. He loves the excitement. And *I* really like him. He makes me laugh.'

'If you really like him,' Paul countered, 'tell him to come home.'

Sayna threw her head back in laughter. 'To you? Ha! Why, I don't blame him for leaving.'

'I love him,' Paul declared. 'I'll take care of him. No matter what. Unlike you!'

'He doesn't need taking care of,' she waved him off. 'He can look after himself very well. Better than you ever can.'

'At least I don't take him on drug deals!' bellowed Paul at her.

She narrowed her eyes at him. 'Oh, you're so square! Between you and Dum Dum you're the real dummy!' She gave a toss of the head and walked away.

One day after school, Paul caught a glimpse of Dum Dum on a street corner, standing around with Sayna and her friends. Paul ran across the street to reach them. He found Dum Dum and Sayna arm-in-arm. A lit cigarette was dangling from his lips, and he was oblivious to everything around him. He was telling jokes about his owner Marc, and Sayna kept giggling at them.

'If the cops caught me for all the kisses I stole from you,' he was saying, 'I'd go away for a long time.'

Sayna and the other girls burst out in laughter.

'You always seem to know what to say,' gushed Sayna, stroking Dum Dum's shoulder.

'That's because I only say what you're already thinking,' quipped Dum Dum.

Sayna chuckled again and planted a kiss his forehead. He looked up at her with a bright gleam in his eyes.

Paul was shocked to see him like that. He was completely under Sayna's spell.

In the weeks since Paul had last seen him, Dum Dum had truly become more and more of a real boy. His wish was coming true too fast and seemed out of control. Sayna and her rough bunch had pulled him to their world of drugs, drinking, and gambling.

Like any real boy, Dum Dum seemed to find it all irresistible. Paul knew that he was in danger of losing his friend forever, to the very things he had been trying to escape in the first place.

Paul stopped and stood near them, but Dum Dum didn't even look at him.

'Dum Dum!' Paul shouted. 'Don't pretend you didn't hear me!'

'Christ! Who let the kid in early?' joked Dum Dum to his new circle of admirers. 'Someone tell him the zoo's still closed.'

They all laughed at Paul.

He lunged forward and tried to pull Dum Dum away.

'Hey!' Sayna barked. Her friends all advanced on Paul and surrounded him.

'Okay, okay,' Dum Dum finally came forward raising his hands. 'Easy now. Easy. No need to hurt the kid.'

He put his hand on Paul's wrist and pulled him to the side.

'Watch it now, will ya?' he scolded. Paul could smell the liquor in his breath.

'You've been drinking!' he said accusingly. 'It's not even six o'clock yet!'

'I drink when I can,' Dum Dum shrugged. 'Sayna says it makes me funnier.'

'Well, it doesn't,' disputed Paul. 'It makes you horrible!'

He noticed a rip in Dum Dum's shirt. 'What happened to your collar?' he asked.

'Couldn't be helped,' Dum Dum jerked his head indifferently, just like Sayna. 'Got into a scrape the other night. Some blokes seemed to have it in for me. I had give them the old one-two.'

'That happens a lot when you're drunk,' Paul berated him in turn. 'You do stupid things. And the next thing you know you're in a fight.'

'It's all part of the fun,' replied Dum Dum, wiping his lips. 'Now I know why everybody loves drinking so much. Now I know why Marc never stopped.'

'You *are* becoming like Marc!' hissed Paul. 'You said you wanted to get away from him!

Because he was so awful. Now you're becoming exactly like him! Cursing and fighting and carrying on. I used to think that when bad things came out of your mouth, you were just saying things Marc used to force you to say. Now the bad things are coming from you! You can't blame anyone else anymore!'

Dum Dum was quiet for a moment. Paul saw a tear in his eye.

'I'm sorry,' Paul touched him on the shoulder. 'I didn't mean to make you cry.'

'Who's crying?' Dum Dum yelped and jumped back. 'Dummies don't cry, silly! Only dummies like you think they do!'

Paul walked away, trying not to burst into tears in front of everybody.

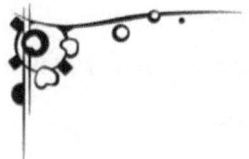

Chapter 20

Paul's friends were very keen to help.

'We'll have to get him back,' avowed Ryan, his ginger eyebrows furrowed in concern.

Every day they met at the playground or one of their houses to plot how.

'We've got to show him he's wrong,' Albert said.

Charlie had brought that day's newspaper. The front page showed a picture of Sayna.

'Two of the boys in her group have been arrested for burglary,' he told them.

'Another one was wounded in a fight with another gang,' read Ryan from further down in the paper.

'We've got to make Dum Dum see!' Charlie pounded the table.

'He needs to know the truth about Sayna!' echoed Nadine.

'First we've got to find him,' Paul said.

'That's easy,' responded Nadine. She flipped the paper to the back page. 'It says here they're always at a park near Calvert Road.'

The next day they made their way to Calvert Road. They walked around until they found a good hiding place. They waited for hours before anything happened.

'There he is!' Nadine finally exclaimed.

Paul and Charlie jumped out to accost Dum Dum.

Charlie whistled and waved, 'Hey, Dum Dum! Come over here!'

Dum Dum turned around to make his way towards them. But Sayna suddenly called out from somewhere, 'Dum Dum, No!'

He spun around and started running the other way. Charlie and Paul took off after him. But they were surprised at how fast Dum Dum had learned to run.

'Stop!' Paul started yelling. 'Help! Somebody stop him!'

But when people saw two boys chasing a dummy, they just pointed and laughed. Drivers slowed down to gape at the trio darting across the busy road.

When they reached the other side, Paul lost sight of Dum Dum. His eyes scanned the crowds but he couldn't find him.

'There he is!' Ryan cried out from across the street. Paul turned just in time to see Dum Dum running down the stairs to the Tube station, behind a bunch of pedestrians.

'Dum Dum! Stop!' Paul called out. 'Wait for me! Dum Dum!'

Some people stopped and glared at him, looking insulted. 'Who you calling Dum Dum?' one man snarled. 'Stop shouting!'

'I'm not talking to you!' retorted Paul 'I'm talking to…'

He pointed to where he had seen Dum Dum. But he was gone.

Another day Paul and Ryan saw him coming out of an empty building. He tried to walk briskly away but Paul caught up to him.

'Where you been?' Paul demanded.

'I'm not telling you,' Dum Dum kept walking.

'Why not?'

'You don't tell Charlie or Albert everywhere you go,' reasoned Dum Dum. 'Real boys don't tell each other everything they do.'

'But it's different with Albert and Charlie,' Paul answered.

'How is it different?'

'I found you.'

'You didn't find me,' shot back Dum Dum. 'I found you!'

'No, I found you!' Paul contended. 'I let you stay in my backpack so you could get away from that awful theatre!'

'So? I owe you, do I?'

'No,' Paul uttered. 'But I don't want you to end up back there. I want you to become a real boy, like you always wanted.'

'I am doing what I've always wanted!' Dum Dum stomped his foot. 'You're the one who's trying to stop me! Living with you is no better than with Marc!'

Paul took a deep breath before saying, 'That's not you talking. It's Marc.'

'Why, yes, it's me!' Dum Dum pointed to his own mouth. 'See my lips moving? Yes! It's really *me* talking. And I'm saying I'm *better* off *without* you!'

Paul leaned forward to grab him. But Dum Dum jumped back and ran away.

Ryan came up to join Paul.

'We've got to make him listen,' Paul said. 'He doesn't know what risks he's taking.'

'It's none of our business now,' Ryan replied. 'We can't force him.'

'But he doesn't know what he's doing!' fretted Paul. 'He thinks he's a real boy now and he can think for himself. But he can't.'

'If he really wants to be a real boy,' said Ryan, 'maybe has to find that out for himself.'

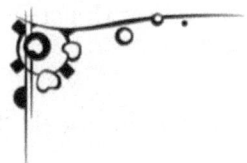

Chapter 21

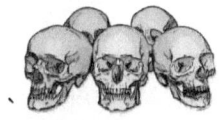

In another part of the city, Dum Dum was oblivious to all of Paul's worries, and was having the time of his life. He and Sayna's friends would stay up all night playing pool, drink and talk about the places they'd broken into.

But one night they were coming out of the bar when Sayna froze in her tracks. 'Uh-oh.'

'What's wrong, sweetie?' Dum Dum asked.

'I think that bunch might be waiting for me.'

'Why?'

She pulled Dum Dum into a doorway and they peered out at the group hanging around at the corner.

'That's Mickey,' Sayna whispered. 'The one holding the bat. That's Dosido next to him in the torn shirt. That big one is Screwball and the bald one is called Guillotine.'

'Why would they be waiting for you?' Dum Dum touched her shoulder.

'Seems they're still cheesed off about the stuff I pinched from them.'

'Don't you worry petal,' he patted her cheek. 'Old Dum Dum's here to protect you now.'

They were living in one of the upper rooms of an abandoned hospital that was once a workhouse. The ground floor was overrun with greenery, littered with old hoses and bedpans, empty medicine cabinets and rusty bedsteads with peeling white paint.

The old operating room still had its swinging doors and Sayna said the large room with metal cabinets used to be the morgue. She told Dum Dum she often heard creepy noises from down there, and was too scared to go downstairs by herself.

One day they came out the front door to find the group waiting for them.

'Where's that stock you swiped?' Mickey demanded, swinging his bat.

'Your book is overdue.' Guillotine stuck his head out from behind him. 'Time to pay the fine!'

Dum Dum and Sayna ran back inside.

The young men raced in after them, shouting up the stairwell, banging their clubs and bats on the walls. 'We'll get it back one way or the other!' Mickey bellowed.

On the upper landing. Dum Dum and Sayna pressed themselves into a corner, Sayna clinging tightly to his arm.

Finally Dum Dum ran down the stairs to confront them. They all fell on him with their weapons, shrieking and cursing. Sayna covered her ears and cowered on the landing.

But the knives broke on Dum Dum's wooden body, the bars bounced off and fell to the ground.

While Screwball was staring in disbelief at the bent blade in his hand, Dum Dum swung his foot back and gave him a kick in the knee.

'Ow!' Screwball hopped around clutching his knee. The others tried to get hold of Dum Dum, but he leapt around punching and kicking, just like he'd seen drunks do in the pubs after their shows.

Finally, the boys had had enough, Mickey grabbed his bat and ran out. The others followed.

And so Dum Dum became a hero in Sayna's world. Soon everyone knew what Dum Dum had done. He used all the tricks he'd learned from Marc and his friends, talking like a thug and scheming behind people's backs. With every new mischief he grew in Sayna's eyes.

One day Mickey's gang come back. Sayna looked out the window and saw them coming.

'They've got guns,' she whispered. 'You can't possibly beat that.'

'Don't worry about me,' Dum Dum said. 'I haven't run out of tricks yet.'

He went to the door.

'Where you going?' Sayna asked.

'I'll just go fetch some old friends,' he told her and left.

It was almost night by the time he got back. Sayna opened the door and helped him drag in a large leather bag that looked big enough for him to fit in.

'Boy, you took forever,' Sayna whined.

'It's a long way,' Dum Dum answered. 'And I didn't want anyone to stop and ask what I have in my bag.'

'What *is* in that bag?'

Dum Dum pulled it closer to the door. 'You'll see.'

'I've been cooped up all day,' Sayna got up and went to the window. 'You fancy taking me out for a walk?'

Dum Dum was too busy fumbling with the bag to answer. Then she said, 'Oh, Lord!'

'What's wrong?'

'They're here again!'

'Good,' said Dum Dum hoisting the bag. 'I can't wait to see them.'

'Don't go down there!' Sayna whispered. 'They'll kill you!'

'They tried that before,' shrugged Dum Dum and went out the door. He hauled the bag to the ground floor and took out its contents.

They were skulls he had borrowed from the cellar near Paul's building. He positioned them in various places in the dark, deserted rooms, putting the scariest ones on the metal drawers of the old morgue. They looked eerily bright in the shadows. Dum Dum grinned to himself.

The swinging doors parted and Mickey and Dosido burst in.

'Hey, there's that gonzo!' Dosido spotted Dum Dum. They all scattered to catch him.

Dum Dum ran around in circles, making sure he led them through the empty rooms, round and round until they were in the old morgue. It was completely dark now.

'Why it's good of you boys to come and visit,' said a voice from somewhere.

'Who said that?' gasped Screwball, his head swivelling from side to side.

'Why up here!' said the voice again. 'Look above you! Are you blind?'

They all looked up and saw the first skull. They started withdrawing towards the exit.

'Now meet my brother and sister,' said the voice again.

The boys almost bumped heads as they turned this way and that. 'Where? Where?'

'Behind you, dozy! Right here near the door!'

At last they saw skulls leering down at them.

'This is spooky!' uttered Mickey. 'Let's get out of here!'

Crazy laughter started to fill the abandoned rooms. The skulls all seemed to be mocking them as they ran from one room to the other, terrified. But wherever went there were skulls leering down at them from the shadows.

'They're everywhere!' Mickey cried out. 'Quick! Get out!'

They fought over who would go out the swinging doors first, then they all tried to squeeze through at once, until they all burst out like a cork from a bottle.

Dum Dum stood at the doorway laughing.

He took a long time to gather the skulls and put them all in the bag. Then he went up to rejoin Sayna.

'So these are your old friends,' she giggled when he showed her the skulls.

'Yes,' Dum Dum zipped up the bag. 'Now I have to take them home.'

Soon Dum Dum's reputation grew. He started to enjoy the games, the money, the fear others had of him.

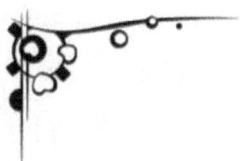

Chapter 22

One day, Charlie came to school with a newspaper.

'Read that!' he shoved it in Paul's hands. The front page showed pictures of a gang being rounded up by police somewhere in London. Paul and his friends passed the paper around, reading the article.

'That description sure sounds like Dum Dum,' Albert remarked.

'We've got to get him back!' Ryan said.

'But how?'

They all wracked their brains for a long time.

Suddenly Albert yelled, 'Ginger!'

Charlie turned to him. 'What about Ginger?'

'She might be our only chance to get him back,' explained Albert.

'But I don't even know where she is,' lamented Paul.

'That's just it!' uttered Albert. 'you've got to convince Dum Dum to search for her! She was the reason he ran away in the first place.'

The next day they went to all the places mentioned in the newspaper. They sneaked into pool halls, pubs and private clubs, dressing up in their parents' clothes to pass for grown-ups.

Outside one club they heard two drunks talking.

'That Eastern girl sure is going places with that midget boyfriend of hers,' said one drunk.

'He's a bit odd-looking,' replied the other drunk. 'But he certainly knows a few tricks. You never know if it's him talking or the guy next to him.'

Paul pulled Charlie aside.

'They're talking about Dum Dum,' he whispered. 'The "Eastern girl" is Sayna. The midget is Dum Dum.'

Charlie nodded. 'So they're just somewhere here.'

A week later Paul read about a fight between two gangs in some abandoned hospital. The article mentioned someone who sounded like Dum Dum again. He wrote down the hospital's address.

A few days later, he and Charlie went there. They searched through the overgrown wards and went up to the upper rooms. There they found the windows shattered, the door hanging by one hinge to the jamb.

There were dark stains on the walls, along with some sickening slime.

'Look!' Charlie pointed at something on the floor.

Paul went over and picked it up.

'It's one of Dum Dum's ears!' he bawled. 'We've got to find him and put it back in!'

Charlie put a hand on his shoulder. 'This proves he really was here. Don't worry. We'll find him.'

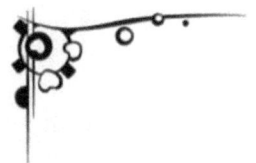

Chapter 23

The next time Paul returned with Charlie to the abandoned hospital, it was already being torn down. The roof had been taken off and there was a mountain of junk behind the building. The two boys walked around to the back and dug through a mound of debris. At last Charlie pulled out something. It looked like a leg.

'It's him!' cried out Paul. He pounced on the spot. He swept all the rubbish aside like a crazed ferret until he managed to free Dum Dum.

Paul brushed the dirt away and took out his handkerchief. He used it to wipe Dum Dum's arms and clothes. But Dum Dum's eyes stayed closed.

'Dum Dum!' Paul shook him. There was no response.

'Put back his ear!' Charlie said.

Paul took the ear out of his pocket and stuck it back on Dum Dum's head. Then he tightened the ear that was already there.

'Dum Dum! Dum Dum!' whispered Paul into each ear. 'Wake up!'

But Dum Dum just lay there, like a dummy made of wood.

'Oh no!' groaned Paul. He looked down at Dum Dum, motionless as a rock.

Paul began to wonder if it had all been just his imagination.

'Maybe we should take him to a doctor,' Charlie suggested.

'A doctor wouldn't know what to do with him.'

Paul picked up Dum Dum and they walked to the street corner. He felt strange carrying Dum Dum like this, without him complaining or wriggling.

Several buses went by as they tried to decide where they should go.

Suddenly Paul brightened up. 'I know where to take him!'

'Where?'

'To my uncle Matthew!'

They sat in the upper deck, Paul cradling Dum Dum like a baby.

But when they got to Matthew's shop it was closed. They rattled the door and knocked on the glass. But there was no one inside.

'I forgot,' said Paul. 'He was going on a trip.'

Charlie clucked his tongue. 'That could be a problem.'

They looked around hopefully for someone who might help them.

Then Paul remembered something. 'I know where he keeps a spare key!'

They ran around to the back.

Paul put down Dum Dum and hitched up his pants. 'Quick! Help me up.'

Charlie clasped his hands to give Paul a boost. Paul scrambled onto the bars until he could reach the space just behind the doorway light.

'Got it!' he said and jumped down. He picked up Dum Dum again and unlocked the shop. They dashed inside.

Charlie gazed up at the glass counters and the confusing array of tools hanging from the walls.

'You're not thinking of doing it ourselves are you?' he asked.

'We don't have time to wait for my uncle,' Paul replied, laying Dum Dum down on the long wooden table. 'I've seen him do it. I know which tools to use.'

Charlie looked doubtful.

'Well, come on,' Paul urged, taking down saws and hammers. He put them down next to Dum Dum.

'What's this for, then?' Charlie took down a large clamping device and turned it over in his hands.

'I didn't see my uncle use that,' replied Paul. 'So we probably won't need it.'

Charlie put it back.

'But whatever we do,' said Paul, 'we shouldn't use a chisel.'

Charlie gazed at Dum Dum's motionless figure on the table. 'I suppose we better get busy, then.'

They started patching up Dum Dum, continually throwing glances out the window in case someone came in. Even they were surprised at how quickly they worked.

Soon Dum Dum looked slightly better shape than when they'd found him. They sat him up to look him over.

'I think his feet might be on backwards,' Charlie pointed out.

And that wasn't the only problem. Paul raised Dum Dum's hands and tried to move the fingers. They were stiff.

'Uh-oh.' Paul looked horrified. 'What have we done?'

Charlie took one of Dum Dum's arms and moved it up and down.

'You listen,' he said to Paul.

Paul pressed his ears against Dum Dum's chest while Charlie continued testing the limbs.

'Sounds all rusty inside,' Paul said, looking panicked. 'Soon he won't be able to move at all!'

They put down Dum Dum down carefully and watched him for several moments. There were no signs of improvement.

'I'm afraid we need some help,' declared Charlie.

'Obviously. But who?'

'Uncle Rupert.'

'No!' shouted Paul.

'We have no choice!' Charlie retorted.

'But he'll just ruin everything!'

'How?'

'He's going to see Dum Dum isn't an ordinary puppet. He's going to tell my mum!'

'Right now Dum Dum seems just like any ordinary puppet,' observed Charlie. ' And he needs fixing.'

'What if Dum Dum talks while Rupert is here?'

Charlie glanced sadly at Dum Dum. 'I'm not sure he'll ever do that again.'

'That's what I'm really afraid of,' uttered Paul, fighting back his tears.

He tried to move Dum Dum's arms again, hoping to see his eyes open, trying everything to make him come back to life.

'Okay,' he said at last. 'Let's call Rupert.'

By the time Rupert arrived it was getting dark.

'My , my, my,' he tutted. 'What a tip you've got here.'

'Uncle Rupert, please!' Charlie said. 'We'll explain later. This is an *emergency*!'

Rupert picked up Dum Dum and scrutinized him with a ferocious look. He turned him over several times, making all sorts of disgusted noises.

'Wrong! Wrong, wrong, wrong, wrong, wrong!' he chimed at different pitches as he fiddled with every inch of Dum Dum.

'Hand me those tools, would you?' he said and proceeded to labour over Dum Dum. Every now and then he would look up from the table to tell the boys what they had done wrong. He put his hands inside Dum Dum, made him turn his head, flutter his eyes and move his lips.

'Ah! There's the problem!' Rupert finally proclaimed.

He groped in the back of Dum Dum and made him snap his jaw a few times.

Paul looked up without much hope. But he caught Dum Dum winking at him.

'You did it!' he jumped up with a cry.

'Of course I did it,' Rupert said smugly.

'Uncle Rupert!' gushed Charlie. 'I never knew!'

'Now, now, now, boys,' Rupert raised his finger. 'It's almost nine o' clock. Time to run along home. Quick supper and off to bed. Enough of puppets and what not. Tomorrow's a school day.'

He walked to the door and turned around, looking closely at the place for the first time. 'Say, how did you boys get in here? Do you even have permission to be in here? '

'It's a long story,' Charlie said with a smile.

Rupert thought about it, then shrugged and left.

As soon as he was gone the boys danced around happily with Dum Dum.

'I feel as good as new,' Dum Dum said. 'Though for a while there, it felt like my feet were pointing backwards.'

Paul and Charlie laughed.

'And even my ears feel right,' Dum Dum touched the sides of his head.

'Do they?'

'Yes!' Dum Dum nodded. 'They've never been this snug before. I swear I've never heard this good!'

'Neither have I!' shouted Paul with joy.

'Paul,' said Charlie from the door. 'It's late. Let's go home.'

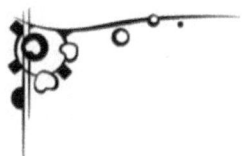

Chapter 24

Long after he'd brought Dum Dum home, Paul didn't stop worrying. He couldn't help thinking there was something different about Dum Dum.

'Does he look okay to you?' he kept asking Charlie.

'He looks fine,' Charlie would shrug. 'What's bothering you?'

'I don't know,' said Paul. 'I'm afraid he's just turning back into an ordinary dummy. The real Dum Dum is gone.'

Before they went to bed each night Paul would quiz Dum Dum.

'Can you still do magic tricks?'

'Sure I can,' the puppet assured him.

'Can you still do different voices?'

'Why wouldn't I?' Dum Dum replied in Paul's voice.

It startled Paul for a moment. But when he recovered he resumed his questioning.

Dum Dum finally snapped, 'Will you stop pestering me with these questions?'

'I just want to make sure you're back,' Paul told him. 'All of you.'

Dum Dum looked at his hands and bent down to see his feet. He patted his stomach, moved his head up and down. 'Yup. I'm all here.'

But Paul was still anxious. 'Are you sure?'

He picked up Dum Dum's wrists and released them. They fell limply to Dum Dum's sides.

'See?' he said 'You seem just like a regular dummy again.'

'So do you,' retorted Dum Dum.

Paul looked at him. He saw the twinkle in Dum Dum's eye.

He jumped up and hugged Dum Dum. 'You *are* back!' he cried. 'Now I believe it!'

A few nights later Paul woke up to see Dum Dum sitting upright on the bed.

'What you doing?' he asked.

'I just remembered something,' Dum Dum whispered, 'I've got to go find Ginger!'

Paul jumped out of bed with a cry, 'Hurrah!'

His mum pounded on the wall. 'What's the matter?'

But Paul couldn't contain his joy. He shouted again, 'I love you mother!'

'Aw shut up!'

Paul was impatient to start searching for Ginger. The next day he gathered maps and train schedules and laid them out on the kitchen table. 'So where would they be now?'

'Blackpool, no,' Dum Dum moved his finger from one point of the map to another. 'Bournemouth and Scarborough are out.'

'How do you know?'

'Ginger's owner started out in those places,' revealed Dum Dum. 'She's made too many enemies there. She swore she'd never go back.'

Paul took out a big Road Atlas. 'So where else could they be?'

Dum Dum closed his eyes and seemed to meditate. Suddenly his eyes opened. 'Ginger's owner often went on travelling fairs. She could never resist a carnival.'

'That's a start,' said Paul. 'Now where do we know that has a carnival?'

Dum Dum drummed his fingers on the table as he tried to think. He suddenly sat up, 'Why, Valta, of course!'

Paul scratched his chin. There's no place called Valta.'

'Of course there is!' Dum Dum insisted, pulling the Road Atlas towards him. Paul sat down and searched with him. After a long time he gave up. 'See? It doesn't show any place called Valta!'

'It wouldn't, naturally,' shrugged Dum Dum. 'What kind of nut do you think would put it on the Road Atlas?'

'Then how would we know how to get there?'

'That's what *my* map is for,' Dum Dum answered, searching in his pocket.

Paul gave him a blank look. 'What map are you talking about?'

'Remember the map I showed you the first time we met?'

'The one some puppets gave you at a pawnshop?'

Dum Dum nodded, still fumbling in his pockets. Then he suddenly froze. 'My God! It's not here!'

'Where could it be?' Paul jumped up with a cry.

'I don't know!' Dum Dum put his head in his hands. 'So many things have happened! I forgot all about it!'

They ran into Paul's room and turned it upside down. 'My mum cleaned up in here,' Paul moaned. 'She might have thrown it out!'

Dum Dum let himself fall the floor with a pout. He looked heart-broken. Paul was afraid he'd lose him all over again.

He lunged under his bed to search. But he still couldn't find it. He threw the closet doors open and yanked out all the clothes. Dum Dum waded through the heaps of Paul's things strewn everywhere. Then he saw the corner of Paul's memory box. He bent down to pick it up.

After a few moments he cried, 'Aha!'

'What!'

'It's right here in your book of nursery rhymes!'

Paul ran over to look. Indeed it was, stuck between two of Daniel's favourite verses.

'Yay!' Paul waved Dum Dum's map like a flag. 'Now we can go find Ginger!'

They ran out to the kitchen and held the map against the Road Atlas.

'But I still don't see how you can get to a place called Valta,' Paul said. 'The railroad on the atlas ends here, and I don't see how it connects to the railway on your map.'

'See here, where the two pages overlap?' Dum Dum put his finger in the crease between the two large sheets. Paul pressed Dum Dum's map against the fold. His eyes widened: at last he saw how the railway lines joined up

'There it is!' he cried. 'No wonder I didn't see it before. It was hidden by the crease!'

They were both excited.

'I guess that means we might be going on a trip!' cheered Paul.

'Maybe we should tidy up your room first,' answered Dum Dum.

As they got ready for bed that night, Paul looked at Dum Dum's map again.

"I can't believe you can get to Valta on an ordinary train,' he whispered. 'Then how come no one I know has ever been there?'

'Not everybody has a friend like me,' smiled Dum Dum.

Paul quietly got things ready for their journey. When he saw his friends at school, he asked them to meet him at Charlie's house.

'I'll need you all to cover for me,' Paul told them. 'If my mother finds out I've gone off without telling her, she'll have my guts for garters.'

'Why don't you just tell her the truth?' Albert suggested.

'She'd never believe me,' said Paul. 'Besides, I don't want her to know about Dum Dum.'

They pondered the problem for several moments.

'I know!' Charlie finally burst out. 'You could join me and my family in Wales. We're going there for two weeks.'

'Ginger isn't in Wales,' Paul pointed out.

'I know,' said Charlie. 'But you could pretend you're there while you're actually out looking for Ginger!'

'She'd never let me go for that long,' Paul hung his head.

Nadine thought very hard.

'That's it!' she exclaimed at length.

'What's it?' they all turned to her.

'Let's put Dum Dum on the phone,' she proposed. 'He could put on mother's voice and tell Paul's mum she's inviting him to come with us to Wales.'

Paul mulled over the suggestion. 'Mum's been thinking about going to Cyprus or something. But she didn't have anyone to leave me with.'

'There you go!' Nadine snapped her fingers.

'But would she believe Dum Dum?' Ryan said.

'She won't *know* it's *Dum Dum*!' Charlie answered. 'She'll think it's my mother calling.'

'She might not believe Paul or any of us,' said Nadine. 'But she'd believe our mother.'

They all thought about it.

After a while they started nodding.

'Yes.'

'Yes.'

'Maybe.'

'It just might work.'

So they gave Dum Dum the phone and called Paul's mum. They snickered quietly as Dum Dum spoke in the exact same voice as Charlie's mother and asked for permission to take Paul to Wales.

When Dum Dum put down the phone they all crowded around him.

'What did she say?'

'What did she say?'

'She said, aw, all right then!' Dum Dum repeated in the voice of Paul's mum.

They all jumped up and cheered.

'You're going to find Ginger! You're going on an adventure!' they all applauded and danced around.

When they settled down, Paul summed up, 'Now the only problem is getting train tickets.'

Charlie and Nadine ran to their rooms. They came back with envelopes.

'This is from our Christmas money,' Charlie said. 'We can give you some for the trip.'

They both counted out some bills and handed them to Paul. Albert and Ryan reached into their pockets and did the same.

Paul thanked them and put the money away. 'Now we have to hurry home and pack.'

They said goodbye to everyone and left.

Nadine waved to them from the front door. 'Give my love to Ginger when you find her!'

'I've never been to a carnival before,' said Paul as they were walking to the corner.

'Dum Dum grinned at him. 'Now you will.'

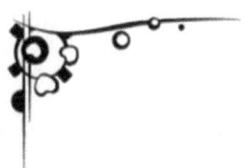

Chapter 25

Dum Dum waited at the stairwell while Paul went home to get his bag. His mum walked him to the front door.

'Should I give you some money?' she said worriedly.

'I've still got some from Christmas,' fibbed Paul.

'Will that be enough?'

'Of course,' Paul assured her. 'We'll be in the woods most days. There won't be much to buy up there.'

She lingered at the door. 'Will you be okay without seeing the doctor?'

'There's nothing wrong with me, mum,' Paul said. 'I don't need to see a doctor all the time. I was sick before. But now I'm better.'

'Well, all right, then,' She bent down and gave him a kiss. 'You take care of yourself.'

'Why don't you take that trip to Cyprus with Jeremy?' Paul said.

His mum was taken aback. 'How'd you know about that?'

'I heard you talking on the phone. Sounds like you really want to go.'

'It's for a bit of work as well,' justified his mum. 'It's not all fun and games, you know.'

'I know,' Paul nodded. 'But fun and games are ok for grown-ups, too, you know?'

'Well, look who's talking,' she smiled at him.

Paul ran to the stairwell and picked up Dum Dum.

At Charlie's they knocked on the side door and Nadine let them in as they had agreed. She led them to the farthest rooms in the house so her parents wouldn't know what was going on. It was such a secret they couldn't risk eating in the dining room. So Charlie brought sandwiches and they ate them on the beds. They talked in whispers about Paul and Dum Dum's plans.

At last Charlie and his sister got up to say goodnight.

'Have a safe trip!' Nadine whispered at the door.

'Call us when you get back,' Charlie murmured solemnly and left. Paul locked the door behind them and lay down to get some sleep.

He must have been sleeping for hours when he felt someone shaking him. He opened his eyes to see Dum Dum standing next to him.

'What?' he mumbled sleepily.

'Time to go,' Dum Dum uttered impatiently.

Paul peered out the window. It was still completely dark.

'We'll go in the morning,' Paul muttered and turned over.

'No. It might be too late in the morning,' Dum Dum insisted. 'If we're going to find Ginger, we better go now.'

Paul had no choice but to drag himself out of bed.

They opened the door softly tiptoed through the dark house. They felt their way back to the side door, then Paul slid the lock open. They stepped out.

It was the middle of the night. The wind was cold and their footsteps were the only thing Paul could hear for miles around. The street lights reflected in Dum Dum's eyes. He looked happier than Paul had ever seen him.

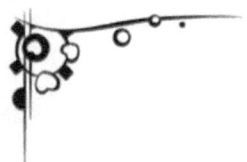

Chapter 26

By the time they got to the station, there was a train waiting to go. They ran to join the rush of passengers towards the platforms. When they got to the third car, their way was blocked by a large cart of bags being unloaded into the carriage.

The conductor directed the passengers to their cars. When he turned his back, Paul nudged Dum Dum, *Go!*

They squeezed between the weary travellers, most of whom were so sleepy they weren't sure they really saw a boy running up the aisle with a dummy.

The train was crowded. Paul and Dum Dum moved through clusters of people, looking out for the ticket inspector, picking up food left by other passengers.

'I told you we should get tickets!' whispered Paul.

'It would have taken too long!' Dum Dum murmured back.

The made their way to the restaurant carriage. Paul grabbed an uneaten sandwich left on the table. 'Why don't we just buy our own?' Dum Dum asked.

'I don't want them to see you,' said Paul. 'Besides. We might need the money later.'

A little girl noticed them. She opened her packet of biscuits and held it out. 'You want some?'

Paul and Dum Dum took a few each.

'Thank you,' said Dum Dum

The little girl gasped and opened her eyes wide.

'Mum!' she tried to get her mother's attention. 'Mum, mum! He said thank you. Look at the puppet. He really talks!'

Paul tried to inch away. But the girl's mother was too busy talking to her husband.

The girl turned back to Dum Dum. 'Where are your strings?' she asked.

Dum Dum nodded his head towards Paul. 'He's the one with the strings.' He raised his hands behind Paul and pretended he was making Paul move and talk.

The girl squealed with delight. She called her brothers over. 'Hey, look!'

They all gathered around Paul and Dum Dum.

'Go on,' said the eldest boy. 'Make him talk.'

Dum Dum turned to him and said, 'Who, me or him?'

'Whoa!' yelled the boy. 'Do that again!'

Dum Dum put on a little show in the corner of the dining car. The children hooted and laughed at his antics, while Paul anxiously watched the children's parents or any other grown-ups who might notice.

'Where are you going?' asked the little girl.

'We're going to a carnival,' Dum Dum told her.

'Where?'

'In Valta.'

The name seemed to puzzle the girl. She said, 'I've been to a carnival. We saw people on stilts and bears riding on bicycles.'

Just then Paul heard the ticket inspector calling out: 'Tickets, please! Tickets!'

He pulled Dum Dum towards the door.

It was several moments before the girl realized they were gone.

'Where did they go?' she asked her brother.

'She climbed up on the stool and nudged her mother's arm. 'Mummy where did they go?'

'Where did who go?' her mother turned to her.

'The boy with the doll.'

'What boy with the doll, dear?'

The girl and her siblings looked at each other, gazing up and seeing nothing but adults all around them.

Several cars away, the boy with the doll they were looking for was running as fast as he could. He and Dum Dum were pursued through the aisles by the ticket inspector's relentless call. 'Tickets, please! Tickets, please!'

They stopped to catch their breath, but another inspector appeared from the opposite direction.

'Hey! You there!' he shouted. 'Show me your tickets!'

The bolted way and that until they found a door and slipped out. They lowered themselves carefully onto the couplings, clinging to whatever handhold they could find. Their feet dangled mere inches above the sleepers.

They waited long enough to make sure both inspectors were gone.

'You think they're still there?' Dum Dum asked

Paul pulled himself up and looked through the window. 'No,' he said. 'We're fine!'

He turned to help Dum Dum up, opened the door and they sneaked back in.

They found the carriage strangely silent. There didn't seem to be anyone there. They crept down the passage until they reached a metal door. It was unlocked. Paul opened it very carefully and peeked inside.

In the darkness all he could see were piles of luggage and a jumble of boxes.

'Let's go!' he beckoned for Dum Dum to follow him in.

They groped around in the dimness and found places to sit. 'This is a good place,' whispered Paul. 'No one would think to look for us in here.'

'Well, what do you know?' said a voice from above them. 'We've got company.'

Paul wheeled from side to side. 'Who said that?'

'I did,' answered the voice.

'No, I did!' declared another voice from somewhere in the gloom.

'Let's get out!' Paul jumped up and pulled Dum Dum back towards the door.

'Calm down! Calm down,' came the voice from above them again.

'Who are you?" demanded Paul in a frightened voice. 'What are you doing in here?'

'Same thing you are,' chuckled the other voice. 'Come back and sit down. We can all have a nice little chat.'

Paul and Dum Dum exchanged glances. Dum Dum shrugged.

'Okay then,' Paul decided. 'But we need to see you first.'

He fumbled on the wall until he found the light switch.

'Ow!'

The overhead light revealed two puppets on the top racks. They were on either side of the compartment. One was short and round with long furry ears. One ear hung down over the edge of the shelf. The other served as his pillow.

The other puppet was lanky and wearing striped socks that reached up to his waist. He propped his horse's head lazily on one hand.

'Where you fellas headed?' asked Dum Dum brightly.

'Home,' answered the round one.

'From where?'

'Xircupolis,' replied the one with the horse's head.

'Xircupolis?' uttered Paul.

The short and fat one nodded sadly. 'One stop away from Valta. Our owner couldn't keep his mouth shut and we were sent packing.'

'You were going to Valta?' Dum Dum said.

The horse-faced puppet moved his head up and down. 'Yes. We were supposed to have our debut at the carnival. But alas! Our owner shot himself in the foot.'

'Along with our careers,' lamented the rotund one.

'We're heading to Valta ourselves,' Dum Dum told them.

'*You are?*' the horse-headed one sat up so abruptly his head bumped the ceiling. 'Ow!' he rubbed it gently.

'You got a gig in the carnival?' the short puppet peered down at Dum Dum.

'No. But we're meeting someone there.'

'Who?'

'Ginger,' Dum Dum revealed.

'*You know Ginger?*' the horse thumped his head on the ceiling again.

Yes! Dum Dum nodded his head with gusto. 'You know her, too?'

'Do we know Ginger,' chortled the one with bunny ears. 'She's a star! She's the biggest act going to Valta! That's why the show master was hoof-happy, kicking everyone out left and right he didn't like. Because he knew that anyone who's in the same show as Ginger is going to get a leg-up in their careers.'

'If you'll pardon the pun,' said horse-head.' Te-hee!'

'So Ginger *is* in Valta!' Dum Dum beamed at Paul.

'Not quite yet,' said Stripey Socks.

'Why not?' Dum Dum asked.

'Her troupe is doing a few rounds up and down the line before they end up in Valta again,' the other puppet informed them.

He and his companion stared at Dum Dum with interest. 'You do know how to get to the V-X-V Line,' don't you?'

'I've got a map,' Dum Dum showed them.

'Did you get that after they changed the routes?' the long puppet squinted down at the piece of paper in Dum Dum's hand.

'What routes?' Dum Dum asked nervously.

'You can't transfer to the V-X-V Line the old way anymore,' the puppet disclosed.

Paul and Dum Dum exchanged worried glances.

'What's the new route?' Paul asked.

'Here,' the lanky puppet started to climb down. 'Let me show you.'

Suddenly they heard someone moving outside.

'Quiet!' hissed the squat puppet from above them. He stretched his ears to their full length to listen.

Paul flicked the light off and everyone withdrew into the shadows. After a moment or two, the door flew open. A head poked in and looked around in the murk. At length it withdrew and the door slammed shut once more.

There was a lot of movement back and forth outside their door. They listened to the voices and endless footsteps to make out what was going on. None of them dared come out of their hiding places.

Soon Paul and Dum Dum found comfortable positions between two large containers. They stretched out among the bits of freight and soon they were dozing off.

Paul didn't know how long he'd been sleeping. Someone was shaking him.

'We're getting off!' said the horse-faced doll.

'You never showed us how to get to the Valta Line!' said Paul.

'You stay on for a couple more stops,' whispered the puppet hurriedly. 'Then you transfer to the other train.'

'What other train?' Dum Dum poked his head around.

'You get off this one and walk to the end of the station,' explained the chubby marionette. 'Then you go down on the tracks and cross to the sixth platform.'

'Then?'

'Then you wait for the first train that comes.'

'Okay,' Dum Dum nodded.

After several moments they felt the train slowing down. They crawled forward for a few minutes before finally coming to a stop.

'Goodbye now,' the two puppets rushed to the door. 'Good luck!'

Paul and Dum Dum heard them snickering and hee-hawing as they ran off to join their owner.

Paul and Dum Dum waited in the darkness until the train was moving again. They stayed behind the stacks of luggage until they had counted two stops. Passengers came on or got off at each station, thudding past their door with their luggage.

Once or twice someone came in to retrieve their packages, before rushing out once more. But Paul and Dum Dum stayed out of sight. Soon, they were underway again, and Paul started to panic. 'Did they say two stops or three?'

'I think they said the sixth one,' answered Dum Dum.

'No,' said Paul. 'I think they said two more stops and then go to the sixth platform.'

They carried on like this until at last they felt the train slowing down. They were approaching the next station.

'This is it!' Dum Dum whispered. Paul stepped to the door, but waited until the carriage had come to a complete halt.

Then, as soon as they were stationary, he threw the door open and hissed, "Let's go!'

They shot out of the train before all the other passengers could get out of their seats.

They walked to the end of the station as the two puppets had instructed. Then they climbed down and crossed to the sixth platform.

It was strangely quiet. Only then that they notice: no one else was getting off their train. It just stood there, the engines running, the lights dimmed as if everyone on board was asleep.

They waited for a long time, but no other train came. In fact, the whole station was deserted. Some of the windows were broken, and everywhere was thick with dust and cobwebs.

They had no idea where they were, or if any trains were coming at all.

'Maybe those puppets got it all wrong,' Dum Dum began to worry.

'Maybe we should have stayed on that train,' said Paul.

'Maybe we better get tickets this time,' said Dum Dum.

'There's no one to buy tickets from,' replied Paul, glancing at the dark, deserted gates across from them. 'I'm not even sure this station is still working.'

'We can still get back on,' Dum Dum nodded towards the train they had just left. Its engines were still gently chugging away, no one moving in or out.

They were just starting to cross the tracks towards it when they were startled by a shrill train whistle. There was a loud thumping on the rails, and an old locomotive wheezed and rumbled into the station.

The pair didn't have time to climb back onto the platform. The train came to a stop just inches from them. All they could see in the gap between the train and the walkway were the feet of passengers and their luggage being rolled away. They saw some strange boots and what looked like duck's feet walking across the breach above them. They glimpsed a bunch of little children's feet. They seemed to be following a goose.

It was still very dark and Paul couldn't believe his eyes.

'What kind of place is this?' he murmured.

Finally, the crowd thinned and they clambered onto the platform. They craned their necks to see the name on the train's front. "VALTA," it proclaimed in great bold letters.

'This is it!' Dum Dum cheered. This is it!'

They ran to the last carriage and sneaked aboard. It was empty. It looked so old some of the compartments had trees growing in them.

Paul and Dum Dum tiptoed past the sleeping conductor. Snoring a few seats away from him was a tall figure under a thick tiger's fur. On the floor by his side were a safari hat and a long, shiny shotgun. On the rack above him was a battered suitcase crammed with elephant tusks, the largest ones sticking out of the sides.

Paul opened the door to one compartment. It was empty. Dum Dum climbed on to the luggage rack. Paul curled up below him and they both went to sleep.

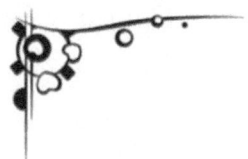

Chapter 27

When they woke up, sunlight was streaming in through the window. The train had stopped.

'Where are we?' Dum Dum whispered.

'I don't know.'

Dum Dum rubbed his stomach. 'I'm hungry.'

'Let's get out,' Paul sat up. 'I think I can smell coffee.'

There was a lot of noise from outside. They could hear laughter and music.

Dum Dum swung down from the rack. 'Let's see where we've ended up!'

They crept out of the quiet train and walked out of the station.

After a short stroll, they found themselves on a large square. A massive cathedral that Paul had never seen before towered over them.

'Are we back in London?' Dum Dum said with disappointment.

'No,' said Paul. 'This is not London. Let me see the map.'

Dum Dum took it out and gave it to him. Paul studied it for a long while.

'This must be Valta, then!' uttered Dum Dum.

Paul finished looking. 'No. Valta is still a long way away.'

Dum Dum looked crest-fallen. 'Then where *are* we?'

'I don't know,' said Paul, looking around helplessly. A man wearing a tall multi-coloured hat appeared a short distance from them.

'Excuse me,' Paul called out. 'What is this place called?'

'Why, don't you know?' replied the man in disbelief. 'You're in the magnificent city of Vierris!'

Paul was puzzled. 'Vierris?'

'Yes,' nodded the man. 'It's where the Vierris Wheel was invented, you know!'

He walked off, balancing the tall hat on his head.

'I've never heard of a place called Vierris,' Paul frowned.

'Why don't you check on the map?' Dum Dum suggested.

Paul did. 'Well, you know what?' he looked up beaming. 'It *is* here!'

'It is?' Dum Dum peeked over Paul's arm.

'It's the first town in the V-X-V Line!' Paul showed him. 'That's Vierris, then all the other towns, then Xircupolis, then Valta!'

'Yes!' Dum Dum cried. 'We're on the right track!' It was a place where people drank beer from early in the morning until late at night. They sat around the square with their tall glasses and enjoyed the cool air and sunshine. The sound of violins floated everywhere as Paul and Dum Dum wandered around. They found a spot where statues climbed down from their pedestals and sat down to drink tea. They had long discussions with each other at the cafés, gossiping about other sculptures. After they'd had a few drinks they would climb back to their places and resume their frozen poses.

Some people stood for hours watching to see if the stone figures moved a finger or blinked an eye. Others even left glasses of beer or wine on the pedestals to see if the statues touched them.

Now and then one of the visitors would hold up an empty glass, shouting, 'See? I told you he's alive! This glass was full when I put it down!'

Paul and Dum Dum stopped to watch a small man playing an enormous guitar. His small hands chased each other up and down the strings as a clown walked on a tightrope above them. The clown maintained his footing even as he walked through the top of a fountain. He shivered a little and let out a hoot as the cold water gushed up to his waist. But he kept his steady progress towards a high wall on the other side of the square.

'Look at that wall!' said Dum Dum.

It seemed to stretch out for miles, running all along one side of the city.

'I wonder what's on the other side,' Dum Dum mused.

'I don't know,' said Paul. 'I don't remember seeing it.'

'We must have passed it when it was too dark to see.'

People stood and watched as the clown came closer and closer to the wall.

When he was only a few steps away, a policeman blew his whistle. A bunch of them ran up and shouted for the clown to turn around. The clown ignored them and kept going. One of the lawmen threw up his truncheon and made the clown lose his balance. He flailed his arms to stay upright, but finally fell to the ground.

One of the waiters at the cafes ran inside to call an ambulance.

They heard a siren screaming towards them. After a tense interval it reached the square, and two orderlies rushed out with a stretcher. But the clown suddenly jumped up. He ran away laughing.

Paul and Dum Dum looked at each other and shook their heads. 'What a crazy place!'

After they had bought some ice cream, a slender man with pale hands approached them. He dangled a beautiful bracelet before their eyes.

'This is yours,' he declared.

'It is?' Dum Dum came forward.

'If you can grab it from me,' said the man.

Paul and Dum Dum tried to snatch it from his hands. But the man moved it around so fast the bracelet kept slipping out of their grasp. One moment it would flash right next to their faces, the next it would be in the other hand. He passed it around so quickly it almost seemed like he had three hands.

'Hold out your hand,' he told Paul.

Paul did as he asked. Then the man lowered the bangle in Paul's palm.

'Now close it.'

Paul did.

'Now open it again.'

Paul spread out his fingers to find that the trinket had vanished.

'Now where is it?' demanded the man.

Paul shrugged. 'I don't know.'

'Look in your pockets,' ordered the man.

Paul searched.

'How about here?' The fellow patted Paul's front and back pockets. 'Or here?'

But they both came up with nothing.

'There it is!' the man finally pulled the bracelet from behind Dum Dum's ear.

'I didn't do anything!' Dum Dum held out his hands. 'I swear!'

'Of course you didn't,' smiled the stranger. 'I guess this is not your lucky day.'

He put the bracelet back in his pocket and walked away. He turned one last time to wave to them with both hands. As he was withdrew into the crowd Paul saw a third hand come out and raise the man's hat.

'Want more ice cream?' Dum Dum asked.

'Sure!' Paul reached in his pants for some change.

'Hey!' he brought up his empty hand. 'Where'd our money go?'

'You had it just now,' said Dum Dum.

'I did. But it's not here anymore!'

'I didn't take it,' Dum Dum stepped back.

'Well someone sure did,' frowned Paul.

Dum Dum looked aghast. 'It's all *gone*?'

Paul opened his palms to show the few coins he had left.

'Uh-oh.'

They sauntered about, trying to figure out what to do. On the other side of the cathedral there was a very tall man in a multi-colour suit. He was shooting balls into a large multi-colour hat lying upside down on the ground. It looked like the hat worn by the man they had seen before.

'Is that the man we talked to?' asked Dum Dum.

Paul stared. 'He looks the same. But he didn't seem that tall when we saw him.'

'This *is* a very strange place,' remarked Dum Dum.

A crowd gathered to watch the man pitch one ball after another into the hat. He tossed so many that his arms got tired. But the large hat never seemed to fill up.

In time he threw his last ball and walked over to the hat. He turned it over.

Instead of balls, doves burst out and flew up over the roofs. The crowd applauded.

Paul took out the two remaining coins in his pocket. He handed them to Dum Dum. 'Put that in his hat.'

'But this is all we have left,' protested Dum Dum.

'We'll get some more,' insisted Paul. 'He deserves it.'

So Dum Dum trotted across the square to drop the coins into the tall man's hat. The spectators laughed and pointed to see him. Some of them clapped their hands. The tall man saw the coins and beamed down at Dum Dum. He made several deep bows.

Dum Dum rejoined Paul and they disappeared into the throng.

They saw a monkey playing an accordion. Women stepped in front of the ape and started to dance with each other. Pigeons gathered around the accordion player, and some of them cried at the strains of the sad music.

As they walked away Dum Dum tugged at Paul's wrist, 'Look!'

There was a man levitating up the side of a building. When he reached the top he disappeared.

When they looked down again, they saw a man in an old overcoat stride to the middle of the square. He pulled something out of his jacket.

'Now watch this!' he called out, moving the object from side to side for everyone to see. It was a piece of brown cardboard. He folded it into two.

Nothing happened for some moments. But when he raised it high above his head, an amber liquid started pouring out of it.

People gasped. The liquid kept flowing until a pool had gathered at the man's feet. Birds started swooping down and drank the pale yellow water off the cobblestones.

'A glass!' the man shouted. 'Someone bring me a glass!'

A waiter from one of the cafes dashed up to him with a goblet. The man poured the solution from his piece of cardboard into it. He offered it to the waiter, who took one gulp and cried out, 'It's beer! Very good beer!'

Everyone scrambled to get glasses. They fought to get them filled from the torrent in the man's hand. He poured barrels of beer into people's glasses, taking their money with one hand while holding up the gushing cardboard with the other.

Everybody kept coming back for more, until they were all drunk and started fighting with each other. Some of them fell asleep on the street corners and in doorways.

Soon the man selling the beer put his piece of cardboard away. He began rifling through the pockets of drunks sleeping on the ground near the fountains. He ran off snickering.

In the end, even the birds flew down and tried to lick up the beer spilt on the cobblestones. They started flying in crazy circles, smashing into windows, breaking crystals and plates on the café tables.

The waiters tried to chase them off with their napkins. But most of them were also drunk and they fell over each other in their battle with the birds.

Dum Dum and Paul watched them laughing, and almost didn't notice when a loud whistle blew from somewhere.

'What was that?' said Dum Dum.

'I don't know,' answered Paul. 'And I don't care.'

They were having too much fun.

Soon another street performer walked up to them.

'Watch this,' he swung a gold fob watch by its chain.'

'No, no,' Paul and Dum Dum drew back, wary from the last time.

'You don't have to do anything, the performer shook his head. 'Just watch.'

And before their eyes he pressed the timepiece against an unopened champagne bottle. His jaw quivered with the effort, but at last they heard a clink in the bottle.

'Et voila!' he held it up before them. The fob watch was inside, the second hand still moving.

'See?' he grinned. 'It's still tells the time!'

'What time does it say?' Dum Dum asked Paul.

Paul squinted at the face of the watch behind the rising bubbles of champagne.

'It's time to go back!' he yelled.

For a moment they were confused which way they had come from the station. They ran in one direction, then spun around to go in the other. Finally they staggered into the station.

'We got off on the last track, remember?' panted Paul. 'We'll have to go there again.'

But when they reached the platform the train was gone.

'That must have been the train whistle we heard,' said Dum Dum.

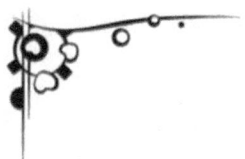

Chapter 28

There was still plenty of daylight left. So they started walking. They followed the railway as it wound its way across the city.

But soon the light began to fade, and they knew they had to hurry. They kept going at a brisk pace until they came to a very high wall.

'The railroad passes over it,' Paul observed. 'We can't find that train again unless we can get past this wall.'

They tried every way they could imagine. Paul stacked several broken crates they found lying around. They climbed on them and tried to reach the top. But the pile made a rickety ladder, which always collapsed just as they were about to reach the summit.

The wall was just too high and sheer, they couldn't even get up a quarter of the way.

'We might have to spend the night here,' Paul threw up his hands.

They were looking for places to bed down when suddenly they heard heavy footsteps coming their way.

'Guess who's coming!' said Dum Dum brightly.

Paul looked down the street and saw a towering figure teetering towards them. It was the very tall man in the multicoloured costume.

'WELL, IF IT'S NOT MY FRIENDS FROM THE SQUARE!' he bellowed cheerfully when he came near.

Paul and Dum Dum stood staring up at him.

'IS THERE ANYTHING I CAN HELP YOU WITH?' asked the man.

'Can you maybe help us over the wall?' said Dum Dum.

The tall man shook his head admiringly at Paul. 'My boy, I really don't know how you do it. I've never seen anyone work like you with a puppet!'

Paul and Dum Dum exchanged smiles.

'And when you made him run along and throw the coins in my hat,' continued the man in his booming voice. 'I swear it was pure magic! There was nothing I could do to rival it!'

Dum Dum swivelled his head back and forth between the man and the wall.

'Oh!' exclaimed the colourful giant. 'Now let's get you both over this nasty wall.'

He lifted Paul up and placed him on top of the partition. Then he plucked Dum Dum from the ground and put him in Paul's waiting arms.

'Thank you!' they chorused up at him. The man dusted off his hands and took a deep bow. He tipped his hat at them before he turned and walked a short distance away. He raised one leg over the wall as if it were some kind of low railing.

Once he was on the other side he unbuttoned his shirt and began taking off his multicoloured clothes. He stuffed hem all into his big hat. In a blink of an eye he was transformed to a man of normal size. He put on his grey clothes on and disappeared into one of the alleys.

'What a strange man!' uttered Dum Dum.

'What a strange place!' echoed Paul.

They looked down at the landscape below them. They saw how the wall stretched out for miles, dividing the city into two distinct parts.

On the side they had just left, everything was bright and colourful, with sweet music soaring over the houses, and flowers blooming everywhere.

On the other side everything was dark and grey, the buildings dingy and crumbling. In the alleys below them Paul saw beggars shambling in their ragged clothes, picking weakly amongst the litter, sitting down to rest in the smelly ditches. There were children with them, their faces black as the soot on the tenements and they stumbled around like drunks. They got up only to fight with the mangy dogs whenever scraps of food were thrown over the wall from the other side.

'I wonder who built this wall,' Dum Dum said.

'They built it so one place would be always bright and clean,' said Paul. 'And the other would always be dark and dirty.'

'Why?' Dum Dum asked.

'I don't know,' Paul shrugged. 'That's something they never taught us in school.'

They got up to see a bit further into the distance.

'Look,' Dum Dum pointed to the railroad far away. 'The tracks go through the fields. Then it keeps going and going.'

'Valta is that way,' Paul gestured. 'That's quite a long walk.'

They took a long time to find a safe place to climb down. There was still enough light to explore a little. So they went off to wander, trying to find the best place to catch the train. It was dusk by the time they reached the river. There was a barge being loaded.

'Let's get on!' urged Dum Dum. 'I've never been on a boat before.'

Paul seemed alarmed at the suggestion. 'No! Trains are better.'

'But there are no more trains!' pointed out Dum Dum.

Paul borrowed the map again. 'Yes there is!' he tapped a spot further away from Vierris.

'It'll take us till tomorrow to get there,' argued Dum Dum. He poked his finger on another site. 'Look! there's the river! It goes all the way to Valta.'

Paul tried to pull away. But Dum Dum grabbed his wrists and heaved with all his might, until they were near the gangway.

'Come on!' he hissed at Paul. 'While no one is looking!'

At last Paul gave in. Dum Dum ran aboard the barge and Paul followed him.

They found places to hide in among coils of rope and oil drums.

When they heard someone coming, they retreated deeper into the vessel, between the chains and containers outside the engine room.

It was already dark, and the piles of carpets in the hold looked very inviting. They lay down like sheiks in the desert. The warmth from the engines and the steady hum lulled them.

Soon they were asleep. They didn't feel the vessel push off and start floating down the river.

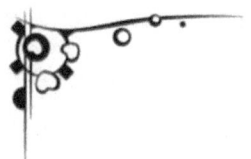

Chapter 29

When they opened their eyes, the huge doors were wide open and the hold was filled with bright light. Most of the cargo had been removed and the engine had stopped running.

'What place is this?' asked Dum Dum.

'I don't know,' Paul said. 'But we'll find out.'

He unfolded their map. After poring over it for some moments, he proclaimed, 'It's a place called Udavescht.'

They tiptoed to the opening and listened. Under all the din of the work going on around the pier, they could pick out something else.

'I can hear music!' whispered Dum Dum.

'Let's see where it's coming from!'

They rushed out over the gangway and made their way from the wharf.

The first thing they saw was a man flying above them, holding onto an umbrella. They followed him until they reached the plaza. As soon as they got there they heard a woman scream.

They were shocked to see a headless woman running, making wild desperate gestures but not making a sound.

'I thought I heard someone screaming,' Dum Dum said.

Then they heard the shriek again. Only then did they see a man chasing the woman. In one hand he was holding an axe, his other hand was clutching the woman's severed head, which kept screaming.

The crowd laughed as the man pursued the headless woman over the park benches, while the head in his hand went on shouting, 'Stop him! Somebody stop him!'

Each time she screeched the throng laughed even more. Soon Paul and Dum Dum were laughing along.

'Look!' Dum Dum pointed across the street.

There were enormous creatures that looked like dragons walking towards the intersection. When they got to the corner they split into two, the head and forelegs going in one direction and the hind legs and tail taking a more roundabout route. When they reached the other junction they joined together and become one creature again.

Paul and Dum Dum sauntered about with the rest of the townspeople. They stopped in front of a woman growing out of a tree. When they looked away for a moment, her branches had quickly turned into arms.

They stepped around her for a closer look. They knelt down to touch the tree's roots and feel its bark. But when they looked up again the woman was gone. All they saw in front of them was an old tree at the edge of the plaza.

They passed a juggler who kept juggling even while he was doing cartwheels. When he had done two circuits of the square he stopped and put away the balls. He pulled other things out of his vest and tossed them up.

The heads of onlookers went round and round to follow the circle of objects he kept pitching and spinning around.

'They're eyes and ears!' pointed Dum Dum with excitement. Paul realized that the man was now juggling ears, noses, eyes and mouths.

An assistant came up and placed a glass jar on the ground near him. The juggler swirled the objects one last time and made them land in the jar. They formed a smiling face.

The crowd applauded.

Just by standing there and talking, Paul and Dum Dum were mistaken for performers. A small pack of spectators started to gather around them.

They laughed every time Dum Dum said something. Unaware they were being observed, Paul put his hands in his pockets. Dum Dum did the same.

Their little audience clapped their hands.

'You think these people are watching us?' Paul said to Dum Dum.

'Yes, I think they might be,' Dum Dum winked.

The crowd chuckled and shook their heads in awe.

'Well, we better do something entertaining,' urged Paul.

'I don't know if they're already drunk,' answered Dum Dum. 'But I'll do my best.'

He started dancing and singing songs. Paul followed his lead.

They performed several numbers, Paul copying every move Dum Dum made. Their viewers roared with approval and started throwing them coins.

Paul and Dum Dum scooped them up and stuffed them in their pockets.

'See?' Paul said. 'I told you we'd get more.'

They ended up performing again and again. During breaks they would run to the park around the corner and discuss what to do next. Dum Dum would show Paul the tricks he knew, then they would run back to the square and resume their little show.

In one skit Paul would pretend to be angry and walk away. To spite him, Dum Dum would do a jig by himself and start singing drinking songs.

Paul put a bag over his head and Dum Dum would say,

'I looked just like that when he brought me home from the shop. Then he took me out of the bag and I started talking. He's been trying to send me back ever since.'

Their listeners guffawed. Everyone loved them. By the end of the day word had spread about the marvellous duo. Admirers came up and formed rings around them.

'I've never seen anyone so young perform so well,' gushed one woman. 'Even the puppeteers at the theatre can't do half the things you do.'

'You can always see them pulling strings or moving the doll's head,' another put in.

A third one bent down and cooed at Paul, 'But with you it's like real magic!'

'How long have you had this puppet?' a young lady asked Paul. 'He's so cute!'

Dum Dum turned his head all the way round to give Paul his smug grin.

A showman from the other side of the plaza had been watching them intently. He broke away from his own group and approached them.

'You can make a lot of money with talent like that,' he addressed Paul. 'I could use you in one of my shows. If you join my caravan I can make stars of you both!'

Paul and Dum Dum looked at each other.

'No thank you,' Paul demurred. 'But we prefer to travel on our own.'

'Think about it,' pressed the showman. 'I'm offering you a *very* rare opportunity.'

He tipped his hat and walked away.

More and more people came to see the amazing boy ventriloquist. They begged to have their pictures taken with Paul and Dum Dum.

While everyone was fussing over them, Paul noticed a scruffy group of kids watching them from across the road. They gathered between the buildings, keeping their distance from everyone else. Their faces were painted all different colours, and they kept holding plastic bags to their faces.

Paul would watch them stagger around like they were drunk, chasing each other on the pavement with raucous laughs. There were no grown-ups with them, and they roamed the town like a pack of painted hyenas.

When they drifted near one of the cafes, the waiters jumped up shouting and shooed them away.

'Those kids remind me of Luke and Cy,' Dum Dum said when he saw them. 'Except their faces are all different colours.'

'Maybe they work as clowns,' Paul guessed.

One day a reporter from the local paper came to the square. He came with a surly photographer who took several pictures of Paul and Dum Dum.

'I've heard so much about you,' the reporter prattled to Paul. 'Could I please have an interview?'

Paul didn't know what that was, but he let the young man lead them to a corner café and seat them at a table. The man ordered lunch and took out a pencil and notebook. As soon as their food was brought, the inquisitive fellow let off one question after another.

'Is your father a ventriloquist, too?'

Paul didn't know how to answer.

'At what age did you start being interested in ventriloquism?'

Paul didn't know what the man was talking about, so he lowered his head and ate his sandwich.

'Who taught you how to make your puppet talk so well?'

'He did,' Paul inclined his head towards Dum Dum.

'He did?' the reporter opened his eyes wide. Then he realized something. 'Oh! How cute!'

He wrote furiously in his notebook.

'Where are you and your parents staying?' the man put the pencil between his teeth to wait for Paul's answer.

'Parents?' Paul gulped down the rest of his sandwich. 'Er, uhm, they're not with us.'

'They're *not*?' the man's eyes widened again.

'I mean, they're uhm...'Paul looked to Dum Dum for help. 'They're out shopping somewhere.'

'Where?'

'I don't know.'

The man sucked on a tooth, and decided it didn't matter. 'Anyway, won't your mother be so proud when she sees your picture in the paper!'

The mention of his mother horrified Paul. He put down his glass.

'Actually, I'm not very hungry....' he started sliding out of his seat.

How about your cake?' the newsman sat forward. 'It's coming now! Just a few more questions. Please!'

Paul knocked the chair over as he bolted away from the café and Dum Dum followed him.

The next day they saw their picture on the front of the newspaper.

"A VISIT FROM THE YOUNGEST MASTER VENTRILOQUIST EVER!" the headline proclaimed.

'I hope my mum doesn't see that picture,' murmured Paul.

'You look good in it,' smiled Dum Dum. 'So do I!'

'She has no idea we even left London,' groaned Paul. 'If this paper ever gets into her hands, both our heads will come off!'

But when they got back to the square everyone recognized them. People pointed and clapped their hands.

They were forced to perform newer and newer things.

They poked fun at each other for laughs.

'He just says whatever I think and claims he thought of it," taunted Paul.

'That's not half as bad as what he does,' Dum Dum responded.

'Oh yeah? Like what?'

'You do all sorts of wicked things,' Dum Dum defied him. 'Then you claim you were just sleepwalking!'

Paul shot him an angry look.

'Well? Isn't that true?' pressed Dum Dum. 'People got tired of your excuses. So you got me! Now you have someone else to blame.'

People laughed. But Paul yelled in real anger, 'That's not true!'

'Sure!' Dum Dum winked at the audience. 'If he wasn't sleepwalking, then the dummy must have done it!'

'That's a lie!' cried out Paul.

'Lie? Dummies don't lie,' Dum Dum looked to everyone for support. 'They just say what their owners really think.'

The spectators cackled.

"You're lying!' shrieked Paul. 'Shut up!'

'I'll shut up if you shut up,' Dum Dum crossed his arms.

Paul lowered his head and went quiet. Dum Dum did the same.

The whole place erupted in applause.

Later they bought some apples and ate them under a big tree.

'You should stop betraying me in front of people!' Paul scolded.

'How did I betray you?' Dum Dum answered.

'You talked about my sleepwalking,' accused Paul. 'You weren't supposed to. It's personal.'

'That's exactly what Marc used to say to me,' Dum Dum responded. 'You're becoming more and more like him.'

'Well, maybe you're making me into him!' spat Paul. 'Maybe you make everyone into a bad person like Marc!'

'I'm only as bad or as good as you are!' retorted Dum Dum.

'No you're not!' Paul jumped up. 'You're your own person! I don't make you do or say the things you do! You say them yourself! You're already more of a real boy than you think!'

'That's not my fault,' Dum Dum got up and dusted off his hands.

'But some things are!' said Paul. 'Some things *are* your fault. You've got to start being responsible for yourself! That's part of being a real boy!'

They walked off in different directions.

For dinner they bought some bread and cheese with the coins they had collected. When night came, the plaza became deserted. They looked for a place to sleep.

'I think we'd better find the train station,' Paul said. 'In case a train comes in.'

They walked around for hours until they found the station. But there was no one there.

It seemed like an old, disused building.

'They don't even have a timetable,' noted Paul.

They looked at the empty tracks.

'I don't think any trains will be stopping here,' said Dum Dum.

Paul checked their map again.

'The train hasn't stopped here in years,' Paul revealed.

'Does it stop anywhere near here?' demanded Dum Dum.

Paul traced the lines on the map for a long time.

'Here!' he finally burst out.

'Where?'

'It says the V-X-V line stops at Danubia,' Paul told him.

Dum Dum's head spun from side to side. 'Where's *that*?'

'That's the next town.'

Dum Dum's eyes went as wide as saucers. 'So we'll *have* to *walk*?'

Paul nodded.

It was a cold night and they looked for warm places. The church was locked and all the shops had their shutters down. The doorways were too narrow for them to huddle in. So they trudged around for a long time, trying to stay warm.

And then they saw a fire glowing brightly in the distance.

'I can smell food,' uttered Paul happily.

They were drawn irresistibly towards the spot flickering in the blackness. They stumbled around until they reached the blaze.

It was in an empty alley between abandoned buildings.

'Hello?' Paul called out. 'Hello! Anybody here?'

At first, there was no reaction. Then they noticed dark figures emerging from the vacant structures. They formed a curious, silent ring around Paul and Dum Dum.

'We're by ourselves,' Paul said timidly. 'We don't have a place to stay.'

'That's a nice little fire you got there,' Dum Dum added. 'Can we join you?'

The reticent creatures in the shadows twittered among themselves. But none of them spoke or moved closer.

Then slowly, one or two of them came near. One face, then another appeared out of the murk. Soon all the others came out into the light to peer at their visitors.

'It's true!' the smallest of them breathed. 'He can really talk!'

They all crowded in to gape at Dum Dum.

'There are no wires or strings!' proclaimed one child to the others.

'It's true what everyone says!' another voice pealed out of the shadows. 'It's really magic!'

The tallest of the boys came forward to see for himself.

'I also eat real food, too,' said Dum Dum, rubbing his stomach. 'That is, if you have any to spare.'

The tall boy nodded and a bunch of smaller ones rushed off to one of the buildings.

They came back bearing a pan of beans and some bread, still warm from the fire.

Paul and Dum Dum gratefully took it and sat down to eat. The children stood around, watching in amusement as Dum Dum devoured his share of the food.

'He really can eat!' another child uttered in wonder.

'I never saw a puppet that can do that!'

'I can drink, too,' Dum Dum turned to them. 'Beer, juice, anything that goes *glug glug glug*.'

Paul glowered at him.

At another signal from the large boy, a group scurried off and brought out some water. Paul and Dum Dum drank hungrily.

'Where are your parents??' Paul asked.

'We have none, ' the leader told him. 'We were all left on the streets. Some of us ran away.'

He stepped closer so Paul and Dum Dum could see him clearly.

'My name is Green,' he said, pointing to the paint marks on his cheeks. 'I'm called that because I always have green paint on my face.'

He gestured to all the others still standing half hidden in the dark. 'This is our family.'

One by one they came forward into the light. Paul and Dum Dum saw that their faces were all painted different colours.

'Why do you paint your faces like that?' Paul inquired.

They all laughed and one of the smaller kids ran to bring back bags from somewhere in the darkness.

We don't want to paint our faces,' explained Green. 'It just gets like that when you sniff paint all day.'

'What is everyone else called?' Dum Dum asked.

Green pointed to the other kids around them. 'He's called Yellow, he's Blue and he's Black and that one there is Brown.'

He explained that they called each other by the names of the colours on their faces. There was also Red, there was Silver, and there was a big hulking kid called Violet.

'I love sniffing blue paint,' said the boy they called Blue. 'Because after a while everything looks blue. And I feel like even my insides are blue.'

'What's so good about sniffing paint?' asked Dum Dum.

'It makes you feel like you're flying,' answered the one called Silver. 'You forget about food and the cold and missing your pets.'

'If you miss your pets,' said Paul. 'Why don't you go home?'

'This *is* our home,' Violet answered, stretching out his large arms to indicate everything around them. 'We can go wherever we like. 'Sometimes we live in our shaft, and when that gets too cold we can go to our other home under the bridge. We can sleep in the church and ring the bell if we want.'

The other kids snickered.

Brown stepped forward to say his piece, 'See? Have you seen any place as big as this? This is all our home. It's bigger than any castle!'

'But where do you get paint?' Paul said.

'We buy them from the market in Danubia.'

Paul recognized the name. 'You *know* how to get to *Danubia*?'

'Of course,' uttered Yellow. 'That's where some of us were born. But we stay here because our parents keep looking for us over there.'

'Is there a train station in Danubia?' Paul questioned.

'Of course! That's how some of us got here,' Gold told him. 'They climbed on the train from somewhere and ended up here.'

Can you show us how to get to Danubia?' Dum Dum chimed in.

'Better than that,' said Black. 'We'll walk you there!'

You can show us some magic!' piped in Orange.

They walked and talked all night, which was good because it stopped them thinking about the cold and their hunger.

When they reached the train station in Danubia, it was starting to get light.

'You know,' Dum Dum said. 'Maybe I'm beginning to see why it's good to sniff paint.'

'Here,' one of the bigger boys pushed a bag of paint on Dum Dum's face 'Let's see if you can still do magic after that!'

The other boys stopped him. There was a scuffle and finally Green intervened.

They all stood in one long line and waved goodbye to Paul and Dum Dum.

'Thank you,' said Paul.

'Thanks for the paint!' Dum Dum waved to them.

They all waved back snickering and trudged back the way they came.

When they were gone, Dum Dum and Paul stumbled into the station. The platform guard saw the paint in Dum Dum's face and blew his whistle.

'Get out!' he shouted. 'This place is not for you paint sniffers!'

'We're not paint sniffers!' Paul shouted back.

The guard charged forward waving his stick, 'I'll have you thrown in jail if you're not careful!'

Paul and Dum Dum ran. They hid in the bushes and waited for the station guard to leave.

When he did, they crept to the board to check the schedule.

'There!' Dum Dum pointed to the column of departures. 'The V-X-V train!'

Paul squinted at the listing. 'Yes. But that doesn't come till midnight.'

'Midnight? Said Dum Dum. 'What are we going to do till then?'

Chapter 30

They started by exploring the town. They weren't looking for anything in particular, but after a while Paul was enticed by a wonderful aroma.

'That bread smells so good!' he gushed. They followed the scent until they stumbled upon a small bakery. They marched up to the window and peeked inside.

'Do we have any money left?' Dum Dum asked.

Paul took out their coins and counted them. 'We certainly have enough for some bread.'

'What a pretty little sparrow!' Dum Dum pointed upwards. Paul raised his head and saw a bird cage hanging above the door.

Dum Dum seemed entranced by the creature fluttering from one side of its enclosure to the other, cheeping at everyone that passed. Now and then it jutted its bill out between the wires.

'All right,' Paul pushed the door open. 'We'll get a loaf and try to get some more money.'

Dum Dum stayed outside and watched him go up to the counter. Paul gave his money to a fat man in a baker's cap. The man whipped up a large sheet of paper and wrapped Paul's loaf.

Another customer arrived and left his bicycle near the entrance. The bicycle was just high enough to allow Dum Dum to reach the bird cage. He climbed up.

Paul came out clutching the warm loaf like a newborn baby. When he saw Dum Dum reaching up for the birdcage, he almost dropped the bread.

'What do you think you're doing!' yelled Paul.

'She wants to get out!' Dum Dum answered.

'Come down right now!' ordered Paul.

'No!'

Before Paul could stop him, Dum Dum opened the bird cage.

The sparrow shot out, circled above them with sharp, happy chirps, before flitting away into the clouds.

The baker saw what was going on and came out running. 'Ah! What did you do? What did you do that for?'

Paul and Dum Dum scuttled down the road. The baker thundered only a few inches behind them, shaking his fist. 'Don't come back! You miserable paint-sniffers! I'll wring your necks if you ever show up here again!'

Paul and Dum Dum didn't stop running until they reached the edge of the small town.

There they saw a large clearing. A dozen or so trucks were parked in a massive ring around the open space. They stopped to catch their breath.

'I sure wish you hadn't done that!' panted Paul.

'I had to,' Dum Dum protested. 'She was begging me to.'

'No she wasn't. You were just imagining it.'

'Listen to you!' Dum Dum countered. 'Are you just imagining me talking to you?'

Paul thought for a moment, and was forced to admit, 'No. I guess not.'

They were interrupted by a friendly cheep. They looked up to see the sparrow wheeling above them as if to say hello. It whizzed off again after a few turns, whistling in joy.

'See?' Dum Dum looked after it. 'She didn't want to be in that cage. Just like I didn't want to be with my old owner Marc. I just did for her what you did for me.'

Paul kicked a stone and nodded.

'Now, she's up there somewhere,' Dum Dum beamed up at the sky. 'Looking for adventures. Like me and you.'

'You're right,' Paul put his hand on Dum Dum's shoulder. 'But that means we won't be able to go back there to catch the train.'

They walked towards the trucks. They saw people packing up costumes and taking down two colourful pavilions.

'WHY, IF IT'S NOT MY FRIENDS FROM THE SQUARE!' boomed a man's voice from behind them.

The turned around. It was the showman they had seen at the plaza.

'The magnificent boy ventriloquist!' blared the man in his powerful voice.

Paul and Dum Dum recognized some of the performers from the square. They were piling puppets, costumes and props into trunks, then loading them into the trucks.

Paul realized that the ring formed one long caravan. They saw the headless woman and the dragons that split into two parts and came back together again.

'You can make a fortune with my group,' the showman cajoled Paul. 'More than you ever could on your own. You'll be famous before this trip is done.'

Dum Dum's eyes lit up when he saw the beautiful female puppets being stacked into one box.

'Where are you going?' Paul asked the showman.

'Oh, well we go from town to town,' the man answered with a wave of his cane. 'Until we join up with all the others for the Carnival in Valta.'

'*Valta*!' Dum Dum blurted out in excitement. He nodded his head like he wanted it to come off.

The showman laughed. 'You never cease to amaze me!' he gave Paul a disbelieving shake of the head. 'And I'm sure a lot of people will feel the same.'

Paul started to step away. 'No. We'd rather go by train.'

'Train?' the showman smiled with disdain. What train? In this *town*?'

'There's one coming through here tonight,' Paul held firmly.

'Are you *nuts*!' Dum Dum started to shout.

The showman chuckled. 'Well, if you can't make up your mind, you could at least sell me the dummy. I have performers who will work wonders with him.'

'No!' said Paul.

'Yes! Yes!' Dum Dum started jumping up and down. 'Sell me! Sell me! I want to go with him!'

The showman threw his head back in laughter. 'That's what I love about you two! You never stop working on your act. This one you're doing right now will go down *marvellously* in front of audiences!'

'It' not an act!' snapped Paul. 'We really *don't* want to join you.'

'Yes, we do!' Dum Dum piped up again. 'Didn't you *hear* the man? He's *going* to *Valta*. That's where we're going to find Ginger! And he's got lots of pretty puppets in the meantime!'

'I'll tell you what,' the showman bent down and fixed his eyes on Paul. 'Why don't you stop arguing with yourself for a minute? Part of you wants to be rich and famous. But another part of you is afraid. You're using the dummy to voice out your real dreams. But you're using your own voice to express your fears.'

'I'm not…' Paul tried to challenge him but the showman was already walking away.

They left the clearing and found another place to sit down. Paul unwrapped the bread and they started eating.

'Why won't you go with them?' Dum Dum demanded. 'It's the best way we'll find Ginger.'

'I don't trust him,' Paul maintained.

'Why not?'

'He has a red nose.'

'His nose is no redder than yours!'

'But his is big and red,' Paul pointed out. 'My mum said never to trust a man with a nose like that. She says my dad's nose was like that.'

'you're just being silly!' Dum Dum leapt to his feet.

'No I'm not!'

'Anyway, it's me he wants,' declared Dum Dum. 'But he thinks you're the one making me talk. He doesn't *know*. Without me you wouldn't be able to work in any show!'

Paul jumped up, too. 'Without me you'd just be a piece of wood!'

They finished eating and ambled back towards the tracks. 'As soon as we hear the train,' Paul said, 'we run to the station. It'll be late. The baker won't be looking for us any more.'

They waited until it got dark. But then it started to rain.

'It's getting cold,' Dum Dum shivered.

'Let's go under that tree over there,' said Paul.

They stood under the tree and waited for the rain to stop. While the downpour continued they saw the caravan winding around the corner and turn away from the town. It juddered past them like a long heavy chain and suddenly came to a stop.

The door of the lead truck opened and they saw the showman leaning out.' This is your last chance!' he called out to Paul. 'You'll never get another one like it again!'

'No, thank you!' Paul yelled back.

'Goodbye, then!' the showman waved and shut the door. The caravan started to move once more. It crept forward a few yards before coming to a halt again.

'Now what do they want?' Paul muttered. He looked around for Dum Dum.

A window opened on the last truck. Paul saw someone waving to him. '*Goodbye!*'

He suddenly realized it was Dum Dum.

'Wait!' he ran towards the convoy shouting. 'Wait!'

The door on the lead truck flew open. Paul jumped in.

Then caravan snaked out through the rain, like a wet caterpillar pushing its beam of light into the darkness ahead.

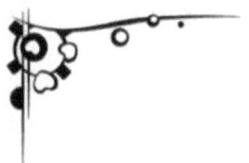

Chapter 31

Paul and Dum Dum woke up to a warm day. They sat up on the berth in the rearmost truck. Through the blinds they could see that the caravan was already positioned in a huge circle. Green, yellow, and blue pavilions were pitched in the middle.

Beyond their ring they could see part of the new town they were in. Its narrow buildings were painted all different colours, with overflowing gardens tumbling onto the street.

They climbed out of their truck. Dum Dum followed Paul until they found a long table set up under the green pavilion.

Members of the troupe were busy having breakfast, reaching over each other for slices of bread, cheese, and ham; drinking coffee or milk that they poured from the big metal pots.

Dum Dum and Paul pushed their way onto the table and filled their plates. The performers sitting around them were so tired and hungry no one took notice of Dum Dum eating beside Paul.

After a few moments the showman appeared wearing his silk top hat. He clapped his hands and announced, 'All right, everyone! Let's get ready for showtime!'

People emptied their plates and spread out to do their work. They took out the stalls and smaller tents and started putting them up. When they had finished, the area around the trucks looked like little village. They had made a make-believe settlement outside a real one.

The showman surveyed the results with satisfaction. Then, waving his cane, he called out: 'Laszlo, Flora, Theo and Wiggenclutz, let's go! Let's wake up this town and drum up some enthusiasm!'

A small gaudy group gathered to join him for the little expedition. Before they set off, he took Paul aside, 'Now I want you to try and attract everyone's attention. Make them want to come see our show.'

They marched to the town centre with Wiggenclutz, the tall clown, beating a tiny tin drum. Behind him were the three midgets Theo, Flora and Laszlo. The two men were blowing trumpets twice their size, while Flora clapped gigantic cymbals. In the rear behind Paul and Dum Dum was the headless lady wearing a patched up frock coat, followed by her partner, who carried her head in a hat box. Further behind them were some assistants bearing props, chairs, and costumes.

Paul sidled up next to the showman and asked 'What's this place called?'

The showman shrugged, 'I don't know.'

'How can you not know?' countered Paul. 'You got us here! How could you get here if you don't know what it's called?'

'That's just it,' the showman held up his hands. 'I don't know how we got here. We were just travelling in the night, and when we woke up in the morning we were here.'

'I don't believe you,' griped Paul and walked away.

The midgets in front of them kept tooting their horns and ringing their bells, while the showman and the headless lady waved to bystanders. Soon children and dogs, along with several townspeople were trailing after them.

When they got to the square, Wiggenclutz bent down so Flora could climb on his back. She clambered onto his shoulders and smacked the cymbals on either side of his head.

The crowd laughed as Wiggenclutz made his head quiver like it was vibrating from the crash. Some town dwellers stopped playing their guitars and stood up to watch. The headless woman stepped forward.

She took off her coat to reveal a shiny red dress. Her bare shoulders were draped with a shawl made from the

reddest feathers. She spread out her hands and started to
dance, beating out the rhythm with her heels, while the
midgets stood around her, clapping to the tempo. The town's
dwellers were hypnotized by her movements, and marvelled at
how she moved about so surely, though she didn't have eyes to
see.

She picked up the shawl and twirled it above her
shoulders like a lasso, while her body spun around in the
opposite direction. She whirled so fast her skirt was like a
scarlet disk that was about to fly out of the square. She threw
out her feet this way and that, stomping on the cobblestones.

She ended her dance in a frozen pose, with her fingers
spread out in front of where her head should be. At that
moment her partner opened the hat box so her head could
peek out and shout, '*Ole!*'

The crowd applauded with gusto, and were still
clapping when they heard the heavy thudding of hooves.
Everyone jumped aside as a man in a matador's outfit
appeared, running in front of an angry bull. Everyone looked
for a place to hide, leaving he headless woman standing alone,
not knowing where to go. Her partner jumped back and threw
the frock coat over her, before the bull could see her red dress.
At last a few men ran out of the shops and cornered the bull.
They tied it up with ropes and led it away.

The showman laughed. 'Sometimes the locals like to put on their own show.'

He signalled to Paul, who came forward with Dum Dum to do their routine.

A man stopped pushing his barrel across the road to watch them. People in the taverns came out to the street, still holding their hefty, frothing glasses, chortling to see the boy with his puppet.

An old woman bent down to pinch Dum Dum's cheeks. 'Ow! Those cheeks are a lot harder than they look!'

Out of the corner of his eye Paul noticed a group of loutish youths coming out of a tavern, lurching and singing out of tune. All the hilarity surrounding Dum Dum drew their attention and they came closer. They grabbed Paul and put a hand over his mouth.

Dum Dum leapt up and hollered, 'Let him go!'

He ran around waving his hands. 'Let him go!'

The audience laughed even harder. The thugs realized it was no use holding Paul, so they released him. They began to chase Dum Dum instead.

Dum Dum darted around the square, yelling, 'Help! Help! Don't just stand there and laugh! This is for real!'

His pursuers spread out until they finally caught him. Dum Dum cried out even louder. 'No! Let me go! No!'

His screams brought a policeman to the square, who chased the hoodlums away with his stick.

Paul dusted himself off and walked across the square to join Dum Dum. The throng on the pavement went wild with cheers.

'Hey, what are you all applauding him for?' protested Dum Dum. 'He doesn't do anything but stand there!'

The crowd was even more enthralled. There were whoops of 'Bravo! Genius! What a virtuoso!'

Dum Dum took several bows, saying 'Thank you! Thank you! Thank you!'

The crowd roared with laughter.

Finally, the showman snapped his fingers. It was a signal for his assistants to bring out table and put it in the middle of the square.

'And now, ladies and gentlemen,' he declared, 'you shall meet the star of this evening's show.'

He motioned with his other hand and another aide came forward. He was holding a female figure. He placed it on top of the table.

'Ladies and gentlemen!' announced the showman. 'May I present the IN-COM-PA-RABLE...THAUMINA! The amazing half-woman!'

Along with all the townspeople, Dum Dum felt his jaw drop to see the woman whose body only went down to her waist. She was regal and stylish, and her eyes sparkled with magical power. She raised one arm like a real diva to receive the ovation.

'Oh, many, many thanks for your most gracious welcome!' She spoke in the most sophisticated voice Dum Dum had ever heard. 'I look forward to fulfilling your most intense wants and longings this evening. Please come to our show!'

Everyone was bewitched with her elegance, and her ability to speak despite having only half a body.

'You'll see more of Thaumina,' promised the showman, 'and much more. Tonight at six o'clock!'

As they made their way back to the caravan, the showman walked next to Paul. 'Thaumina might need your help tonight,' he murmured

How?' Paul asked.

'I want you to throw your voice and speak through her crystal ball.'

'How should I do that?'

'Why the same way you throw your voice to make him talk,' the showman pointed to Dum Dum.

'I don't have to do anything to make him talk,' Paul told him.

'But you must!' insisted the showman.

'No, I don't,' vowed Paul. 'He was like that when I found him. I never had to do anything.'

The showman looked confused. He nodded towards Dum Dum. 'Can he throw his voice, then?'

'Certainly,' Paul replied. 'He knows more about voices than I do.'

The man slowed down and looked very closely at Dum Dum.

'But can he do a woman's voice?' he said to Paul. 'Like Thaumina, for example?'

'Of course I can,' Dum Dum answered him in Thaumina's voice.

The showman stopped walking. He looked a little spooked. After some moments he brought his hands together.

'Very well, then, he nodded to Paul. 'You're on with Thaumina tonight. You sit with the dummy on your knee, and he's going to speak through the crystal ball.'

'In Thaumina's voice,' stressed Dum Dum.

The showman stepped around to look Dum Dum over. He didn't seem to find what he was looking for.

'Ptscha!' he said and walked away.

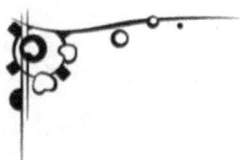

Chapter 32

As soon as they reached the caravan Dum Dum said, 'Now let's go find that wonderful half woman!'

They asked the other members of the troupe where to find Thaumina. One of them pointed to a violet trailer with veiled windows and glittery stars painted on its sides.

They went up to the door and knocked.

The door flew open and Thaumina leaned out in her dressing gown. 'Come in!' she chimed.

Paul and Dum Dum climbed in after her.

The trailer's interior was lined with rich dark velvet, festooned with silk scarves and exotic furs. One of the windows served as Thaumina's booth. She would sit on a high stool and part the heavy curtains. To anyone standing outside she looked like a normal woman with strikingly bright eyes. The black hair that went down to her waist made her look even more mysterious. From outside no one could tell she was only half a woman.

Paul and Dum Dum walked around the trailer in amazement, examining the sparkling crystals, the Ouija Boards, the ancient talismans scattered on the tables. Dum Dum saw a deck of cards and grabbed it.

'Good!' he said, shuffling the cards. 'Let's deal a few hands!'

'Put that down!' ordered Thaumina. 'Those aren't playing cards!'

Dum Dum stopped shuffling. 'Then what are they?'

'They're Tarot cards, dummy!'

Dum Dum put the deck back on the table.

'Sit down, boys,' Thaumina chimed again as she moved around on her hands, using her arms like crutches to swing herself forward. When her hands were busy doing something else, she managed to somehow balance herself on her waist, righting herself whenever she tilted too much to one side. She propelled herself to one corner and rummaged in a drawer.

'Here,' she gave a list to Paul. 'These are the predictions you'll read tonight.'

'You *already* have them?' Dum Dum said. '*How?*'

Thaumina rolled her eyes. 'Well, I can see the future, can't I?'

She sat down with them.

'Here,' she said to Paul. 'If you see me holding up my index finger you read number 1. If you see me scratch my temple with my pinkie, then read number 4.'

'Wait, wait, wait,' Paul dithered. 'You already *have* the predictions *written* down?'

'Of course!'

'How?' asked Dum Dum.

'Well,' Thaumina pressed a finger in her cheek, 'if it's a woman she'll be asking when she's going to get married. If it's a man he'll ask if he's going to win the lottery.'

'What if it's a kid?' said Dum Dum.

'A girl will want to know if a certain boy likes her.'

'And a boy?'

'A boy will want to know when his brother is going to die.'

They went through the list, and practiced throwing Dum Dum's voice through the crystal ball.

After dozens of repetitions they got it perfectly.

Thaumina would close her eyes, and Dum Dum would speak in her voice, making it sound as if her voice were coming from inside the crystal ball.

'That's it!' Thaumina raised her fist in jubilation. 'They're all going to love that!'

She put the crystal ball aside for a while, and they all sat back for a rest.

'How come they made you without any legs?' Dum Dum asked.

'To keep me from running away, I guess,' Thaumina replied.

'Why would you run away?' Paul asked in turn.

'*Can't* you *see*?' Thaumina gesticulated wildly. 'I don't *belong* in this *place*. 'I'm not a mule who can travel in box cars and sleep on hay!'

She placed a dainty hand on her chest, *I belong in* the *theatre!*'

'But I thought you were going to Valta.' Dum Dum said.

'Valta!' she turned furiously towards him. 'Oh, don't make me laugh!'

She put her hand on her chest again. 'I'm no mere circus performer!' she shrieked. 'I belong in Paris! London! Rome! Just like my mother!'

Dum Dum turned to her with wide eyes, 'You *have* a *mother?*'

'Why, of course!' she replied. 'Don't you?'

'No,' Dum Dum shook his head. 'I was made by an Italian carpenter.'

'Ha!' spat Thaumina. 'I'll have you know my *mother* was a *famous* diva. And I *look* just *like* her!'

'Your mother also had no legs?' Paul leaned forward to look at her.

'Why, yes! She was the one who made it fashionable to have no legs!' Thaumina made mad, impassioned gestures. 'Her name was Thauma! She made all the men in Europe pant for a girl with no legs. And so they made me like this!'

With passion like that, Thaumina always brought the house down everywhere she went. Their show that night was an enormous success. People gathered in front of the makeshift stage and listened to Dum Dum speaking through the crystal ball. The eerie voice that seemed to be coming out of the glass told every old maid from the town that she would soon find love, and all the adolescent boys that the girl they liked might finally change her mind about them.

Long after the show was over, teen age boys kept sneaking back to Thaumina's booth to ask her questions about their future.

When they were all gone, Dum Dum stole out of his berth and went to her trailer. He was so enchanted with her wit and proud beauty that he forgot the time.

It was hours after midnight when he crept back to join Paul at their berth.

'So would you consider running off with a girl who's got no legs?' he whispered.

'I would have to look in the future to answer that,' responded Paul with a yawn. 'But first, I need a good night's sleep.'

Dum Dum climbed onto the rack above the window. He couldn't sleep for a long time. At last he said softly, 'If Thaumina wants to leave this show, maybe we should help her.'

'But we *have* to find *Ginger*,' Paul objected. 'Besides. The showman will accuse us of stealing her.'

Dum Dum didn't answer. Paul thought he must have fallen asleep. Then he felt the caravan starting to move again.

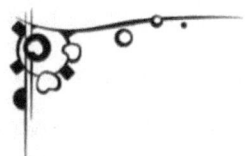

Chapter 33

The next day they woke up to yet more unfamiliar surroundings. They saw one of the caravan drivers as they climbed out of their truck. 'What's this place called?' asked Paul.

The man shook his head. 'It's not my business to know what any place is called. They tell me to go, I go. They tell me to stop, I stop.'

Paul took Dum Dum by the wrist. 'Come along. I don't like the sound of this bunch.'

'But aren't we going to eat?' Dum Dum motioned towards the other performers sitting around the big breakfast table.

Paul pulled him away from the gathering. 'I think we better look after ourselves for a while.'

They hurried towards the road just as the showman came out and started ordering everyone to get to work. Soon the stillness was shattered by the noise of the tents and the booths being put up. The pair kept walking until the caravan was out of sight. After a while they reached the town. The main street opened up before them.

It was an even stranger place than the one they had visited the day before. Outside one café they saw three heads on a table talking to each other.

'Please pass the butter,' said the first head.

'There's no more butter,' answered the second head.

'Now how can you expect me to work all day if I don't get enough to eat!' the first head blew up.

The three heads all started yelling, grabbing the saucers and forks with their teeth and hurling them at each other.

Finally the whole table rose and floated above the pavement. Under the table cloth Paul and Dum Dum noticed three pairs of legs. They walked away from the café and disappeared into an alley, the three heads still howling at each other and carrying on.

Paul examined the street corner they were standing in. 'This looks as good a place as any to start working,' he decided.

They stood side by side and watched the passers-by for several minutes.

'There's a tall one,' said Paul of a gangly citizen walking by.

'Yes,' Dum Dum agreed. 'He looks like a ladder wearing clothes.'

A little girl giggled and pointed out Dum Dum to her mother. They stopped for a moment to watch the pair. Dum Dum waved to the girl. She giggled again and pulled her mother's hand. 'Did you see? Did you see?'

Then a midget appeared from the other side and shambled towards them.

'Hey, you!' he jabbed his finger at Paul. 'You'se taking my spot!'

Paul and Dum Dum exchanged looks.

'He's pretty pugnacious for someone his size,' scoffed Paul.

'I could probably lick him without sitting on your shoulders,' chuckled Dum Dum.

A crowd started to gather around them. There were chants of 'Fight, fight, fight! Fight, fight, fight!'

'Is that right?' the midget put his hands on his hips. 'Who you going to lick?'

Dum Dum raised his fist and pointed to it, 'You ask him!'

The midgets hooted and threw down his hat. 'You never seen a contortionist before, have you?'

'A contor-what?' Dum Dum said.

But the man had already stretched up to his full height. He glowered down at them like a man standing on a roof.

Paul grabbed Dum Dum's wrist, 'Run!'

They scurried between people's legs until they lost sight of the angry performer.

On the next street they saw a policeman.

'What's the name of this town?' Paul inquired.

'Oh, a visitor,' the policeman tipped his hat and made a bow, 'Welcome to Fiorenci, *signori.*'

Paul thanked him and they walked away. They found a short flight of steps in one lane and sat down. Paul took out their map and hurriedly scanned it.

'There!' he said, pressing his finger on a spot. Dum Dum leaned forward to see.

'Fiorenci!' Paul read out the name. 'It's in the completely opposite direction from Valta!'

Dum Dum's face turned pale. 'So we're not headed towards Valta at all?'

'No!' moaned Paul. 'That's why they wouldn't tell us the names of the towns. I knew that showman was lying!'

Dum Dum put his head in his hands. 'So what do we do now?'

'I don't know!' wailed Paul. 'I knew you could never trust a man with a red nose!'

They got up and walked around, trying to think of a solution. Then in the distance they heard a noise.

'Was that a train whistle?' said Dum Dum.

'I hope so!' Paul replied. He looked at the map again. 'That's right!' he exclaimed. 'It says here there's a station near Fiorenci where the Valta train stops!'

They had been walking for nearly an hour when Dum Dum abruptly stopped. 'Can't we just go back and say goodbye to Thaumina?'

'No!' said Paul. 'Once that showman sees us again he'll never let us go.'

'But she wanted to leave him, too,' pleaded Dum Dum.

'*No!*' Paul refused to give in. 'She's a princess. She'll do all right without us.'

At last Dum Dum gave a shrug and they resumed their march. They plodded along without talking until they reached the edge of the town.

Paul slowed down and took something out of his jacket. 'Good thing I kept some of the bread from yesterday.'

He broke it in half and they ate while they were walking. Dum Dum kicked at the stones on the path, looking down-hearted.

'There's the station!' Paul suddenly uttered. It was just beyond a junkyard and an empty field. 'We're going to make it!'

But Dum Dum stopped to turn around again. 'Did you hear that?'

Paul cocked his head to listen. 'Hear what?'

'I thought I heard someone shouting behind us,' muttered Dum Dum.

'You probably just imagined it.'

They resumed their advance until they heard something again.

Dum Dum turned to look behind them. 'Somebody said darling.'

'Where?'

'Back there,' Dum Dum pointed down the long curve of tracks they'd just passed. Up ahead of them the station was only about fifty yards away.

A frightened look came into Paul's eyes. 'It might be one of the showman's assistants! I told you he wouldn't let us get away!'

Dum Dum looked worried, too. 'You really think so?'

'Of course, I do! Hurry!' Paul started sprinting towards the station. Dum Dum took off after him. They saw an empty shed one side of the junk yard and dashed into it.

It was full of bare tubes and rusty gears from old locomotives. They squeezed between the blackened fragments of metal and empty oil drums. There was only a little light streaming in through the cracks in the tin walls. They kept still and listened out for several moments.

Soon they heard someone moving outside.

'Who do you think it is?' whispered Dum Dum.

'Ssh!'

'I saw you two go in there!' a woman's voice came from the front of the shed. 'You naughty, naughty boys!'

Dum Dum turned to peek at Paul.

Paul nodded and hissed, 'Yes! It *is* her!'

They climbed out of their holes and threw the doors open.

'Thaumina!' Dum Dum jumped out with outstretched arms.

'You dreadful pair!' Thaumina glowered at them. 'That's no way to treat a lady! Sneaking away without even saying goodbye!'

'I wanted to, I swear!' pouted Dum Dum. 'But he wouldn't let me.'

'You're just as guilty as each other!' Thaumina barked. 'You both deserve to be punished.'

'How?' Paul meekly came forward.

'Well, you'll have to take me wherever you're going.'

Paul and Dum Dum look at each other. Dum Dum nodded with a happy grin.

'But..but,' stalled Paul, 'we'll need to jump on a train,'

'So? All the more reason to take me with you,' said Thaumina. 'It won't cost you any more if I come along!'

Paul was still reluctant. 'But how're you going to hold on?'

'I'll hold her!' offered Dum Dum.

'Nobody has to hold me,' Thaumina said with a flick of her hand. 'Just hoist me through the window and I'll take care of myself. I found you, didn't I?'

As they were arguing, a train thundered around the bend, making the ground rattle, wheezing to a stop several yards from them.

'Quick!' yelled Paul. 'Run for it!'

Dum Dum picked up Thaumina and they scooted towards the platform.

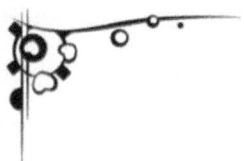

Chapter 34

The last of the passengers were squeezing into the carriages by the time the three of them got there. The conductor was shouting '*Aaaaaaall* aboard? *Aaaaaall* aboard?' as he walked along the train.

Paul and Dum Dum crouched behind a group of travellers and hunted for a way to get on.

'There's an open window!' pointed Thaumina. 'Just throw me in there.'

'No,' said Dum Dum. 'You're sitting with me.'

'Stop arguing!' snarled Thaumina. 'Just sling me over and be done with it!'

Paul snatched her from Dum Dum and did as she asked. She disappeared inside.

Dum Dum held out his hands. 'What'd you do that for?'

'There's no time to argue!' said Paul and spun around to climb onto the couplings. The train was starting to move by the time Dum Dum had clambered into position and squeezed in next to him.

They held on for several miles, counting the villages and farms that streaked by. Everything went dark as they entered a long, winding tunnel. The wind inside was so powerful they were almost blown off.

Then they came out on a high, rickety bridge. Through the wooden slats of the sleepers below them they saw the thin ribbon of water flowing between huge boulders hundreds of feet under the train. It wasn't until they got to the other side that Paul started to breathe again.

Dum Dum looked around as though he couldn't believe they had made it. Then he said, 'Maybe we should go check on her.'

Paul carefully raised himself up to the glass on the door and looked in.

'Why the next car is almost empty!' he said.

Dum Dum's face lit up. 'Let's go in and find her, then!'

Paul shook his head. 'It's easier to get caught if there's three of us. If she's by herself the conductor might think she belongs to one of the passengers.'

Dum Dum looked deflated. 'How many more stops before we get to Valta?' he asked.

Paul took out the map. 'Quite a lot.'

'Good,' nodded Dum Dum. 'That means we've got a chance to show Thaumina around. She'll be great in our act.'

'We can't do that!' objected Paul.

'Why not?'

'The showman's going to say we stole her. He'll have the police looking everywhere for us!'

'He doesn't know where we are,' countered Dum Dum

'It won't be hard to find out,' said Paul. 'How are we going to hide her? She's half a woman, Dum Dum! How long will it be before word spreads about two boys carrying around a woman with half her body missing?'

'We'll just say she had an accident or something.'

'That's not the point,' answered Paul. 'Besides, I thought we were going to find Ginger. How are we going to do that if we have Thaumina with us?'

Dum Dum thought for a moment. 'Well, Thaumina's just half a girl. 'She can have half of me, and Ginger can have the other half.'

'Now you're talking like a real dummy,' declared Paul.

'Thank you.'

'Anyway. No more arguments,' Paul decided. 'We have to get rid of her before we reach Covaria!'

'Covaria?' said Dum Dum. 'What's that?'

Paul pointed on their map. 'That's the next station. We'll be there in the next hour or so.'

Dum Dum tried to reach for the door handle above him. 'We better go and find Thaumina, then!' He turned the handle and tried to open the door.

Paul pushed it shut. 'No, Dum Dum! We don't need her. Let's just jump off now!'

'We've got to at least say goodbye,' Dum Dum defied him. He yanked at the door with all his strength. 'We tried that before. And look, she found us!'

Finally Paul had to let go, and Dum Dum skipped inside. Paul had no choice but to follow him.

Careful not to be seen by the conductor, they traversed the entire breadth and length of the rolling train without catching sight of Thaumina.

They went down a second time and Paul recognized the window where he had thrown her in.

'She should be somewhere around here,' he said. 'Where could she have gone?'

Dum Dum started to panic. 'I told you we should keep her with us! Now someone has stolen her!'

They retraced their steps one more time and they found themselves at the dining carriage. And there, surrounded by adoring passengers, carrying on as if she were still in her own trailer, was Thaumina.

Her listeners laughed at her jokes, gasped at outrageous predictions, and kept asking her about their futures. While she peered into the palms of a string of old ladies, a waiter brought her one drink after another in tall martini glasses.

Paul and Dum Dum watched her in amazement. 'She was supposed to stay out of sight!' hissed Paul.

'She can't help it,' Dum Dum whispered back. 'She's so classy. A dame like that always *needs* to be *seen*.'

Among the group surrounding Thaumina was a skinny young man with thick tortoise-shell glasses and a goatee. He hung on to every word she said and devoured her with his eyes.

'So where is this engineer you keep bragging about, Theodore?' Thaumina finally addressed him. This was the moment he had been waiting for, and he jumped up.

'Well, if the ladies would excuse us,' he pulled her chair out. 'I can take you to see him right now.'

He scooped her up and carried her out of the dining car.

'Where's he taking her?' Dum Dum strained like a dog on a leash. 'Where is he taking her? Stop him! Stop him! What's he going to do with her?'

'That's none of our business,' shrugged Paul. 'If she wants to go with him, let her. We've got to get off this train anyway!'

'No!' cried Dum Dum. 'No!'

'Ssh!'

'He might be a mad murderer!' Dum Dum whispered. 'He might kill her and throw her off the train!'

'*Kill* Thaumina?' sneered Paul. 'I doubt there's anyone in the world who can do that!'

'We've got to save her!' shouted Dum Dum. He wriggled out of Paul's grasp and ran into the next carriage. Paul sighed and rushed after him again.

They followed the trail of Thaumina and her new friend, and wound up right at the locomotive.

Through the glass door they saw Thaumina already chatting with the engineers. She was sitting on the console, regaling Theodore and the engineers with theatrical accounts that involved waving her arms in large arcs and showing a series of silly expressions on her face.

It made her listeners throw their heads back in laughter and slap each other on the back. Paul and Dum Dum were even more dumbfounded when the man at the wheel got up and let Thaumina take over the controls. They guffawed even louder when she made the train swerve.

Dum Dum tapped on the glass to get her attention. Paul did, too, but Thaumina was too engrossed in her new audience. Then they heard the door open in the carriage behind them. The train conductor was coming their way.

"He's going to see her!" exclaimed Dum Dum.

'He's going to see *us!*' added Paul. 'Quick!'

They pushed out the door and manoeuvred to get back onto the couplings. They sat still for several moments, listening out for signs of the conductor.

'I think he's gone,' Paul said at last.

'Let's see about Thaumina,' Dum Dum said. He pulled himself up on the handrails until he was on the roof of the speeding train.

'What're you doing?' shouted Paul.

But Dum Dum's feet had already disappeared above him. Paul clambered up after him. He crawled forward until he saw Dum Dum inching towards the edge. Before Paul could stop him, Dum Dum had lowered his head over the side to look through the windows.

Inside, Thaumina was in the middle of telling another story. '...So I pulled the curtains open,' she was saying. 'Then I saw...'

She caught sight of Dum Dum's head hanging upside-down through the glass.

'*Argh!*' she shrieked.

'And you saw *argh*?' one engineer laughed.

'What I'd give to see *argh*!' quipped the other.

Thaumina recovered enough from her shock to say, 'Gentlemen, you know I just realized I haven't been to the Ladies'.'

'She needs to go to the Ladies',' the engineers winked at each other.

'Now if you would be so kind,' said Thaumina, 'as to put me outside that door.'

The engineers exchanged amused glances once more, but one of them lifted Thaumina and planted her outside the door.

Thaumina quickly moved to the other side and leaned out.

Dum Dum had just returned to his position on the couplings.

'There you are!' he cheerfully welcomed her. He grabbed her and held him firmly on his side. She wriggled to see where they were going.

'Why, I believe we're arriving at a station,' she announced.

'Yes. It's a place called Covaria,' Paul informed her.

Thaumina leaned her head out further for another look.

'Oh how sweet!' she cried out. 'A welcoming party! I suspect someone knew we were coming.'

'They did?' Paul craned his neck to see for himself.

It was true. The station was in fact full of people, and some of them were wearing uniforms.

'Why they even have my name on the posters!' Thaumina squealed in delight.

'What posters?' Dum Dum asked.

The train shuddered and blew out puffs of smoke, and at last they came to a stop. Then they saw what Thaumina meant.

Huge posters hung from the station's walls. Big block letters announced the theft of an automaton named Thaumina. Two boys are believed to have stolen her and were last seen leaving Fiorenci.

'Why, there's even a reward!' cooed Thaumina, reading the sign. 'How flattering! Who would have thought that cheapskate cared so much about me? I told you that show is *nothing* without *me!*"

'*Ssh!*' murmured Paul. 'They're searching the train!'

They sat very still and dared not make a sound for the next several minutes. They heard all the passengers being asked to get off, and the policemen came aboard and searched through the carriages.

The trio leaned out of sight when someone opened the door above the coupling and poked his head out.

It seemed like several hours before the lawmen finally gave up looking. They all got off and the train started moving again.

'Now we're criminals!' Paul glowered at Dum Dum.

Thaumina looked from one to the other.

'Well, all this has been a lot of fun, boys!' she said dusting off her hands. 'Now, why don't we go back to First Class?'

'Fugitives don't ride in First Class!' Paul glared at her. 'You go there if you want to. We'll be fine here.'

'Why, Theodore won't mind,' Thaumina cajoled. 'He's got empty seats all around him. He'd be happy for some company.'

'Who's Theodore?' Dum Dum blurted out.

'Why he's one of the passengers, darling,' Thaumina answered. 'He's rich and wants to marry me.'

'Marry you?' scoffed Paul. 'You're *half* a *woman*.'

'So what?' Thaumina shot back. 'It's the only half he cares about.'

'But what about the showman?' said Paul. 'He obviously wants you back.'

'Oh Theodore will figure that out,' Thaumina waved her hand. 'He's fallen totally, irrevocably in love with me!'

'He's not the only one,' Dum Dum gave her a look of pure adoration.

'Of that I have no doubt!' Thaumina touched her forehead with the back of her hand. 'I'd be terribly shocked if it were otherwise!!'

Just then the door from the locomotive flew open. The three of them froze.

'Thaumina, my darling!' Theodore reached out with both arms. 'Thank God! I was terrified those awful policemen had taken you!'

'Theodore!' Thaumina tried to calm him down. 'Not now!'

He leaned down to try and grasp her. 'Come into my arms, my darling!'

'No, Theodore!' she leaned away. 'Not now, please! We're in a rather delicate situation!'

They made so much of a racket someone opened the other door. It was the conductor.

'Hey, you there!' he shouted to Theodore. 'Don't do that while the train is moving! Get back to your seat!'

Theodore lunged forward to seize Thaumina and disappeared back inside. The conductor turned his gaze to Paul and Dum Dum.

'What are you two doing there?' he yelled, stretching down to grab one of them. Paul tried to crawl up to the roof to get away. Dum Dum jumped up and latched onto his legs.

'Hey! You two!' the conductor screamed after them. 'Come back here, right now!'

They managed to get on the roof, but had to lie face down because of the thick clouds of black smoke the engine was spewing out.

'Where'd he go with her?' Dum Dum tried to see upside down through the windows again.

'Forget her!' Paul said. 'She'll be fine without us.'

Paul squinted through the diesel haze.

'Better hold on,' he said. 'There's a sharp turn coming up.'

But they reached it sooner than he thought. The train veered suddenly and sent the pair flying over the underbrush.

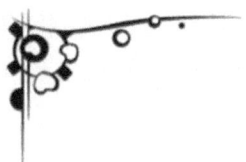

Chapter 35

The clacking of the train's wheels echoed on the tracks long after it had disappeared over the horizon. Paul raised himself up to a sitting position and looked around. They were miles from anywhere. He got up and started picking spores and thistles out of his hair and clothes. Then he rummaged in the brush to find Dum Dum.

He found his foot and pulled him from the brambles, wiping away the dirt from his face. Then Dum Dum jumped on to the roadside and swung his head from one side to the other. He gaped helplessly at Paul. 'It's really gone?'

Paul nodded. 'Maybe it's for the best.'

'Are you *nuts*?' cried out Dum Dum. 'We've lost Thaumina and we've probably broken a few bones, and we're in the middle of nowhere! And you say it's for the *best*?'

'Calm down,' Paul replied. 'It's not that far to walk. At least we didn't fall off at the last station. Or we'd be in prison right now.'

'She's worth going to prison for,' Dum Dum bickered. 'Besides. We sure could use the reward.'

Paul shouted at him, 'Everyone thinks we stole her, you Dum Dum!'

'Don't call me Dum Dum.'

'But that's your name!'

'Aw, shut up!'

They dusted themselves off and started following the railroad.

'After a while Dum Dum stopped. 'What's that?'

'What's what?'

'I can hear music,' Dum Dum craned his neck towards some trees. 'Someone's playing a fiddle.'

Paul listened for a moment. 'You're right! I can hear it, too!'

It was a playful tune, starting slow and then going faster and faster. Then it would stop abruptly. They could hear people laughing.

'Let's go have a look,' said Paul.

They slogged past the trees and found a narrow dirt path. After several minutes they came upon the source of the sound.

There was a little boy playing his fiddle in front of a thorn brush. A group of people were gathered around him. They kept laughing and clapping their hands.

But they were not watching the boy.

Paul and Dum Dum came closer and saw a man with a long beard standing in the thorn brush. He was inside the brush as though it were some kind of cage. Each time the boy played a tune, the man would dance, cutting himself on the thorn brush. That was what the cluster of villagers were watching.

'Why doesn't he stop dancing?' remarked Dum Dum. 'He must know he's hurting himself each time he moves in there.'

'I..don't..think…he can…stop,' Paul tried to say. The boy had started playing the fiddle again and Paul couldn't stop himself from dancing. Soon Dum Dum was doing the same.

'I never even knew I could do the jig,' Dum Dum chuckled as his limbs moved of their own accord. They made him cavort and bump his hips like he'd never done before. Soon the villagers had turned to watch them. They were pointing their fingers and jeering.

'I…can…feel…myself moving towards the thorn brush,' Paul struggled to say. He couldn't stop his body from prancing towards the bristly thicket.

'Stop him!' Dum Dum yelled at the villagers.

'Stop!' Paul screamed at the boy. 'Stop playing!'

But the child kept bowing the strings until all the villagers began joining in. They threw their bodies this way and that, bopping and jumping like small children. They moved in circles, hooting and kicking up dust. Someone grabbed Paul and Dum Dum by the crooks of their arms and whirled them about from one partner to the other. They danced round and round in endless loops.

'We've got to leave!' shouted Paul.

'I'm trying to!' Dum Dum yelled back.

Their spinning ring of dancers got bigger and bigger, as more and more villagers took part. Soon Dum Dum and Paul are being smashed against fences and shrubs, trampling flowerbeds and destroying sheds.

The villagers ignored the damage they were causing, reeling like one giant human carousel that couldn't stop. Dogs and other animals scampered out of their way.

At last Paul broke free. He dashed towards the boy and grabbed his bow and fiddle. He ran away from the mob and threw the bow as far away as he could.

In the sudden silence the villagers slowed down to a halt, and rested with their hands on their knees, gasping to catch their breath.

Dum Dum bolted towards Paul.

In a short time, some of the men had recovered.

'Give the bow back!' one pointed at Paul. Paul grabbed Dum Dum by the wrist and they fled across glade. They sprinted until they saw a thick growth of scrub.

'Quick! Jump in there!' ordered Paul.

'No!' Dum Dum balked. 'Not another thorn brush!'

'It's *not* a thorn brush!' cried Paul.

They both jumped into the bush. They sat very still for several moments. Soon they heard the villagers thundering towards them. They tramped around for a long time, trying to find Paul and Dum Dum. The two stayed where they were and didn't dare make a sound.

At length, the mob gave up and trudged away.

It became quiet again.

'They're gone,' Paul finally whispered.

'*No!*,' murmured Dum Dum. 'There's still someone there.'

'Where?'

'Just behind us,' said Dum Dum. 'I can feel them poking around.'

'Nobody's poking around,' said Paul.

'Someone is!' vowed Dum Dum. 'Can't you feel it?'

Paul felt around quietly for a moment. Then he uttered, 'You're right! I can feel it, too!'

The whole bush seemed to be writhing.

'It's moving! It's moving!' Dum Dum shouted in fright. The brush all around them was alive. It wasn't a bush at all. It was a large mound of snakes.

The pair jumped out and looked for a way to escape. They went in the opposite direction to the way the villagers went, picking the snakes out of their clothes and flinging them every which way they could.

'Look at all the trouble your Thaumina got us into,' Paul grumbled.

'She won't be my Thaumina much longer if we don't find her soon,' answered Dum Dum.

'We're not going to find her!' responded Paul.

'But we have to!'

'No!' Paul stood his ground. 'We came here to look for Ginger. It's either Ginger or Thaumina. You can't have both!'

They followed the tracks without talking for a long time. Then Dum Dum went off to the side.

'What a pretty little bottle,' he said. He bent down to pick it up. There was something glowing inside.

Dum Dum held it up to his ear. 'I think it's talking!'

'What's it saying?' asked Paul.

'He wants me to open the bottle,' Dum Dum told him. 'He says he's trapped inside.'

'Give me that!' Paul snatched the bottle out of his hand. He held it in front of him and stared at it. The light inside was throbbing as if it were trying to say something. Paul wheeled around and hurled the container over the trees.

'What did you do that for?' whined Dum Dum.

Paul dusted off his hands and said, 'Sometimes you just got to stop yourself from picking up pretty things!'

It was late afternoon by the time they reached the outskirts of a town. They saw houses with strange turrets and the shells of abandoned barns. On the hillsides there were structures that looked like gloomy castles. They walked over a very old wooden bridge covered with moss.

'What is this place called?' asked Dum Dum.

Paul slowed down to consult their map. 'It's called Grüm.'

'Grüm?' echoed Dum Dum. 'What kind of name is that?'

'How should I know?' said Paul. 'This map is full of weird names.'

A train station loomed into view. It was a dark stone building with pointed arches and gargoyles all around the roof.

On the platform they made out a young girl waiting. Her hair was so long it trailed on the ground several feet behind her. People had to traipse over the long tresses like it was a precious carpet they mustn't step on.

A short distance away on the same platform was a girl with skin as white as snow. She seemed to be eating a beautiful red apple, but a dwarf kept trying to snatch it out of her hand. She would push him away and keep on trying to finish her fruit. Paul and Dum Dum counted half a dozen dwarves in the crowd waiting for the train.

'This place looks full of bizarre people,' observed Dum Dum.

'Good,' said Paul. 'Just the place we're looking for.'

They counted the blackened gargoyles on the roof of the station building until they reached a corner. There they saw another bunch of people.

At their centre of it, to Paul's dismay, was Thaumina. She had set herself up behind an upside down apple crate and was peering into the palm of an old lady. Her seat was an upturned bucket, and the novelty of a woman's half body perched on a pail only attracted more onlookers to the horde already gathered around her.

Paul rolled his eyes. 'She *just* can't *keep* out of *sight*, can she?'

'But look,' defended Dum Dum. 'She's already making some money!'

Thaumina traced lines on the woman's palm, muttering things that made the elderly lady giggle.

Thaumina's client rested on a footstool borrowed from a shoe maker, almost tipping it over each time she shifted her weight. She wore a purple velvet hat with shiny silver trimmings, like the ones Paul had seen on large paintings in a museum. Her earrings swung and glittered each time she moved her head, like crystals on a great chandelier on a windy night. Everything Thaumina told her seemed to make her titter like a little girl.

There was already a line of ten people eager to have their fortunes told. A few steps from them stood a white-haired chauffeur in an impressive uniform, waiting by the door of a gleaming antique limousine.

Some of the bystanders overheard Thaumina's predictions and they laughed along. People stared at her in wonder, puzzled how such a fanciful creature could be alive. For once Dum Dum felt eclipsed.

He stepped forward and declared, 'Thaumina, my lovely!'

'Not now!' she held up her hand. 'I'm busy!'

She turned her attention back to the wrinkled hand in front of her. She was so intent she didn't hear the peal of a siren and the clanging of bells. Thaumina remained oblivious to the commotion when the police car pulled up. Several lawmen jumped out.

They pushed their way through the crowd. 'Excuse us! Make way please! Police business! Excuse us now!'

Paul pulled Dum Dum back against the wall.

'Thaumina!' Dum Dum hissed across the space. 'Thaumina!'

At last she heard him and looked up. But by then the policemen were only a few paces away.

"Oh dear,' the old lady got up. 'I think we might have to continue this somewhere else.'

Paul and Dum Dum had no idea what Thaumina had been telling the old woman, but she scooped up Thaumina and carried her to the limousine.

Thaumina poked her head over the woman's shoulder and motioned for Dum Dum and Paul to follow.

The white-haired chauffeur opened the doors for all of them.

Once they were all seated, the chauffeur started the engine and pulled away. From the back of the vehicle, Paul and Dum Dum saw the policemen pick up the apple crate, turn it over and closely inspect Thaumina's upturned bucket. They were questioning the shoe maker and other people when the station disappeared from their view.

'What happened to Theodore?' Dum Dum asked.

'Oh, I had to send him off for a while,' Thaumina replied. 'He was getting *too* possessive! I mean, the man just *would NOT* let me *out* of his *sight!*'

They drove up the hill until they came almost to the very top. Then the chauffeur pulled in through a tall black gate topped by sharp spear heads. The old lady's home turned out to be one of the forbidding castles they had seen from below.

When they got inside, they found the walls bare, the corridors chilly and littered with animal droppings. Everywhere was full of cats, dogs, rabbits, and tramps.

The old lady led them to a large bright room where all the furniture had been pushed against the wall. There were so many animals there was barely enough room to stand.

Rabbits were hopping about, dogs snarling at the cats, and the tramps lay around on the marble floor, smoking hand-rolled cigars or playing cards. Some of them had pitched tents in parts of the room, and were chopping some of the furniture to throw into the fireplace.

'Please feel at home,' the old lady said. 'As you can see, I just can't resist adopting people.'

'It's not the people that's the problem,' said Dum Dum. He watched fearfully as the cats and dogs sniffed him out, trying to make out what kind of creature or food he was.

'Oh, don't mind them,' the old lady said. 'They'll get used to you soon enough.'

'We might not be here that long,' Paul told her.

'Oh? You're headed somewhere, are you?'

'Yes!' Paul said. 'We're trying to catch the carnival in Valta.'

'Oh a carnival? How nice! But in Valta?' the ld lady touched her cheek. 'I don't think I've ever been to that place.'

'You wouldn't have,' said Paul.

'Why?' asked the lady with an anxious expression.

'You need a special map to get there,' said Dum Dum.

'Really now? And how did you come by this map?'

'He got it from someone we met in a pawnshop,' explained Paul.

'Oh how wonderful! the old lady said. 'Come, you can tell us all about it over dinner.'

'Over dinner?' Paul and Dum Dum exchanged looks.

'How about them?' Dum Dum nodded towards the animals.

'Oh, don't worry about them,' the lady waved her hand. 'They'll be fed right here. Us people can eat in the dining room.' She put two fingers in her mouth and let out a piercing whistle.

'That means you, too!' she hailed the tramps. 'Come on! Chow!'

They followed her in a ragged file as she waddled through the draughty halls until they reached the dining room. She seated them on heavy square chairs with carved back rests. The food was brought in on silver trays by footmen wearing the same uniform as the chauffeur. Paul and Dum Dum couldn't believe the size of the portions.

They ate three full courses, and when they were finished, the old lady motioned for the sweets to be brought in. Cakes, pies and meringues were rolled in on silver carts, until no one could eat any more.

The old lady pushed her plate away and began to doze in her chair.

'So, what exactly are you planning to do in this carnival?' Thaumina asked.

'We're looking for a friend of Dum Dum's,' Paul volunteered.

Dum Dum shot him a nasty look, but Paul went on, 'She's a star in the carnival.'

Thaumina's eyes flashed. 'A *star*? In a carnival?' She turned her nose towards the ceiling. 'Ha! I didn't know there was such a thing!'

'But she *is*,' maintained Paul. 'She's a really classy girl.'

'Shut up, Paul!' barked Dum Dum. 'You haven't even met her.'

But Thaumina was intrigued. 'Come to think of it,' she waved her cake fork around. 'It might be something to make a splash at some carnival.'

She batted her eyelashes at all the men around the table. 'I daresay I could make quite an impression there.'

'Why don't you?' Dum Dum egged her on.

'Don't waste your time,' said Paul. 'It's not the theatre.'

'But I thought you said she was such a big celebrity, this friend of yours...'

'You can be even bigger,' Dum Dum urged her some more. 'Why don't you come with us?'

'No, she can't!' Paul slammed his fist on the table. It woke up the old lady and she blinked around the room, trying to rejoin the conversation.

'If she comes with us,' ranted Paul, who's going to take care of Theodore?'

'Ah! Theodore!' Thaumina yawned.

The old lady chuckled. 'Goodness, you're making me even sleepier.'

'Tell you what,' she gestured for the table to be cleared. 'Why don't we continue this discussion tomorrow? I'm sure we could all use some sleep.'

As the plates were being put away, she got up and stumbled to the door. 'Good night, everyone.'

Everyone said good night back and she left the room. After a few minutes everyone followed suit. A servant carried Thaumina upstairs to join the old lady. Paul and Dum Dum went off to find beds in the other rooms.

They took two ends of a large four-poster bed, and closed the tasselled velvet curtains for some warmth. They left the door open so the dogs could come in and sleep under them.

'You shouldn't have blabbed like that about Ginger!' Dum Dum upbraided Paul.

'You shouldn't keep promises you can't keep,' Paul shot back.

'I didn't promise anything,' Dum Dum said.

'You did! You said we were going to find Ginger. Now you've stumbled on another pretty thing and you're forgetting all about Ginger.'

'But I think Thaumina should go to Valta,' Dum Dum pleaded. 'She really could be famous. She deserves a chance!'

'In the first place,' groaned Paul, we'd probably never get her there. The police will spot us and take her back to the showman. We'd be lucky if they don't throw us in prison.'

Hours later Dum Dum was smiling in his sleep, and a comforting buzz wafted up to them from all the tramps snoring downstairs.

Suddenly everything exploded. The cats screeched, the dogs leapt up and made a deafening racket.

Dum Dum ran out into the hall. He saw a figure creeping around in the dark. He grabbed a chair and slammed it against the shadow's head.

'*Ow!*' he heard a grunt and the figure fell down with a thud.

Bright lights came on. The old lady came out with Thaumina, wearing matching dressing gowns of Turkish silk.

The intruder pushed himself up with a whimper. From inside his jacket he pulled out a large bouquet of roses.

'Theodore!' Thaumina cried out. 'You came back. I knew you wouldn't be able to resist!'

Theodore rubbed the side of his head with a wince. You know 'I'd go to the ends of the earth for you, my lovely!' he said.

'Oh, you!' Thaumina jumped on to the floor and bounced into Theodore's arms. They sat on the floor, murmuring to each other like doves.

The dogs settled down, the lights were put out, and everyone went back to sleep.

The next morning Paul and Dum Dum came down to find Thaumina having breakfast with Theodore.

'Oh, good morning!' Thaumina chirped as they walked in. 'We have an announcement to make!'

'What's that?' mumbled Paul sleepily.

'Theodore and I are getting married!'

Dum Dum's jaw dropped. 'What about me?'

Thaumina smacked her lips after a sip of coffee. 'Well, you boys can go on to your carnival. After our honeymoon, Theodore and I can go and see you.'

Dum Dum lowered his chin to his chest.

'But what about the reward money?' said Paul.

'Oh dear,' Thaumina brushed her brow with the back of her hand. 'I didn't think of that.'

'Why don't we call the showman?' suggested Dum Dum 'Tell him to pick you up from here. Then he can give the reward to the old lady.'

'That's a wonderful idea!' declared Thaumina.

'You think so?' Dum Dum gawked at her, like he expected a pat on the head.

Theodore suddenly grabbed Thaumina's shoulders. 'But then he'll take you away from me!'

'Hm.' Thaumina rested her chin on her hand. 'I didn't thank of that, either!'

They were in a bind. Thaumina counted out time with a teaspoon on her saucer.

At length Theodore burst out, 'I know!'

'What?'

'What?'

'What?' they all turned to him.

'I'll give you the reward myself,' he said. He took out his wallet and started counting out the money. He placed the wad of bills on the table and looked around. 'Anything else?'

'Well,' said Paul. 'We'll need to get back on the train.'

They piled into the old lady's limousine and drove back into the town. They got off at the train station and looked at the time table.

'There's a train coming at 2:00,' said Theodore. 'I can get you tickets for that.'

He went inside to get them.

'We've got a while before 2:00,' said Paul. 'Let look around.'

They ambled about the steep streets that branched out in all directions. At one corner they stopped to look in a shop window.

Dum Dum's face lit up. 'That's Ginger's!' he cried.

'What's Ginger's?'

'That's her Irene Castle cap!' Dum Dum pointed through the glass. 'And here's her ostrich feather dress! She'd never part with that.'

They stepped back to read the faded wooden sign above their heads. It was a pawn shop.

They went inside.

'Where did you get that ostrich feather dress?' Paul asked pointing to the window.

The pawnbroker adjusted the tiny round glasses on his nose and peered at Paul and Dum Dum.

'Why, that was brought in by a young lady a month or so ago.'

'Did she have a girl puppet with her?' Dum Dum poked his head over the counter.

'Why, yes in fact she did,' replied the pawnbroker. 'She even tried to pawn the puppet, too.'

'And you didn't take it?' asked Paul.

The old man shook his head. 'This is a small town,' he said. 'No one's likely to be interested in a ventriloquist's puppet. But the cap and ostrich feather dress might fit little girls or babies.'

'Where's that young lady now?' asked Paul.

'Well, the old man scratched the top of his head, 'she asked how much a train ticket to Xircupolis would cost. So I gave her enough for that, then a bit more for some drink.'

He winked at them behind his penny-sized spectacles.

'Xurcupolis?' Paul and Dum Dum exchanged looks. They thanked the man and hurried out of the shop.

On the corner outside, Dum Dum blurted out in excitement, 'So they were here! Ginger was here! We're on the right track!'

'That's a sign, Dum Dum,' Paul said. 'We're doing the right thing.'

'But if they went to Xircupolis,' Dum Dum mused, 'maybe that's where we should go!'

They heard the town clock tolling.

'It's almost two o' clock!' gasped Paul. 'We'll be late!'

They ran to the station. As soon as they got to the entrance, Theodore came out to meet them.

'I've got your tickets!' he announced.

'Can we go to Xircupolis instead?' asked Dum Dum.

'Too late,' Theodore answered, handing them the stubs. 'That's just one stop before Valta. You can always get off earlier if you want.'

Paul studied the vouchers. 'First Class!'

Theodore gave them a smug grin.

The train was chugging, ready to leave. The conductor started shouting, '*Aaaaaaall* aboard! *Aaaaaall* aboard?'

Dum Dum ran towards the first carriage.

'Wait!' Paul abruptly held him back.

'What's wrong?' Dum Dum said, swivelling his head this way and that.

'I just want to make sure there's no police,' Paul responded.

They looked for a few more moments. But no uniformed men appeared. So they bolted onto the nearest car and grabbed their seats.

In a few moments the train was moving. Theodore and Thaumina were on the platform. He held her up so she could wave to them. Through the thud of the wheels they could hear her shouting, '*Bye, bye dahrlinks!*'

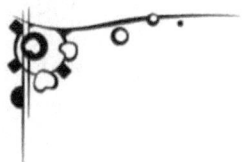

Chapter 36

As Grüm receded further and further behind them, Paul did his best to comfort Dum Dum.

'She'll be happier with Theodore,' he coaxed. 'She won't have to ride on train couplings any more.'

'She could be with us now!' Dum Dum whimpered 'Sitting there, splendid as ever!'

'She can sit in a chair all her life,' reasoned Paul. 'But we can't carry her around forever. Besides, how're you going to explain her to Ginger?'

Dum Dum looked out the window for several moments. At last he gave a defeated sigh, 'I guess you're right.'

'Now it's time we thought about Valta,' suggested Paul. 'What are we going to do when we get there? How are you going to win Ginger back?'

'That's easy,' Dum Dum gave him a smug wink. 'I just go *Zing!*'

'She may have learned a new song,' Paul dissented.

'If *that* fails,' countered Dum Dum, 'I could always do *Sway*.'

Snapping his fingers and swaying his body between the armrests, he started to sing: '*When marimba rhythms start to play…*'

He gave Paul a haughty grin. 'A few bumps of my hips and she's back in my arms!'

Suddenly they felt a jolt, and the train began to shake. They seemed to be slowing down.

'We're stopping already?' Dum Dum asked.

Paul hurriedly looked at their map. 'It's too soon.'

'Then why are we--?'

There was a loud explosion. People screamed as the wheels began to screech and the carriages wobbled wildly from side to side.

'What's happening?' All the passengers panicked. 'What's happening?'

'Hold on!' yelled Paul. There was a terrifying racket, then at last they came to a halt.

People craned their necks to see outside windows. 'Why are we stopping?'

The door from the front of the carriage opened and one of the engineers came through.

'Ladies and gentlemen,' he proclaimed. 'There's been a problem with our engine. We don't know how long it will take to repair. Please make yourselves comfortable. Another train is on its way so you can continue your journey. Our deepest apologies!'

Slowly, the travellers got up from their seats and streamed out of the cars, grumbling. Dum Dum got up on his seat to look out.

'That was a short ride in First Class,' lamented Paul.

'Doesn't matter,' Dum Dum said, 'We're here!'

'What?'

'We're in Valta!'

'We can't be,' uttered Paul. 'Valta's still miles away!'

'Then what do you call that?' Dum Dum pointed out the window.

Paul peered through the dusty glass. Jutting out behind some buildings was the top of a large colourful tent.

'You're right!' he shouted. 'Let's go!'

They jumped out of the train and jogged towards the tent. As soon as they rounded a corner they heard the strains of an accordion. They got even more excited.

'You hear that?' Dum Dum beamed.

'Yes,' nodded Paul. 'It's an accordionist.'

'No, I mean the tune he's playing. You recognize it?'

Paul listened for a moment. He *did* find the melody somewhat familiar. 'Could it be...?'

'It is!' exulted Dum Dum. 'It's *Zing*! Ginger's *trademark song*! She's *here* somewhere!'

They dashed across the street to find the fairground.

They ended up in a little lane. They followed it around the back of an old mill. Then Dum Dum saw the top of the marquee again.

'That way!'

They changed direction, aiming for the jauntily striped crown that appeared now and then between the houses.

But when they got there, they found the pavilion empty. There was nothing around it but puddles and litter. They saw the charred remains of wooden stalls, and blackened pillars without a roof.

They came near and saw the holes in the tent's fabric. Under the tattered awning sat the lone accordionist, playing with his eyes closed.

Paul stopped in front of him.

'Where's the circus?' he asked.

The man stopped playing and opened his eyes. "Gone. Long ago. They all left.'

'When?'

The performer squeezed a few mournful notes from his instrument before he answered, 'After the accident.'

'What accident?' demanded Dum Dum.

The man stretched out the accordion and let the air out in one tired *whoosh*. 'There was a lady who got shot out of a cannon in one of their numbers,' he explained. 'Something went wrong and the curtains caught fire. It spread to the stage and up the poles. Everyone had to run for their lives.'

'Do you remember a girl puppet in the show?' quizzed Dum Dum. 'Named Ginger?'

'Yes! Of course!' the musician nodded his head. 'She was their biggest star! Everybody loved her! That's why I learned most of her songs.'

'You know if anything happened to her?'

'I don't know, ' the stranger clucked his tongue. 'There was smoke everywhere. I just grabbed my instrument and ran. When I came back all I saw was this.'

They all looked up at the singed material clinging to the poles.

A short distance away, Paul noticed another settlement. They could see the braids of smoke rising from its low brick structures.

'What's that place called?' Paul pointed at it.

'Why, that there is Lutzenvelde,' the stranger told him. 'I'm not surprised you don't know. It's not even on most maps.'

Dum Dum looked in his map. 'It is on mine.'

'Well yours is a very special map then,' remarked the performer.

Paul motioned towards the little hamlet.' Do you ever go there to play?'

'Ha!' scoffed the fellow. 'Who wants to fall asleep for days?'

'Why would you fall asleep for days?'

'It's those bakeries of theirs. The smell makes you sleepy. And when you eat the bread, all you can do is sleep.'

'Don't they ever have any shows over there?' queried Paul.

'They did. Until the accident. Now all they have is the market.'

'what market?'

The accordion player pointed with his thumb.

Dum Dum and Paul trudged across the scrubland to reach Lutzenvelde. The odour of freshly baked bread enveloped them as soon as they arrived.

'That smell sure is making me hungry,' Paul remarked.

'But we don't want to sleep for days,' answered Dum Dum. 'Like that man warned us. We might get stuck here. That's probably what happened to him.'

'And all those people,' Paul gestured towards the corner.

Dum Dum turned around and saw the inhabitants watching them from their doorways, staring sleepily at them. One of them whispered something, and the others threw their heads back to laugh. But the sound that came out of their moths sounded like crying.

It spooked Dum Dum. 'Let's get out of here!'

They hurried away.

At the edge of the village, away from the smoke coming from the bakeries, they found the market.

Rows of tables were laid out, covered with odds and ends, antique spinners, boxes of flax, dusty paper flowers. Further inside they found stalls selling freshly caught flounders, along with mounds of lettuce and pears.

At the far end of the bazaar they came upon vendors selling discarded fixtures and old pots. Paul and Dum Dum looked through the chair legs, broken chandeliers and door knobs on their counters. It took them a while to realize that some of the items were parts from old puppets. Dum Dum jumped back and covered his eyes.

Paul led him away from the stalls to calm him down.

At last Dum Dum put down his hands.

'We're nothing but bits of furniture for people,' he hung his head. 'They think we're just firewood or something to patch walls or fix their roofs with.'

Paul tried to pull him away, but Dum Dum kept getting drawn to the wares laid out along the aisles.

'This was Cri-Cri,' he commented, inspecting a piece of painted wood. 'She used to sing like a cricket.'

At the next stall he picked up a lamp. He pointed to the stem. 'That's Donatello's leg,' he sighed. 'I'd recognize that knobbly knee anywhere.'

They walked away from the bustle for a while.

'Puppets are just like children,' Dum Dum said. 'Our parents or owners decide everything.'

'Parents can't throw away their children,' differed Paul.

'But with dummies,' Dum Dum responded, 'owners can do whatever they want.'

A seller saw them from the next aisle. He called out and beckoned them over. 'Come this way!' he waved his arms. 'I've got everything you're looking for!'

He was a very big man with a red beard. Paul and Dum Dum walked up to him and he picked up various objects from his counter, holding it for them to inspect one by one.

'My name is Nico Barbarossa,' he tapped his massive chest. 'I collect the best puppet parts in the world. And I sell them to famous sculptors and instrument makers.'

He turned around in his cramped space to show them the back wall. On it hung several wooden pieces of various sizes.

Paul moved to shield Dum Dum from him.

'Some collectors pay top price for instruments made from the rarest wood,' the giant told them.

'This wood, for example,' he lifted one of the darker samples on his right, 'is great for carved legs, for piano stools, antique chairs and the like. They're strong and they don't wobble.'

'These ones, however,' he pointed to the lighter fragments on his left, 'are soft and beautiful. They're perfect for violins! I know because I also happen to be a violin-maker.'

Paul's eyes were drawn to a large poster on the other wall. It showed a debonair Latin puppet, surrounded by beautiful adoring girl puppets. The large letters across the top read: "*PORFIRIO'S HAREM!* THE SHOW THAT WILL MAKE YOU FALL IN LOVE!"

Barbarossa noticed Paul's interest in the poster. His laughter shook the booth.

'He's one of my creations!' he pointed to the Latin puppet on the poster. 'He's famous now. All the girl puppets love him. And all the girls in the audience, as well.'

He leaned forward to wink at Paul. 'I *sold* him for a *fortune*.'

'Which wood is he made from?' asked Dum Dum.

'I made him from the *finest* ebony,' the man proudly told him.

He snapped up an unfinished violin from a glass case. It was made of pale shiny wood.

'Now there's what we call Ivory Wood,' he declared. 'The *rarest* wood in the world! If I could find the extra lumber to finish this instrument, I'll *never* have to work *again*!'

This time Dum Dum tried to pull Paul away.

When they were out of earshot he whispered, 'That's exactly what Ginger is made of. *Ivory wood*. That's why she looks like she's always bathed in light.'

Dum Dum kept glancing back at Barbarossa as they shuffled away.

'At least we know Ginger wasn't hurt in that accident,' he murmured. 'Or that man would have all the ivory wood he needs.'

They stopped in front of another vendor. There was a chair with a mismatched piece of pale wood on display.

'Is that what ivory wood looks like?' Paul pointed.

Dum Dum stepped forward to examine it.

'Hm,' he muttered. 'Maybe Ginger did get hurt after all.'

They hurried back to find the train. 'I hope she hasn't been patched up with parts from other dummies,' Dum Dum worried.

'Why?'

'Because she might not recognize me. She might be completely different now.'

Dum Dum became sullen and inconsolable. As they marched on Paul noticed his shoulders shaking, and he turned his head now and then to wipe something from his eye.

It was mid-afternoon by the time they got back to the train. But its engine had been taken apart, the gears and blocks spread out on the ground. Two of its wheels had been removed.

'I think we'd better forget about the train,' Dum Dum decided. 'We have no time to lose!'

As they hustled away, all they could hear was the *clink, clink, clink* of the workmen's tools, and the foreman's cries of frustration: 'Hurry! Hurry! The passengers are waiting!'

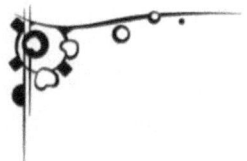

Chapter 37

When the railroad was a long way behind them, they spotted the old woman carrying bundles of firewood.

'Hello!' Paul hailed her. 'Do you know the way to Valta?'

'That's quite a long way,' she said in her creaky voice. 'But it might be a little quicker if you cut through those woods. Just stay on the trail!'

They followed her directions and kept to a narrow track. But it didn't seem to get them anywhere. Before long they were completely lost.

'I'm afraid we're just going around in circles,' groaned Paul. 'I don't think that old woman knows her way through these woods.'

They plodded along for a bit more. Then Dum Dum stopped. 'Wait a minute. I think I see somebody.'

Up ahead they made out a girl walking by herself in the wilderness. She seemed to be barefoot, moving softly over the thorny ground. When they came close enough they noticed she had no hands. A heavy basket swung from the crook of her right arm.

'Excuse me,' uttered Dum Dum. 'Can you show us the way to Valta?'

The girl turned back towards the way she came. She pointed with her left arm. 'You keep going that way until you pass the pond.'

'Thank you!'

'Wait!'

Paul and Dum Dum stopped and turned around.

'You boys look hungry,' she held her basket out towards them. 'Take a pear each.'

The boys plucked out two pears. They thanked her again and went on their way.

When they were a good distance away Dum Dum remarked, 'Did you notice? She had no hands.'

'Ssh!' responded Paul. 'Don't be rude.'

'We've certainly met some strange people since Grüm,' observed Dum Dum.

They tramped across a grassy slope until they saw the pond.

'Let's have a drink!' Dum Dum darted excitedly towards the water. He got down on his stomach and lowered his face towards the pool. But he noticed something shiny at the bottom. He plunged his hands into the cool liquid. When he pulled them out he found a coin in his palm.

'It's full of coins! He cheered.

Paul joined him. They gazed at all the change scattered under the surface.

'Who could have thrown all that in there?' Paul mused.

'Who cares?' Dum Dum pushed him aside. 'Just grab everything you can!'

They scooped up all the money and stacked them in a soggy pile. Then they stuffed them in their pockets and walked on.

Up ahead Paul saw something. 'Quick!' he said. 'I think we're near a road.'

They marched briskly over rotten tree trunks and mounds of rock. It took a while for them to realize they were being followed.

Something was scrabbling in the bushes, cracking twigs in its path.

They kept going until they reached a clearing. Just one last climb and they would be out of the woods.

313

Suddenly there was a loud croak.

Dum Dum jumped back. 'What was that?'

A dark creature leapt out of the grass.

'It's just a toad ,silly,' Paul chuckled.

All at once a whole army of toads poured out of the shrubbery. Suddenly the two found themselves surrounded by toads of all sizes, belching and croaking angrily.

At their lead was the largest toad Paul had ever seen. It was the size of a dog and barked like one, his eyes bulging with anger. They made such a deafening racket Dum Dum and Paul had to cover their ears.

'What do they want?' Paul yelled over the din.

'I think they want the coins back!' Dum Dum shouted in answer. 'It's theirs!'

They quickly dug into their pockets and threw everything on the ground.

The toads pounced on their money. They snatched everything in their jaws and hopped back happily into the forest.

At last, Paul and Dum Dum scrambled up the incline and got up on the road.

Paul patted his pockets. 'Oops! I think I gave them some of the money from Theodore!'

They looked down at the clearing they had just left. There was no sign of the toads or the coins. The glade was still and quiet again.

They had been rambling for miles when they saw a man driving a cart full of milk bottles. 'Are you going to the town?' Paul asked.

'Of course I am,' scowled the man.

'Can we ride with you?'

'No! The cart is full and I'm in a hurry.'

'Maybe we should buy some milk,' Dum Dum whispered to Paul.

'We don't have any money.'

'We should never have picked up those coins from the pond,' Dum Dum clucked his tongue.

'Now we know,' said Paul. 'It wasn't ours to take.'

They trotted after the cart and begged the man to stop.

The carter turned around wearily. 'What do you want now?'

'Just a mile or so,' Paul implored. 'We're really tired.'

The carter picked up his reins and spurred his horse to go faster.

Up ahead they could already see the town, its tall clock tower protruding out of the mist. It was perhaps another half hour's walk away, but their legs were killing them.

And besides, the sky above them was turning grey, and there was the rumble of thunder from somewhere.

They tried to sneak onto back of the barrow as it bobbed along. But the old man spun around in his seat. 'Hey! I told you to go away!'

'Just till we get to town,' Paul bargained. 'We'll help you unload your milk.'

'I said, no!' the man grabbed his whip and started flailing it at them. It cracked in the air all around them.

Paul and Dum Dum covered their faces. Suddenly they heard a shriek from above them.

They lowered their hands to see a sparrow flying circles around the carter. He struggled to hit the bird with his whip but it was too quick and agile. It spurted from his left to his right, then to the back and the front of him. It pecked him on every side of his face.

'Ow! Ow! Ow!' This time he was the one covering his head. He dropped his whip and curled up into a ball, afraid to move.

Then the sparrow started pricking the horse. It neighed and kicked, and finally it reared up to its full height and turned the cart over. The bottles smashed on the path while the beast went berserk and tore out of its bridle. It did a looping jump, still tormented by the sparrow, before it galloped away and disappeared.

Then other birds swooped in to drink the milk spilled on the ground. Paul and Dum Dum seized some unbroken containers and gulped down what was left in them.

When they had slurped their fill of milk off the earth, the birds spiralled up to the sky once more.

'Where are they all going?' said Dum Dum.

Paul looked up at the sky and held out his hand. A large blob of water spattered on his hand. 'I think we're in for some rain.'

The countryside exploded in a massive downpour. The air went white and the ground hissed like a frying pan. Dum Dum and Paul ducked from one tree to another, trying as best they could to stay dry.

'Do you hear that?' Dum Dum pointed upwards.

Paul listened.

Clang clang clang. There was a bell ringing.

'It's the clock tower!' cried out Dum Dum.

They bolted across the fields, following the sound of the bell. Lightning struck several times, and they took shelter under a bridge to wait out the worst of the storm.

When the thunder shower had weakened a little, they ventured out of their refuge. They picked their way through the mud until they found a stream. They followed it until they and reached a row of houses.

They could see the back of the clock tower. They ran and dove under its awning, drenched and shivering. Dum Dum stepped out for a few moments and looked up at the clock tower. 'Thank you!' he called up.

At last the rain dwindled to a light patter. They decided to leave their shelter.

They met an old man picking his way through the puddles. It was getting dark.

For the first time they saw what a beautiful town it was. All the street lamps were ablaze.

'That's why they call this place Gorsveta,' the old man laughed. 'It means the city of light.'

'Who built it?' Paul enquired.

'It was built by prisoners long ago,' the old man disclosed. 'Now we spend our days just to keep the lights going. It keeps us from missing the families we've left behind.'

They strolled together under the bright lights, and the old man told them stories about the town.

'My name is Iosif,' he said. 'Come see my shop.'

He stopped in front of one of the businesses and took out a key. He unlocked the door and waved them inside.

It was a clock shop. The air was full of the ticking of clocks, in all different tones and pitches. It sounded like a noisy bazaar filled only with timepieces, all chattering in their different tongues.

Dum Dum beamed at the old man. 'It's like they're talking to each other.'

'Yes,' smiled Iosif. 'They chatter all day. That's why I love being here. It's a happy sound.'

'It's a shame we don't know what they're saying,' Paul remarked.

'But I do,' Iosif revealed. 'That's how I knew you two were coming.'

Paul looked amazed. 'The clocks told you *that*?'

'They didn't. But the clock tower did.'

Paul was even more astonished. 'He *told* you about *us*?'

'Don't be so surprised,' put in Dum Dum. 'Remember? He kept ringing his bell so we could find our way.'

'They're always talking to each other,' Iosif nodded gravely.

'Who?'

'The clock towers,' Iosif pointed out the window. 'The one here and the one in the next town. Sometimes I listen in. That's how I know they just had a great show there. Tents and clowns and animals. Puppets and everything.'

Dum Dum's face lit up. '*Puppets*?'

'Yes, my dear boy,' grinned the old man. 'When the clock tower saw you, he thought you were from the show. He was ringing his bell to tell everyone a great show was coming.'

'How far is it to the next town?' demanded Paul.

'Oh, it's just an hour or two through the woods,' Iosif replied. 'But wait till tomorrow. By then the bad weather will have cleared.'

Paul and Dum Dum looked at each other. 'But where are we going to sleep?'

'Why, you can come to my house,' Iosif offered. 'I live by myself. So there is always a spare bed.'

That night they had a hearty supper cooked by the old clock maker. They slept on big warm beds with a roaring fire. The next day Iosif joined them for breakfast. Paul told him all about the carnival in Valta.

'When you get to Valta,' Iosif said, 'look up a good friend of mine.'

'What's his name?'

'Collodi. *Signor* Collodi,' Iosif stated. 'But I call him Carlo.'

'Where is he in Valta?' questioned Paul.

'His watch shop is on the main square,' Iosif answered. 'Right next to the clock tower. He's the one who sets the time on it and oils its gears. That's how he and I manage to talk to each other.'

The boys finished their food. They thanked Iosif and set off to continue their journey. Iosif waved to them sadly from the front of his house.

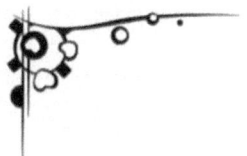

Chapter 38

It was a hot day. They were halfway through the woods when Paul said, 'I'm thirsty.'

'I told you we should have brought some water,' grumbled Dum Dum.

'We don't want to be carrying bottles,' countered Paul. 'Anyway, look! There's a well!'

It was just at the end of the path. They went to it and threw down the bucket. They were pulling up some water when they heard someone shouting.

'Who's that?' Paul looked around.

'Maybe somebody owns this well.'

'No,' Paul leaned over the mouth to listen. 'It's coming from down there.'

They shouted down the hole, 'Who are you? What do you want?'

They heard their own voices echo back at them. But at the end, there came the little cry again, '*Help us! Help! We're trapped Get us out!!*'

'We've got to help them!' said Dum Dum.

Paul peered down to the bottom.

'I'm not going down there!' he backed away.

'Let's go get some help!'

They scampered off.

When they got to another trail they came across an old woman.

'Help!' Paul cried out. 'There's someone in the well! They say they're trapped!'

The woman waved it off. 'That well echoes,' she rasped. This is a strange forest. You hear all sorts of voices. None of it is real.'

She narrowed her eyes at the two of them. 'And what were you doing at the well?'

'We were thirsty,' Paul answered.

'Oh, thirsty, are you?' the old woman smiled. 'I'll give you some water. Would you like some bread as well?'

Paul and Dum Dum nodded.

Follow me,' she turned and trudged up the winding track.

After a while they reached her little cottage. She led them to a pile of logs and handed Paul an axe. 'Here,' why don't you chop me some firewood?'

Then she stooped to pick up a bucket by her front door. She gave it to Dum Dum. 'And you can fetch us some water.'

Dum Dum sauntered back to the well. Then Paul hoisted the axe and started hacking at the logs.

He heaved with all his might, but it didn't do any good. No matter how he tried, the chopper wouldn't bite into the timber. Soon his arms ached from all the swinging.

He ran his finger over the blade. It was quite blunt.

'This axe isn't very sharp!' he complained to the old woman.

'Just keep working,' she ordered.

Paul tried again, but it was useless. After several more attempts, he threw down the axe and scurried into the woods. He found Dum Dum at the well, pouring some water he had just drawn into the bucket the old woman had given him.

But the water kept leaking out into the ground. Dum Dum picked up the container to examine it. He found a large hole at the bottom.

He scratched his head. 'Now how am I supposed to fetch water?'

'And the axe she gave me was blunt!' ranted Paul. 'I kept chopping and chopping and nothing happened.'

'We could chop wood and fetch water for her for years,' added Dum Dum. 'And we'd never get any work done.'

'Maybe that's the idea,' guessed Paul.

Then they heard the noise from the well again. They came closer and leaned down to listen. They could make out a little girl's voice. '*Help! Help! Let me out!*'

'I can climb down on that rope,' Dum Dum reached over for the line.

'No!' Paul grabbed his shoulders.

'Let me go!' Dum Dum struggled. He slipped out of Paul's grasp and almost fell in.

He saw his reflection on the swaying water below, and he pushed hard against the walls to keep from plunging in.

At last Paul managed to pull him out. They both tumbled down on the grass.

Paul sprang up to grab the bucket and the axe. 'I think we better give these back.'

They ran back to the old woman's cottage and knocked on the door.

'Just in time, boys,' the woman leaned out. 'I've cooked your dumplings! Go on. Sit down and eat.'

Dum Dum was so hungry he pushed past Paul and took a seat.

'No!' Paul called from the door. 'Dum Dum, let's go!'

'Wait a minute!' Dum Dum picked up a knife and fork. 'We can't let this food go to waste. It looks delicious!'

'Yes,' the old woman beamed at them. 'After all, you both worked so hard for it.'

Paul gave in and sat down next to Dum Dum. The old lady brought the pot from her stove and started ladling out the dumplings on their plates. They pounced on the hot food. But Paul abruptly threw down his fork and howled.

'What's wrong?' Dum Dum turned to him.

'These are as hard as rocks!'

He leapt up and darted to the door. 'Let's get out of here!'

Dum Dum scuttled out after him. Paul was running up the track.

'Wait!' Dum Dum tried to make him stop. 'Maybe she just overcooked them. I think she's doing some more.'

'No!' Paul sprinted even faster.

When the cottage was out of sight, they slowed down to catch their breath.

'Maybe she could at least put us up for the night?' wheedled Dum Dum.

Paul crossed his arms. 'No!'

'Why not?'

'The blunt axe, the bucket with the hole,' Paul counted with his fingers. 'The dumplings hard as stones. I know this story.'

'What story?'

' That old woman is a water nixie.'

'What's a water nixie?' Dum Dum asked.

'I'll tell you when we're far away from here,' Paul promised.

They had gone past the well when Dum Dum said, 'Maybe we should at least stop and help that girl in the well.'

'No!' Paul kept walking. 'It's all a trick. We'll get pulled down trying to help her. And then we'll be the ones trapped down there!'

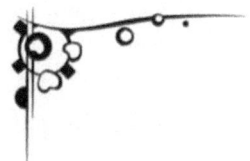

Chapter 39

They slogged through the heavy undergrowth until they were far from the well and the strange old woman.

'How did you know she was a water nixie?' Dum Dum asked.

'Because I've read that story,' answered Paul.

Dum Dum looked at him with awe. 'You know a *lot* of stories.'

'You have to,' Paul pushed forward through the vines. 'Every kid needs to know a lot of them. Nadine knows the most. But you know what my favourite story is?'

'What's that?'

'It's the one about you and me.'

'That's nice,' Dum Dum beamed.

They come out of a dense grove and stopped in their tracks. In front of them was a deep, wide gorge. Paul inched towards the edge and saw the abyss.

'Oh no!' he moaned.

'But there's no gorge in our map,' remarked
Dum Dum.

'Maybe there was an earthquake after the map was
made. Maybe some things changed.'

Dum Dum cocked his head and looked around. 'I can
hear water. There must be some kind of stream or river down
there.'

'Then we'd better get out of here!' Paul shuddered. He
walked away fast.

'Wait!' Dum Dum held him back. 'If it's a river then it
must be on our map. It might take us where we're going.'

'No!' Paul broke away. He moved so quickly
Dum Dum could hardly keep up with him. Paul was so
anxious he didn't realize they were going the wrong way.

"Where's the path?' he suddenly uttered. All they could
see around them were trees and more trees, and mountains of
vines. Paul scratched his head, 'I have no idea where we are.'

'Lift me up,' Dum Dum suggested.

'What?'

'Lift me up to that branch so I can see.'

Paul did as he asked. Dum Dum slid up the branch as
far as he could go. He peered out into the distance for a long
time. Suddenly, he stretched out and pointed at something. 'I
think there's a farm over there!'

'Where?'

'There! You can see the mounds of hay.'

They made their way in that direction.

But by the time they came out of the thicket it was late afternoon. They shambled across the heath until they were at the farm.

But it looked deserted. It was just three buildings around an empty paddock. It was so quiet they could hear the bugs munching on the grass. The tallest structure must have been the barn. All around it were apple trees, ripe fruit dangling out of their boughs, too many to count.

Dum Dum rubbed his stomach. 'I'm hungry.'

'So am I!'

They clambered onto the nearest trees and picked as many apples as they could. They sat on the ground to eat them. By the time they had finished there were still mounds of the fruit left.

'Maybe we should take some with us,' said Dum Dum.

'Let's look for something to carry them with,' Paul got to his feet.

They hunted around the farmhouse for some rope or piece of cloth.

Suddenly Dum Dum let out a cry.

'What's wrong?' Paul ran over to see. Dum Dum's foot was caught in a trap.

Paul slumped to the ground. 'Now we're in even bigger trouble.'

It was early evening when a decrepit old car drove up. A fat man came out and walked towards them. Dum Dum struggled with all his might to wriggle free. Paul tried to part the jaws of the snare but it was too hard.

The fat man stopped and stood over them.

'Ah! Steal my apples, will you?' he bellowed.

'Please,' said Paul. 'We've got some money. We can pay for it.'

'Keep your change, you rascals!' snapped the farmer. 'That's probably stolen money, too.'

'We were just hungry,' reasoned Dum Dum.

'That would probably explain all my missing chickens, too!' the farmer retorted.

'No!' cried Paul. 'We didn't see any chickens.'

'How could you?' the man sneered. 'You stole them all long ago. Every last one!'

'We didn't!' vowed Dum Dum. 'I swear!'

The man chortled and shook his head. 'I've never seen a puppet that could swear and steal chickens as well. Well, now I've got you!'

He released the trap and grabbed Dum Dum by the neck. Then he looped his other arm around Paul and dragged them to the barn.

He threw them inside and locked the door.

As soon as they were alone, the pair lay on the hay and listened. Outside they could hear the farmer trying to start his car. The engine squealed several times but never came to life.

In the end he came out of the vehicle and give it a kick. They heard him tramp past the barn and go somewhere down the field.

They put their ears to the ground and tried to hear everything around them. A horse snorted from somewhere. It hit its hoof against a wall.

'That must be the stable next door,' whispered Paul. 'That might come in handy.'

'Do you know how to ride a horse?' Dum Dum asked.

'No.'

Dum Dum put his head in his hands, 'Now we'll never find Ginger!'

'Yes we will!' Paul reassured him.

'Her owner might already have sold her,' despaired Dum Dum. 'Then how will we ever find her?'

As they were talking, Paul heard something move in the shadows.

'What was that?' muttered Paul.

They peered into the darkness, but couldn't make out anything.

Dum Dum called out, 'Who's there?'

There was a bit of rustling before they got an answer.

Hoot!

Paul gasped, 'What's in *there*?'

'I don't know,' Dum Dum muttered. 'But it looks big.'

They huddled against the far wall. Paul's stomach started growling.

'It's just the apples,' Dum Dum told him. 'Let's try and get some sleep.'

They lay down and shut their eyes. They were both so tired that soon they were snoring.

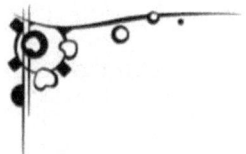

Chapter 40

It became so quiet there wasn't even the sound of the wind. But in the dead of night a long, shrill sound pierced the silence. Dum Dum sat bolt upright. 'What was that?'

Paul stirred and slowly turned over 'I think it was a train whistle,' he mumbled.

'That means the train must be running again!' Dum Dum blurted out.

'Sshhh!' Paul pressed closer to the wall and tried to get back to sleep.

'No!' Dum Dum shook him. 'It's now or never! If we don't move now we'll miss the carnival! We've got to get to Valta! Or we'll never find Ginger!'

Paul turned on his back with a sigh. With a struggle, he pushed himself up to a sitting position. 'But how are we going to get out?'

As they were thinking of a way, a hoot came from above them again. They both glanced at the ladder going up to the loft.

Dum Dum jumped up and started climbing. Paul dragged himself up the rungs.

As soon as they had reached the top, they heard a wild flapping in the shadows.

Strands of hay floated down from the rafters.

Dum Dum crawled forward. He found one of the loft doors dangling by a broken hinge.

'So that's what it was,' Paul reckoned.

Dum Dum pointed to the gap. 'You think we can squeeze through there?'

They managed to lower themselves to the ground, and groped their way into the stable next door.

It was still dark and the horse neighed in greeting, snorting and huffing, towering over them in its stall.

'Why, hello, horsy,' Dum Dum approached with a friendly smile.

'I'm not sure that's its name,' Paul warned him from the door.

'There's a nice little horsy,' Dum Dum cajoled. 'Are you thirsty?' He stroked its sides and hugged it by the forelegs.

'There's a good horsy,' he cooed. He told it stories he knew about horses, all the while stroking its shiny speckled flank. The mare seemed to like it and it pricked up her ears to listen.

Finally they opened the stall door and led the beast outside. She let them walk her out to the road. Dum Dum turned the animal and gave Paul a wink. Paul came forward to boost Dum Dum onto its back.

But the animal refused to be mounted. She shook her whole body and gave an angry grunt.

They took her back to the stable.

'Maybe we should just walk,' Paul suggested.

'It would take us hours to get anywhere,' dissented Dum Dum. 'Someone might see us and tell the farmer.'

They sneaked up to the car left in front of the farmhouse. They tried to go inside. But they couldn't even open the rusty door.

'It's just as well,' Paul threw up his hands. 'Neither of us can drive.'

They rummaged around the paddock until they uncovered an ancient bicycle under the vines.

They brushed the dirt and dried grass off it, and wheeled it out to the roadside. But it was too high for Paul to even reach the pedals.

'Marc used to take me cycling,' Dum Dum bragged. 'He'd run pushing the thing then hop on while it was moving.'

They tried doing that. It took several tumbles before Paul finally managed to get the bicycle rolling.

'Hurrah! Hurrah!' cheered Dum Dum as he ran alongside. 'You did it! You did it! You're doing great!'

He grabbed the rear of the bike and hopped on. It made the cycle wobble, and Paul fought to keep it straight.

It was starting to get light, but most of the way ahead was still dark.

They rode smoothly for quite a long stretch. Then Paul suddenly cried out, 'Oh my God! Oh my God! We're going downhill!'

They went faster and faster, and soon the fields and the trees are whizzing by on either side of them.

'I don't know how to stop this thing!' yelled Paul. 'I can't even make it slow down!'

'Just whistle,' advised Dum Dum. 'That keeps you from falling.'

Paul tried to whistle. But they had come to a place with low-lying branches that seemed to reach out towards them.

They lowered their heads to get past, but one branch whipped Paul on the side of his face and covered his eyes with its leaves. He let out a yelp and they served wildly from side to side.

When he finally brushed off the leaves and opened his eyes, he saw the mouth of the murky tunnel.

'Stop!' Dum Dum shouted. 'Stop!'

'I'm trying!' Paul replied. He kicked against the pedals with all his strength. They plunged screaming into the gloom.

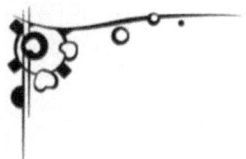

Chapter 41

Paul lay quietly on the ground next to Dum Dum, too scared to even open his eyes. He could hear the bubbling of water somewhere, which frightened him even more.

At last he heard Dum Dum get up. He listened to him walking around.

'Hurrah! Hurrah!' he heard Dum Dum jumping up and down. 'You got us out of there! And you never thought you could!'

Paul got up to see what Dum Dum was so happy about. 'Where are we?'

'Look!' Dum Dum pointed down excitedly.

Paul dragged himself towards Dum Dum. He glimpsed the fast flowing river below them. He nearly fainted.

'Now how are we supposed to get out of here?' he uttered weakly.

'That's easy!' Dum Dum snapped his fingers. 'Where else would it go but downstream?'

'No!' Paul backed away.' We're not going anywhere near that river.'

'Yes we are!' insisted Dum Dum.

Paul nodded towards the mouth of the tunnel. 'We'll have to go back that way.'

'What for?' Dum Dum howled. 'We just came from there!'

Paul took out the map and checked it. 'It says Valta is only two more stops that way. If we find the railroad and follow it, we can be there in a day or two.'

'A day or two!' grumbled Dum Dum.

'Maybe less if we go now! Let's go!'

But Dum Dum would not budge. 'I say this river would be quicker.'

'No!' yelled Paul. 'We're better off staying on land! You never know where the current would take us!'

'Even if we did follow the tracks,' argued Dum Dum, 'it would still take longer than this river!'

'We've got that bicycle,' pointed out Paul. 'I know how to ride it now, remember?'

He strode towards the bushes to pick up the bike. Suddenly he heard a splash. He spun around.

Dum Dum was gone. Paul dashed over to the river bank.

'Dum Dum!' he shouted. 'No! Come back!'

But Dum Dum was already floating downstream fast, waving up to Paul with a smile.

'Oh no,' Paul groaned. He took a deep breath and lunged in after Dum Dum.

At first he panicked and thrashed around in the current. Then he realized Dum Dum was floating like a log. He hung on to him and let the flow carry them down.

They floated for hours, and in time completely lost track of how far they'd gone. After almost a whole day drifting, they washed up somewhere.

They staggered onto the shore, cold and dripping.

'We...b-b-better...get... s-s-some d-d-dry clothes,' shivered Paul.

Dum Dum laughed.

'What's so funny?'

'I thought you were terrified of the water.'

'Well, I am,' admitted Paul. 'But I had to try and save you.'

They trudged further into dry land.

Dum Dum let out another chuckle. 'You thought you were going to save me. But I ended up saving you.'

'I wouldn't have jumped in,' Paul responded, 'if you hadn't gone in in the first place.'

Dum Dum smiled. 'So you learned something, didn't you?'

Paul nodded. 'Yes. The water's not so scary after all.'

'See?' Dum Dum beamed at him. 'We learn something whatever we do. You just have to try.'

They plodded up a barren slope.

'I want to be like you,' Paul remarked.

Like me? Why?'

'You float like a canoe.'

'You want to be like me,' chortled Dum Dum. 'And I want to be like you. I guess we'll be friends for a long time.'

'I hope so.'

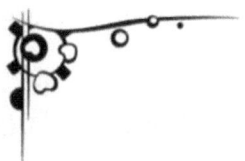

Chapter 42

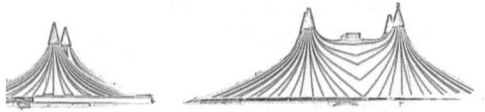

After another hour of hiking they could make out some buildings.

'Where are we?' asked Dum Dum.

Paul slowed down to study their map. 'Oh no! It's all wet!'

Dum Dum leaned in worriedly. 'Is it ruined?'

Some parts are,' answered Paul. 'But there are sections I can still read.'

He pored over the map for a long time. Then he pointed towards the river bank they had just left.

'If the river's over there, that means we should see some towns on this side. I can't read some of the names. But I think we might be just one town away from Valta.'

'One town!' breathed Dum Dum with a gleam in his eye.

'That probably means we're in Xircupolis,' figured Paul.

'We *are*?' Dum Dum swayed with thrill.

'Yes! This is supposed to be the birthplace of the circus,' stated Paul. 'Did you know that?'

'No. But let's go faster!'

They kept going until they caught sight of the beautiful fountains, gushing between rows of structures that looked like pyramids.

'There's the sphinx!' Paul pointed.

'Look at those giant statues!'

There was a great rumbling of hooves from behind them. They jumped to the side just in time, as men on horseback galloped past, racing until they reached a massive fountain, then twisting around it in circles to joust.

On another street they saw people in fancy clothes sitting on the pavement. They were watching clowns and acrobats dancing to the beat of African drums.

'Duck!' Paul suddenly cried.

An orange flying through the air just missed Dum Dum's head. Gangs of children were running around hurling oranges at each other. Paul and Dum Dum picked up some and put them in their pockets.

They tramped on until they were at a wide boulevard. A tall mountain came into view.

Paul paused to examine the map one more time. 'It doesn't make sense.'

'Why?'

'According to this map, that mountain should be near Valta. Not Xircupolis.'

'Who cares?' Dum Dum spread out his hands. 'I love this place!'

Paul seemed fixated on the peak above them. 'That mountain is the reason Valta is the last town on the V-X-V Line,' he noted. 'It's so high the trains all have to turn around and go back the way they came.'

'Stop worrying,' Dum Dum pulled his wrist. 'Come on.'

They roamed around until they saw the clock tower. As they were approaching, it played three merry notes.

'*Just in Time*!' Dum Dum exclaimed.

'Just in time for what?' asked Paul.

'No!' Dum Dum snickered. 'He just played the first three notes of *Just in Time*. That's another of Ginger's songs. So she's really is here! Only she can make everybody sing like that!'

When they arrived at the main square they were greeted by an enormous sign: "GINGER, THE MAGIC GIRL IN VALTA!"

'We're in Valta you dope!' Dum Dum let out a whoop. 'And Ginger is here!'

Paul gazed all around them and uttered, 'And how!'

All the buildings were plastered with posters showing her. Newspapers scattered on the café tables were filled with her pictures and stories about her shows.

There was a gigantic billboard above the square, showing Ginger in all her finery, standing next to her pompous manager in his bowtie and evening tailcoat. The big red letters proclaimed: *DON'T MISS GINGER AT THE VALTA GRAND!'*

They looked across the square at a sprawling hotel. It had gilded columns, velvet canopies, and a hundred marble statues on its roof.

'I guess that's the Valta Grand,' Dum Dum beamed proudly.

'Now the question,' said Paul, 'is whether they'll let us see such a big star.'

'Of course they'll let us see her!' Dum Dum replied. 'We've got money for tickets, don't we?'

Paul cleared his throat. 'That's not what I meant.'

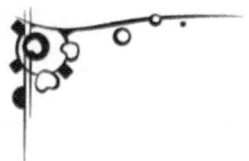

Chapter 43

Hours before the performance, they sneaked into the theatre. They found their way to the dressing rooms, where they slinked past distracted artists scurrying back and forth across the narrow passage. They reached a door with a large shiny star. Dum Dum knocked.

'*Ging*er!' he cooed through the door. 'Guess who's *here!*'

'Later!' Ginger answered abruptly from inside. 'I'm busy!'

Dum Dum heard her giggle and slap someone's hand. 'Oh stop that!' She tittered one more time and Dum Dum raised his hand to knock again.

But a tall figure suddenly cast his shadow over them, wearing a black jacket with a long tail swinging behind him, which made his silhouette look like a giant lizard standing on its hind legs. The man put his hands on his waist to bare his gleaming white shirt.

'And what on earth do you think you're doing?' he glowered down at Paul and Dum Dum.

We kno-kno-know Ginger,' stammered Paul.

'Ha!' The tall man cackled. 'I'm sure you do! Who doesn't?'

I'm an old friend,' Dum Dum squared his shoulders. 'I'm here to see her.'

'Why *of course*, you're here to see her!' smirked the towering impresario. 'That way!'

His smile had turned into a scowl and his thumb was bent like a claw towards the exit.

'We, we used to work together,' Dum Dum tried to say. 'We came all this way to find her...'

The man's hand shot out like an arrow. '*Out!*'

They marched out to the auditorium and found it packed to the gills. The whole town seemed to have come, and Paul and Dum Dum could barely squeeze through the throngs.

At last the show began. The audience twittered breathlessly as the curtains rose.

First came the plate spinners who spread out cross the stage twirling porcelain platters from the tops of thin rods.

Stomping their feet to the music, they formed human pyramids without dropping their saucers or stopping their motion.

They were followed by a fire eater who blew flames over the heads of the crowd. Then he fried a dozen eggs on an enormous pan by blowing flames all over it.

He was followed by a dancer who pranced with a spout of water that moved up and down her arm. She let it slide up to her shoulder and back again, before she made it jump to her other hand.

From there it slithered down to her toe.

She hopped around on one foot for several beats of the music. Finally she kicked the spout of water into the wings, where it disappeared.

She took her bow and the curtains came down.

The audience were clapping and whistling.

Then came the main attraction.

The curtains rose on a darkened stage.

A catchy Latin rhythm started playing from the orchestra pit.

A rich, clear female voice started to sing:

When marimba rhythms start to play
Dance with me, make me sway
Like a lazy ocean hugs the shore
Hold me close, sway me more.

The spotlight came on and focused on one side of the stage.

Ginger appeared in the bright circle, swaying her hips, snapping her fingers.

Everyone was mesmerized, some people murmured, 'Where are her strings? Who's making her move?'

Suddenly the beam of light swung to the other end of the stage.

A silky baritone voice took up the melody:

Like a flower bending in the breeze
Bend with me, sway with ease
When we dance you have a way with me
Stay with me, sway with me.

The light picked out a tall, dusky male puppet as he glided towards Ginger. Her head sprang around towards him, her eyes brighter than the spolight.

She skipped across the distance and flew into his arms. They pressed their heads together and sang:

Other dancers may be on the floor
Dear, but my eyes will see only you!
Only you have the magic technique
When we sway I go weak!

The cymbals crashed on the last word and Ginger's partner stretched to his full height. He had a large, noble head, the thin legs of a *danseur* and the shoulders of a bull.

He was clearly made from all the best parts, and he strutted around the stage, followed by Ginger's adoring gaze.

'I know that puppet from somewhere!' Paul muttered.

'I don't,' Dum Dum gave a dejected shrug.

In front of them, Ginger and her partner crooned away:

I can hear the sounds of violins

Long before it begins

Make me thrill as only you know how

Sway me smooth, sway me now!

As the orchestra played the instrumental part, Dum Dum mumbled in Paul's ear: 'That's supposed to be our song! Why is she singing it with him?'

The pair onstage continued their romantic duet as they whirled across the floor boards:

Other dancers may be on the floor

Dear, but my eyes will see only you.

Only you have the magic technique

When we sway I go weak!

I can hear the sounds of violins

Long before it begins

Make me thrill as only you know how

Sway me smooth, sway me now

As only you know how

Sway me smooth, sway me now!

They finished the number holding hands.

The audience roared with delight as they took their bow.

Dum Dum hung his head like it was too heavy for his neck to hold.

When the applause finally died down, Paul heard a bell ringing frenziedly in the distance.

He nudged Dum Dum. 'You hear that?'

Dum Dum listened for a moment. 'It's the clock tower,' he whispered. 'It's trying to warn us about something.'

The spectacle ended and everyone filed out onto the street.

When they were standing in front of the hotel, Paul declared, 'I just remembered where I know that dummy from.'

'Really?' Dum Dum turned to him. 'From where?'

'Remember the poster?' Paul mentioned.

'What poster?'

'In that market stall. In Lutzenvelde, I think. That big man with the red beard.'

'Who? Barbarossa?'

'Yes, that's his name!'

Something dawned on Dum Dum. 'Why, yes! *Porfirio's Harem*, I think it was called! That's him! The rascal!'

'He's as big as Barbarossa,' observed Paul.

'Yes,' Dum Dum nodded, looking defeated. 'He made a puppet in his own image. From all the best parts!'

Chapter 44

Early the next day, they sneaked into the Valta Grand. But when they got to the theatre, only the stagehands and assistants were there, going back and forth between the wings and the dressing rooms. 'Where could she be?' anguished Dum Dum. 'We need to find her before she goes back onstage with that scoundrel!'

They went up and down the lobby in search of Ginger. But she was nowhere to be seen.

After a while they spotted the showman parading around and giving orders to the hotel staff.

'I don't want anyone going upstairs to bother her!' he dictated. 'No visitors or autographs until after the show!'

He strutted across the foyer and went up the stairs. Paul and Dum Dum tiptoed behind him. When they got to the top floor, they watched him waddle to the very last door in the long corridor and knock.

'Ginger, sweetheart,' he murmured through the door. 'Don't have your breakfast too late! Early rehearsals today, remember?'

They heard a sleepy reply from inside, and Dum Dum nodded excitedly to Paul. 'We've found her! She's in that room!'

They hid behind the couch until three waiters appeared, pushing a cart. One of them opened the French doors on one side of the passage and pushed the cart out onto the balcony. There they threw a large white cloth over a wide wrought iron table. They laid out a sumptuous breakfast.

Then they knocked on Ginger's door.

Ginger stumbled out drowsily in her embroidered nightgown, untangling her hair and blinking in the sunlight. A lone waiter dressed all in white bowed to her and pulled out a chair as she swept up to the table.

He poured steaming coffee into a gold-trimmed cup and put it down in front of her. Then he disappeared back into the kitchen.

Ginger picked up the porcelain cup and brought it to her lips. There were so many breads and pastries in front of her she had to go *eeny, meeny mino moe* with both hands before she could decide where to start.

As she was munching on a second *bichon au citron*
Dum Dum crept towards one of the marble statues. He waited
for the right moment.

A bird flitted with a cheep above Ginger and she
looked up. Behind the statue, Dum Dum started to warble
very softly:

> *Dear when you smiled at me, I heard a melody*
> *It haunted me from the start.*
> *Something inside of me started a symphony...*

He paused to listen as she pushed her chair back and
looked around. Suddenly he jumped out with his hands spread
out: *Zing! Went the strings of my heart!*

The gilded cup fell and shattered on the floor. Ginger
opened her mouth as if she was about to break into song. But
what erupted from her throat was a piercing scream.

A dozen white-garbed waiters swarmed onto the
balcony like angry doves. Dum Dum and Paul bolted towards
the stairs and fled out to the street, the staff and the hotel
manager just inches behind them, shouting and shaking his
fists.

Paul and Dum Dum scuttled as far away from the Valta Grand as they could go.

'She doesn't remember me,' Dum Dum grieved. 'We came all this way for nothing.'

'She just needs time to remember,' Paul consoled him.

'No!' Dum Dum wailed. 'She's been patched up with different parts! Maybe her heart has been put in some other puppet.'

'That can't happen,' Paul reassured him.

'Well, it obviously has!' Dum Dum whimpered.

They walked around until they passed the clock tower.

'I wonder why it was making such a racket last night,' Paul remarked.

'Maybe it was trying to tell us we were just wasting our time.'

They ended up on the main square. Paul slowed down to read a shop sign.

'Collo...Collod...Collodi. Collodi Watches!'

'What're you talking about?' Dum Dum looked up.

'It's Iosif's friend, *Signor* Collodi,' Paul mentioned. 'Remember? He wanted us to say hello.'

They peered through the glass and saw no one inside. Paul opened the door and they entered.

The shop had the same sounds as Iosif's, full of the ticking of clocks and watches, with the occasional *Boing* of the great grandfather clocks, and the bewitching chimes of music boxes in the upper shelves.

A man emerged from a doorway with beaded curtains.

'Welcome, welcome,' he saluted. He had a neat black goatee and a faded old beret.

Paul walked up to him '*Signor* Collodi?'

'At your service!' the man snapped to attention.

'We bring greetings,' spoke Dum Dum. 'From your friend in Gorsveta.'

'Ah, Iosif!' the man delightedly clapped his hands. He didn't seem at all surprised that a dummy had spoken to him.

'So how is my friend Iosif?' He drew them towards the beaded curtains. 'Still keeping well?'

'He keeps listening out for messages from your clock tower,' Paul told him.

Signor Collodi laughed as he led them through the passage beyond the curtains, 'Come, come. You must tell me all about him over lunch.'

They went up a long flight of stairs and came out in a large airy apartment.

'Welcome to my humble abode!' the clock maker swaggered through his own parlour and led them into the dining room. He clapped his hands, and two servants brought out loaves of bread, and plates filled with cheese and ham.

As they were eating, Paul pointed out to the clock tower. 'Why was he making so much noise last night?'

Collodi glanced at the structure outside his window. 'Oh he does that when he sees something he knows shouldn't be happening.'

'Like what?'

'Well you know our famous guests,' Collodi spread out his delicate hands. 'The troupe with the wonderful Ginger?'

Dum Dum nodded his head vigorously. 'Yes?'

'Well, they stay at the Valta Grand. Their rooms are right above the square.'

Paul exchanged glances with Dum Dum. 'Yes, we know.'

'Well, last night,' Collodi lowered his voice to a whisper. 'While the whole town was *enraptured* with the *magnificent* spectacle put on by Lady Ginger and her *splendid* company, something very suspicious was going on.'

'What *was* it?' demanded Paul.

'Someone evidently pried one of the hotel windows open and entered the rooms where the performers are staying.'

Paul gasped, 'Really?'

'They were trying to pull some things out,' continued Signor Collodi. 'Fortunately, some townspeople and myself, alerted by my faithful clock tower over there, ran to the scene.'

'And?'

'We surrounded the villains, and *one-two, one-two*, some of them refused to give up without a fight. But there were many of us. And we nearly caught all of them.'

'*Nearly?*'

The watchmaker spread out his hands in helplessness. 'There was one large man. A giant with a red beard. He rose to his full height, tall as a bear. Unfortunately we lacked the strength to restrain such a man!'

He hung his head in sorrow.

'So they all got away?' uttered Dum Dum.

'Almost!' the watchmaker held up one finger. 'But they left something behind!'

'What was it?'

'Something very vital to their felonious intentions!' Collodi pushed back his chair and got up.

'Come!'

They followed him to the next room.

There was short squat table near the wall. On top of it was a suitcase.

'There it is,' Collodi waved at it.

'What's in it?' Dum Dum inquired.

'There!' Collodi threw the lid open. 'Look for yourself!'

Paul and Dum Dum rummaged through the contents. There were flyers, brochures and posters from Ginger's show.

At the bottom there props, sections of painted backdrops, music sheets and stolen costumes, including Ginger's trademark outfits.

'Looks like they were trying to steal the whole show,' Dum Dum surmised.

'Yes!' Collodi confirmed. 'Some people will stop at nothing to succeed in this thing they call shoe business!'

Paul stared at the suitcase and became lost in thought.

At length he put his hand on the handle. 'Can we borrow this for a while?'

'Be my guest!' Collodi waved his hand.

They thanked him and left with the valise.

'We've got to warn Ginger,' avowed Paul when they were outside.

'We should!' agreed Dum Dum. 'That is, if they even let us near her.'

They roamed aimlessly, thinking. 'But isn't that strange?' Dum Dum commented.

'What is?'

'We thought we'd seen the last of Barbarossa,' said Dum Dum. 'How come he's suddenly here?'

'Maybe Ginger knows the answer,' said Paul. 'Or her new friend Porfirio certainly does.'

Dum Dum winced.

When they got to the end of the boulevard they saw the day's newspaper. The headline announced: "VALTA'S MAYOR TO HOST A DINNER FOR GINGER AND COMPANY."

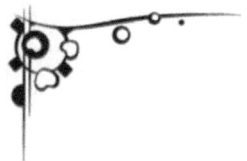

Chapter 45

The next night, Paul and Dum Dum purposely missed the show. While the show was going on at the theatre, they plotted the best way to see Ginger again.

They paid a visit to *Signor* Collodi, who agreed to take them to the mayor's mansion.

It was a big stone building on the outskirts of town, surrounded by a tall vine-covered fence. As soon as they parted the vines to peek inside, a pack of vicious dogs snapped their jaws at them.

Paul held Dum Dum back. 'You're likely to lose your nose that way.'

Dum Dum looked at the distance they had to cover from the fence to the house. He grabbed his head and slumped to the ground. 'We'll never get to warn her!'

They stood around looking for a way to get in, when the dogs started yapping again.

The lights along the driveway suddenly came on. A grey haired woman in a tight fitting black dress strode forcefully to the front.

'They're coming!' she called out to someone in the grounds. 'They're coming! Get those dogs back inside!'

The dog keeper whistled and the pack of canines followed him whimpering back into their kennel.

They heard the screech of wheels and a long convoy of luxury cars came around the corner. The party pulled up into the driveway.

Paul recognized the performers from Ginger's troupe, still in their costumes, as they climbed out of the mayor's limousines. A swarm of servants came to help them out of the vehicles. In the confusion, Paul and Dum Dum were able to sprint through the open gate.

They headed round to the rear of the building.

From behind the hedges they observed as a large, sumptuous dinner was served. The mayor got up again and again to make a toast. They couldn't hear what he was saying, but they could see the guests gesture and laugh at his remarks, as though they were mimes in a mute drunken play.

At last the meal ended and the group broke up into the different rooms of the palatial home.

Paul and Dum Dum came closer to the windows. They looked through every pane but couldn't catch sight of Ginger.

'She might have sneaked upstairs with that Porfirio character,' said Dum Dum.

'You keep looking,' Paul replied. 'I'll go get something.'

'What are you go going to get?'

'Nothing. I'll only be a while.'

Paul disappeared back towards the fence. Dum Dum resumed searching.

At last he glimpsed Ginger sitting by herself in the library, reading a book.

He stared at her through the glass, not sure what to do. After a long time Paul reappeared, dragging something through the flowerbed.

'What's that?' Dum Dum said under his breath.

'Never mind.' Paul said. He saw Ginger sitting by herself inside. 'Where's old Latin chops?' he muttered.

'Probably in the smoking room with all the gentlemen,' answered Dum Dum.

Sure enough, in one of the brightly lit windows they spotted Porfirio, sprawled on an armchair under a cloud of cigar smoke, clowning and puffing away with the mayor and his friends.

Paul and Dum Dum groped along the walls until they found a side door. They opened it and sneaked in. They tiptoed to the library.

Dum Dum stole into the cosy chamber without making a sound.

'You know how to read a book now?' he said brightly to Ginger. 'I can read, too. Left to right. Left to right! All the way till you reach the bottom.'

Ginger looked up and glared at him.

'It doesn't work that way,' she hissed. 'Unless you're reading Chinese!'

She threw the book down with a loud thud.

'You...you read Chinese?' spluttered Dum Dum.

'I might as well be!' snapped Ginger, 'for all the good it's doing me, with all the distraction you're providing!'

'But, Ginger, darling,' Dum Dum came forward, stretching his arms out towards her. 'I'm *not* distracting you. I'm trying to *save* you.'

Ginger got behind a long reading table. She picked up a massive book to defend herself with.

'Will *you* stop *pestering* me, you little *squirt*!' she yelled. 'The only thing I need saving from is you!'

'But, bu-bu but! Don't you remember me?' pleaded Dum Dum. 'Zing! In the truck from Blackpool. We were going to run away!'

'Ha!' she laughed. 'Haven't you heard? I already have a man in my life! My heart belongs to Porfirio! If I had to run away with anyone it would be him!'

'You don't know what you're saying, Ginger,' Paul suddenly appeared at the door. 'You've had an accident.'

'Uh-huh...' Ginger nodded blankly, trying to figure out what he meant.

'They've had to put you together from all sorts of different parts,' continued Paul. 'You may be made up of fragments from different puppets now. But somewhere in there, your heart is still the same. '

Ginger stomped her foot. '*What* on *earth* are you two *talking* about?'

'He's right, Ginger,' Dum Dum inched towards her. 'You may have different hands now, different hair. But underneath all that you're still the Ginger I know. The girl I fell in love with!'

'I'm not the girl you know,' she scoffed. 'I'm a star now! Everybody falls in love with me. But all I care about is *Porfirio!*'

Dum Dum blinked for several moments. Then he started to chant:

'Twas like a breath of spring, I heard a robin sing
About a nest set apart...

'You're right,' Ginger replied.

'I am?'

'I do hear something. And it's *NOT* a *ROBIN!*' she screamed at the top of her lungs. 'NOW *GET OUT!*'

Paul pushed the door shut. 'Ginger, please. Just give us a chance!'

'Open. That. DOOR!' Ginger ordered. 'Open it or you're going to be in *mucho mucho* trouble!'

'One second,' implored Paul 'One second and you'll see!'

He shot out the door so fast Dum Dum and Ginger were left staring at each other. Ginger glanced at the clock, started tapping her foot impatiently.

Before five seconds had passed, the door flew open again. Paul entered with the suitcase from Collodi's house.

He flung it to the floor. 'There! Have a good look! See if we're lying.'

Ginger threw the lid back. Her eyes instantly took in her stolen costumes, the posters and the props form her show.

'Where did you get this?' she demanded.

'They were planning to steal your the whole show,' explained Dum Dum. 'And you were part of it.'

'Me?' Ginger threw her head back in laughter. 'And how were they going to do that?'

Dum Dum pulled out one of the posters and held it up.

It proclaimed: 'THE GREAT PORFIRIO'S HAREM. WITH HIS LATEST CONQUEST! GINGER!'

'Porfirio was just using you,' Paul helped to clarify. 'See? They even printed new posters. They were that sure you'd go along with it.'

'They plotted this for a long time,' put in Dum Dum. 'Porfirio's owner wanted to use your fame to make their own show a success.'

'Look!' Paul yanked out the female costumes, 'They even tried to steal all the girls' clothes.'

'Now why would they do that?' questioned Ginger.

Dum Dum spread out Porfirio's old flyers on the reading table. They showed all of his previous partners.

'They needed dresses for a whole harem, remember?' Paul revealed.

'And you were going to be his newest acquisition,' Dum Dum added.

Ginger's whole body shook with rage.

'*Me?*' she shrieked. 'Me! A *conquest? Me!* In a *harem?*'

She seized the valise and hurled its contents in every direction. Soon the air was filled with bits of the posters and the costumes. Suddenly they heard a train whistle in the distance.

'It's the train!' Dum Dum blurted out.

'Yes!' sputtered Ginger. 'I'm due for an engagement in Paris tomorrow!'

'But you *can't* go,' Implored Dum Dum. 'You belong with me!'

From outside they heard the rumble of many footsteps. Someone knocked on the door.

Paul and Dum Dum moved towards the windows, ready to flee.

'Who is it?' Ginger called out.

'Ginger!' crooned Porfirio from outside. 'The train is leaving soon. Better not be late!'

Ginger looked from side to side. Dum Dum and Paul watched her uncertainly.

She jerked her head towards Paul. 'Alright! Let him in!'

Paul threw the door open. Porfirio samba-stepped into the library, his hips swaying, his lips pursed in a seductive pout. 'Remember my darling,' he crooned: '*Like a flower bending in the breeze*
Bend with me, sway with ease.

The train whistled a second time. At last Ginger opened her mouth.

'The only thing that's going to bend around here,' she uttered, 'is my knee so I can give you a good, solid kick!'

Porfirio staggered back like he'd been slapped. 'Ginger, my precious. Why are you talking to me like this?'

'Well, Porfirio!' Ginger spat out the words. 'Or *Perfidio*, I should say! Get out of my sight! I'm not going to be anybody's conquest! I do the conquesting around here!'

The swarthy Lothario backed out into the hall, stunned.

Ginger lunged forward to slam the door on his face.

Paul and Dum Dum watched silently for several moments. Ginger seemed too drained to talk. She looked down on the floor, breathing heavily, her hair hiding the sides of her face.

In the silence, softly, coyly, Dum Dum began to intone:

All nature seemed to be in perfect harmony
Zing! Went the strings of my heart
Your eyes made skies seem blue again
What else could I do again...

Ginger slowly raised her head. She took a step towards Dum Dum. She looked like she was going to give him a good slap. Then she put her hand on his back. 'Ow!' she flinched. 'Can't you do anything about that damn wire?'

He turned his face submissively towards her.

She gave him a big smile. Suddenly it seemed as though she remembered him. She joined him in his song:

But keep repeating through and through
"I love you, love you"

I still recall the thrill, guess I always will
I hope 'twill never depart
Dear, with your lips to mine, a rhapsody divine
Zing! Went the strings of my heart!

Whatever happened during the rest of that night, the next day was a new beginning. But it was also the end of something. They had come to the conclusion of their quest, and Paul had to get back home.

By mid morning Dum Dum and Ginger had agreed on a lot of things. One of them was that they would leave Valta together.

So they decided to see Paul off at the station.

When they got there, the train to Vierris was at the platform. They waited for it to open its doors.

They walked Paul to his carriage.

'Remember,' Dum Dum reminded him. 'after Vierris you get off the sixth platform and walk to the other end of the station. Then you have to reverse everything we did to get here.'

'I know,' nodded Paul. 'There are things I'll always remember.'

They gave each other a tight embrace, and Dum Dum asked, 'What day is it?'

Paul thought a moment. Then he said, 'Why, I think it's Saturday.'

Dum Dum smiled and puts his arm around Ginger. 'It's true. *A Friday night's wish on a Saturday told, is sure to come true be it ever so old.*'

'Right,' said Paul and got on the train.

'Why don't you take the map?' offered Dum Dum.

'No,' Paul shook his head. 'I don't need it to get back. You'll need it more than me.'

'Thank you,' beamed Dum Dum. 'Thank you for everything.'

'You're welcome,' answered Paul. 'You know you'll always be welcome.'

He walked into his carriage and sat down. Dum Dum and Ginger blew him kisses through the window.

At last, the train pulled away.

Dum Dum and Ginger sang and danced for him on the platform:

Just in time, I found you just in time
Before you came, my time was runnin' low
I was lost, the losin' dice were tossed
My bridges all were crossed, nowhere to go
Now you're here and now I know just where i'm goin'

No more doubt or fear, I found my way.

At the end of their song they spread out their hands and waved goodbye. But Paul was already too far away to see.

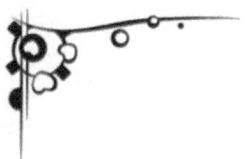

EPILOGUE

Paul sat in the half empty carriage, he suddenly felt something in his hand. He opened it, but saw nothing there. Yet his fingers were tingling as if they had just touched the wire on Dum Dum's back.

He remembered the day he had taken Dum Dum to his uncle's shop. Even an experienced carpenter like Matthew was puzzled by that wire sticking out of Dum Dum's back. Yet that part which seemed to have no purpose was perhaps what made Dum Dum special. It was, in fact, what had made Ginger remember him.

Paul looked out the window with a smile. Like the wire on Dum Dum's back, he used to think his life had no purpose. But in Dum Dum's journey he had played a crucial part.

He turned around as if to grin at Dum Dum. But there was no one there.

The train passed great stretches of open space. As the landscape got dark and more desolate, Paul began to feel lost. He closed his eyes and tried to stop thinking of Dum Dum.

After a moment, he started to feel a warmth around him. And for the first time in a long time, it seemed as if Daniel were sitting right next to him, amazed at everything Paul had done.

Paul's eyes shone as he looked around. Daniel would have been so proud of him. What adventures he'd had!

The train finally pulled into King's Cross station in London, and Paul had to shake himself awake. He made his way drowsily through the crowds to get the bus home.

When he walked through the door he found that his mother was already back from Cyprus. She got up and swept him up in her arms.

'My, that was one long sleepover!' she smiled at him. 'For both of us.'

They had their usual dinner together and Paul went to his room. He felt so lonely when he shut the door.

When he turned off his lamp to sleep, he noticed that the light from outside was shining on something on the floor. Paul stood up to look at it.

The book of nursery rhymes lay there, near the foot of his bed, open at the pages he had first shown Dum Dum.

The beam from outside fell on the second verse on the page. It was the one about the musket and the pipe:

When I was a little boy my mammy kept me in
But now I am a great boy
I'm fit to serve the king;
I can hand a musket
And I can smoke a pipe,
And I can kiss a pretty girl
At twelve o'clock at night.

Paul got back in bed with a look of contentment. Now he was a great boy. He'd had so many adventures.

When he turned over to sleep, he couldn't help whispering, 'Goodnight, Dum Dum.'
As he closed his eyes he thought he heard a voice answer, 'Goodnight, Paul.'

To keep from feeling too sad, he tried to picture Dum Dum. He imagined him being happy somewhere with Ginger, doing all the things dummies do together.

When he woke up in the morning he felt a wetness on his cheek. It was like the dampness on Dum Dum's face when they had embraced to say goodbye.

He told himself only dummiest think that puppets can cry. But he couldn't help thinking that Dum Dum was more human than any boy he had ever known.

The next day he went to Charlie's house. Charlie, Nadine, Albert and Ryan peppered him with questions. He told them little bits at a time, saving the rest for later.

He didn't know how long it would take to tell them everything that had happened. In the end they might think he was just making it all up.

His friends detected no hint of a stutter in his speech. Paul spoke with a confidence none of them had heard before. They also noticed one thing: he seemed a bit more downhearted than when he'd left. As if he had lost a part of himself.

'When can we go and see Dum Dum?' Nadine demanded.

'I don't know,' Paul replied.

'Didn't they tell you where they were going?' Albert was incredulous.

'Not exactly,' Paul explained. 'But there's one problem.'

'What's that?'

'I wouldn't know how to look for them.'

'Why not?' asked Nadine.

'Dum Dum said that as soon as they found somewhere to live, he would change his name.'

'What for?'

Paul answered with a shrug, 'Nobody wants to be called Dum Dum forever.'

END

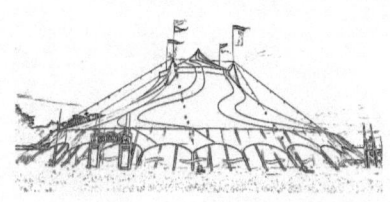